Dirk Bogarde

JERICHO

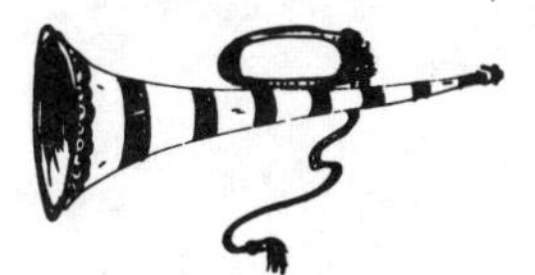

This edition published 1992
by BCA by arrangement with
Penguin Books Ltd.

Set in 11/13½ pt Lasercomp Sabon
Printed in England by Clays Ltd, St Ives plc

A CIP catalogue record for this book is available from the British Library

CN 1721

For

MARY DODD

with endless love

for Thursday teas

Author's Note

There is no such place as Bargemon-sur-Yves, no Saint-Basile, Saint-Basile-les-Pins or any town called Sainte-Brigitte. There is, to the best of my knowledge, no rue de Cayenne in Paris and there has never been, as far as I am aware, a club called Le Poisson d'Avril. All of them are my inventions, along with the characters who inhabit them.

I wish to record my profound gratitude to my editor, Fanny Blake, for her patience with my stubbornness, and in particular to Susan Pink, MCSP, and Doctor Peter Wheeler, who dealt with my questions with infinite kindness. Mrs Sally Betts, once more, has come to the rescue of a very untidy typescript and made it, at least, legible.

D.v.d.B.

CHAPTER 1

HELEN CAME INTO the breakfast-room that morning in her familiar way. I was pretty well used to it: dressing-gown, frill of nightdress below, hair pulled back roughly and secured with an elastic band, slippers which she had long since trodden down at heel.

She carried a tray with a jar of instant coffee, two mugs, a pot of yoghurt for herself, sugar, milk and a small dish of jam.

'Down early. Couldn't you sleep or something?' She set the tray on the table.

I was reading the *Guardian*, I remember, but just photographed, in a blinding instant, her appearance. The normal morning arrival.

I said the kettle had already boiled, so she slopped across, switched it on, stood by the draining-board, hand on the kettle handle.

'You didn't say. Couldn't you sleep?'

'Like a top.'

'Lucky you, I must say, but I didn't exactly turn and toss about. Bloody worn out.'

'Giles all right this morning?' A mild question. I was folding the *Guardian* more times than was necessary. Anxiety perhaps; the end of a union is always unsettling.

She poured hot water into the mugs, then spooned in instant coffee. 'He's fine. Just one of those things kids get.' She switched off the kettle. 'Probably eaten something disgusting at school. School dinners: all chips and jelly-stuff.' Took the kettle back to the stove, stirred the mugs, pushed mine across the table towards me.

Mine had a Mucha print on it, hers a clown with a red nose and a pointed hat. We always used the same mugs: it had become a habit from the start, fourteen years ago.

Her mug and mine. Amazing, considering how much she broke generally, that they had lasted so long. But it was her idea, not mine. Like the whole dreary kitchen: a mixture of the twee and the dreadful. Pitch pine, jars of pasta, bunches of crumbling herbs, a trug basket hanging from the ceiling filled with dusty dried flowers, a rack of graded saucepans, chipped and burned, on one wall, and on another a set of unused jelly moulds, one a fish, one a wreath of fruit and flowers, another a sort of lobster-thing. Tarnished. The tiles which we had chosen together in high euphoria all that time ago for the work-tops no longer gleamed with bright-sparkling light: they were dimmed now by years of fry-ups and quick wipes down with a dishcloth.

'We'll make a country cottage kitchen in dreary old Parsons Green, won't that be super! So cosy.'

She had said. And I agreed. There wasn't much point in discussing things anyway; I was very much in physical love at the time and she could have turned the wretched room into a clinical operating-theatre or a copy of Versailles for all I cared.

The one window looked out on to the 'garden', or, to be more accurate, a yard, thirty foot long with two battered dustbins, a sad May bush, and the rest all concrete, with cracks grown green with moss and damp like an aerial view of the mouth of the Amazon or the Nile Delta.

We hacked it up in the first spring, with great effort, laid turves on fresh earth and made raised flower beds where she planted honeysuckle, fuchsias and some sort of clematis. But it all faded away after a couple of seasons and was neglected. It faced north anyway, and was dank and sunless. We never sat out in it, the cats peed everywhere and it was really all over by the time that Giles and Annicka were born.

I always thought Annicka was a silly name, and said so, but she said it was very unusual and romantic, and screw what the child thought when she was eighteen. Anyway, it would probably be called Anne or Annie – which it was.

I folded the *Guardian* again, watched her eat her yoghurt; she stirred a spoonful of strawberry jam into it.

I didn't like her much.

She looked up as if I had said it aloud, lips sticky with the pink slosh stuff, some sliding down her chin.

'If looks could kill,' she said, wiping the muck off her face with her sleeve.

'I'm not looking. Not killing,' I said.

She hunched her shoulders, tossed her scraggy pigtail, grinned at me across the pitch pine table.

'No need for a killing, is there? I'm going away, willingly, longingly, and you do as you like.'

'Right. I'll do as I like.'

She raised the coffee mug with the clown to her lips, both hands holding it. 'Shan't miss a thing about this place. You're very welcome to it all, every tile and brick. Just my books, a few odds and ends you wouldn't want anyway. I'm very glad we talked things to a head last night, no good dragging on like this, not when love, as they laughingly call it, has dried up like an old pond.'

'No point at all. But you'll let me see the children?'

'It's a friendly separation, sweetie, no harm has been done. You come and see them whenever you want to. Give me a bit of warning; school and all that, you know? Just come down to Mother's when you feel like it, and as this is your house, paid for from your parsimonious pocket, you'll be snug as a bug here, won't you? No kids banging about to disturb your scribbling, and I won't be driven dotty by your ruddy typewriter. Mrs Nicholls will stay on, I bet. Do better for you than I could. And with more enthusiasm. You'll have to give her extra, of course, for meals and so on. She's fab with Lancashire hot pot and mutton stew. You'll get huge.'

'I'll eat out, I expect. Go down to the Grapes.'

'Super potato salad there.' She set down her mug. 'I'll get on to solicitors and things when I'm settled. Or you can. As you like. I'd better see if Annie is awake. She'll be late again. That child has sleeping-sickness.'

She got up, tied the belt of her dressing-gown tightly, and the front-door bell rang. She turned and looked at me accusingly.

'Now, who's that? At this time in the morning?'

'Mail perhaps. It's his time.'

She went out into the hall leaving me looking at the pot of yoghurt with the spoon sticking in it.

The sooner she'd packed and gone and cleared off to her wretched mother in Chalfont St Giles the better. Then I'd be able to think, to try and sort things out, to salvage something from the crumbled debris of a once apparently happy union.

I'd miss the kids, in a way. But nothing else. I could flog the house for a good price and clear off somewhere smaller, without pitch pine kitchens, the chintzy bedroom, the mushy little flowers spattering about the wallpaper.

Falling out of love was every bit as easy as falling in love, it seemed to me. As far as I was concerned, Helen was an empty yoghurt pot . . . there weren't any scrapings left. Love, as she called it, had died over a pretty short period of time. Almost as soon as the carnal interest dried up. Pity.

Finally expired for good last night in the sitting-room with its striped walls, Knole settee, tiddly little tables with bits of Royal Doulton, some fake Louis-junk, and a Magicole fire in the Adam fireplace she'd found in the Portobello Road.

'Real piece of Adam, that. Came from the Adelphi.'

Adam my backside. But she'd liked it and bought it, and had it fitted. So.

'It's the post. A packet for you, hence doorbell. No duty to pay, and a gas bill. That's all.'

'Why no duty?'

'I don't *know* why no duty.'

She looked at the small Jiffy bag in her hand, turned it over a couple of times. Squinting. She'd need glasses soon.

'French stamps. Can't read the postmark . . . Barg-something. No value. It says so on the Customs thing. "Sans Value". It rattles.'

She threw the gas bill and the packet on to the table and went up to wake Annie.

Oh, I had loved her. Fourteen years ago she was vital, attractive to an alarming degree, and knew it with that quiet complacency sexually attractive women have: aware, smiling easily, contained, knowing what she could offer. She was hard to get, which made the chase the more exciting: men were after her like chickens with scattered corn, fighting, scrambling, pushing. She chose me, to my astonishment. I'd not really expected it. Perhaps because I didn't join the others, just stayed quietly away, I intrigued her by my apparent distance – but I wanted her.

And she scented this in an animal way. I thought.

'You're a writer or something?' she had said one evening at some awful party we both found ourselves attending. The Marshalls' place, I remember, celebrating his new book published that week. Poor champagne and lump-fish roe caviar and a fowl in glazed something-or-other.

'I write.'

'Novels? Or terribly erudite biographies of dead people?'

'Bit of both. Depends. Mostly novels.'

'Ought I to know you?'

'Only if you read.'

'I don't. Much. Haven't the time really. I'm with Wright and Steinberger, commercial television. I arrange the "shoots", you know? Locations everywhere, budgeting. I'm out of my mind with travel and figures. One week the Canaries for a Ford commercial, another week Welwyn Garden City for Fairy Liquid – it's all go with me.'

'It sounds hectic. But fun.'

'It's hell. Really. Can you get me a refill of this muck?'

A hired waiter handed us a tray with spilling glasses – not 'flutes' – those god-awful wedding champagne glasses, like inverted umbrellas.

'I'd give it up in a flash, really. I'm getting on, you know; time I had children, a nice little house, get on with a settled life . . . all this careering about is for the birds.'

'Plenty of willing gentlemen about, I'd guess.'

'Guess right. But they are all arse-holes this lot. Commercial TV is the pits. I find it demeaning. Know what I mean? I'm worth more than that.'

She didn't specify.

'The money must be good. Surely?'

'Money', she said with slow deliberation as if she had just discovered the fact, 'is not everything in life. I'd settle for less, really. I mean, look at this lot, all guzzling, red in the face, slapping each other on the back, self-congratulation at every turn, stuffing down that dead bird in aspic as if it was manna from heaven. Couldn't we clear off, quietly? No one would notice if we did, they are too caught up in themselves and Bob Marshall's bloody book. Somewhere peaceful, just us?'

The invitation was clear, the challenge met, we got away easily enough.

'You're not leaving, darling!' Mrs Marshall with back-combed hair and sequins, a glass in her hand, distraction in her eyes.

'I'm off to Malaga at dawn. Must. It's been lovely, really, and this kind man says he'll see me to a taxi. Daren't risk a mugging.'

Mrs Marshall laughed rather loudly so as to be heard above the noise. 'You don't get mugged in Eaton Square, *darling*. But off you go. Sweet of you to come. How lovely! Malaga and all that sun . . .' She turned away from us when someone called her name and we got out.

'Really off to Malaga at dawn?'

'No. The day after. Just an excuse. All right? You mind fibs?'

'Not those kinds.'

We had supper together in a small restaurant in Mount Street, and then went back to my flat near by, and made love all night. Or it seemed all night. She was very good and very experienced, un-shy.

'Practised, I see.'

'Disappointed?'

'A lot seems to have worn off on those trips to Welwyn Garden City, Malaga and the Canaries . . .'

'You mind? What am I supposed to do stuck among a herd of thirty men. Sit alone in some ghastly unit hotel and watch them swill the local beer and brandy and carry on with my crochet in the lounge? Come on, be fair. I'm twenty-seven, I know my way about, I know how to survive too – the hand on the thigh, the arm round the shoulder that slowly slips down to my breasts. I know the messages. "We could make a deal, you and I? £30,000 a year, for full devotion to . . . the job, got it?" I got it. They came from hell those bastards, but you have to play along at my age.'

'I know every nook and cranny of your highly desirable body, but . . .'

She looked at me with lazy indolence, head on the pillow, the morning light just filtering through the curtains.

'But what?'

'I don't know your name!'

'Christ, no you don't, do you? Helen Wiltshire, spinster of Chalfont St Giles, parents' place, and 169 Upper Cheyne Place. And your name?'

'William Caldicott. Writer. Bachelor of Faringdon, Oxfordshire, parents' place, and 687 Mount Street, W1.'

She pulled herself up to a sitting position, dragged her hair back from her forehead.

'Oh Christ! Caldicott! I should have known. I *have* read your books. *A* book. Paperback. About Incas or something?'

'About Argentina actually.'

'Same thing. Oh! Will you ever forgive me? How dreadful! How rude!' She threw warm naked arms around me, and we slid back into euphoria.

Six months later she chucked the job, married me, and we bought the house in Parsons Green and didn't live happily ever after.

I mean, that, in a nutshell so to speak, is that. Over ten years we had. Well past the seven-year-itch time, as they say. Slowly the bed-part began to fade . . . the kids had arrived. Well, Annicka was first, a love child, and Giles a patch-up job. We tried for the poor little sod and made him a sort of bicycle-patch on a slow puncture.

But the tyre went flat anyway.

She missed her crowd, missed the travelling in the end. She'd have traded Parsons Green any day for a trip to anywhere, Corfu, Easter Island, the Falklands even, and she missed the male conversation, still using, as she always had, the coarseness of a unit's language sitting in a bar.

Couldn't blame her really. I'd given her what she thought that she wanted, the house, security, children, before she grew too old. But it really wasn't what she was after, and she gradually found it out. Breast-feeding, disposable nappies, cooking (very badly), yearning for the telephone to ring. For her. One of her predatory gentlemen in television. They seldom did.

And my work suffered too. She hated my being locked away up in the attic I'd converted into an office. Wasn't interested in anything I tried to discuss with her, plot development, characters, research, that sort of stuff. And we foundered, that's all. I hate clutter, and she was a clutterer, careless, letting her hair go, grey streaks, slogging away at the vodka from time to time.

'What else do I do? I'm not constructive like *some* people.' This said with sour heaviness. 'All I am is a bloody nanny-cum-cook-cum-bottle-washer.'

'Not very original.'

'And don't tell me, again, that I talk in clichés, I bloody know I do. I'm a living, walking cliché or whatever it is. Screw you.'

'Well, chuck it. Clear off. Take the kids and go back to mother. Cliché number 1.'

'I bloody well might just do that. Poor Mother. But there's plenty of room since Dad died, a garden for the kids. I could get back to work somehow. I know things have changed, all those Bright Young Bitches in *Harper's* and the *Tatler* have taken *my* place. Still, I'd hire a proper nanny. I could –'

'Well, do. There is no point in going on like this.'

'None at all. We don't even . . .' She had the grace to look at the floral carpet at her feet when she came up with the body blow. 'We don't even like each other any more. Do we? I mean, honestly?'

'Honestly. No. Really, I suppose.'

'Amazed that you took notice. Stuck up there all day with the sodding typewriter, trolling off to your ruddy book-signings, taking that poncey agent of yours out to lunch. At the Caprice, if you please!'

'What's wrong with the Caprice?'

'Nothing's wrong. You've only taken me there a couple of times in all our married bliss, that's all that's wrong.'

'You said that it was too smart, your dress was wrong, and that the food was too rich.'

'Liar! Liar! Liar! I never did. You invent all this guff, the privilege of the novelist, I suppose. Over-active imagination. Lies, all of it, lies.'

'You've had half the vodka.'

'And I'll have the other half, sod it.'

And so it went on. Until last night when we really got down to – cliché – brass tacks: reasonably, sensibly, kindness and understanding smothering my dislike. I refused to lose my temper, took all the blame willingly, admitted wrongs which were not of my doing, offered her a reasonable settlement for herself and the kids for the severance which we both, by this time, desperately desired. When love dies the ashes are cold indeed. Dust. They stick in your craw, like charcoal.

Upstairs, I heard her talking to Annie, the 'understanding mummy' bit she did so well; when she felt like it.

'And we'll have super Hymettus honey with the cornflakes, shall we? It's the stuff I brought back from Greece, remember? When you stayed with Gran in the country last year. Yes, there's enough . . . No. Not for Giles . . . Giles has a beastly tum-tum . . . and two rashers and a poached egg? Or scrambled? Poached . . . okay, and hurry, don't leave the soap in the water, and come down as soon as maybe . . . I'm going to start the eggs. Right? Mummy's lovie.'

All this shouted in a kind voice on the landing. A reminder to me? A warning to Annie.

I picked up the scuffed Jiffy bag. French stamps, of 'No

Value', postmark hard to read, Bargemon-sur-Somewhere, Var. Nowhere I knew, nowhere I had heard of. Pulled off the little yellow plastic sealer and emptied the packet on to the table.

A metal key, five inches long, ancient, not rusty, polished with years of use; wired to the loop at the top, a note.

A page torn from an exercise book, judging by the squares marked on the paper, handwriting rather sprawled, but clear, and disquieting. There was no date.

Mas du Pigeonnier
Bargemon-sur-Yves
Var, France
? Sunday night

Dear William,

A key, you will undoubtedly say. From whence, from whom? From little brother James is from whom.

The key to my house here. You have never seen it, don't know of it, but it has been my refuge, my sanctuary and my life-work (if one can say that) for the last few years. It's rented with three more years to go, all paid in advance. I send you the key because it is now yours, I no longer have need of it, I'm leaving shortly. If you want some years of delight come and get it, but *don't* come looking for me because you'll never find me, I'm not about any longer, or won't be by the time this falls on your front doormat.

I shall have drifted into the blue, as they say, leaving no trace behind me. *Not* a sudden impulse; a thought-out determined action. All I touch seems to turn to dross – my work, my love, my life – so before I take the road to sweet oblivion I will mail this to you and leave you to do fit as you see it.

I have no will, this bit of paper will have to suffice,

and if the lawyers grumble and fuss tell them to bugger off. This is my last will and testament. I am of sound mind and in good health; just got weary of it all.

Show this to my landlord (lady, rather), Mme Sidonie Prideaux, 11 rue Émile Zola, Bargemon-sur-Yves. She'll be fair, she's all paid up. Sad we never really knew each other; but life is like that and the twelve years' difference in our ages didn't help much, did it? You are all that is left of the family, so I leave what I have, not much (nothing in the bank either), to you. Blood is thicker etc., etc. . . . I had a poor innings, but they tell me that the runt of the family usually does. And runt I was!

Goodbye,
James.

He had signed it James Caldicott, officially, presumably for the legal business.

I let it fall against my coffee mug with the Mucha print. Stared out into the hallway, heard Annie hurrying down the stairs, Helen behind her.

'You haven't done my eggs!'

'No. But I've done my face. I'll do your eggs while you eat the cornflakes.'

They clattered into the kitchen. 'And some barley-water for poor Giles . . .'

The door slammed and cut off the wearisome conversation. I stacked the two mugs, the yoghurt pot and the jam on to the tray to give myself time to think before Helen would return, as she was bound to do.

Poor James. The 'runt of the family'. Why did he call himself that, for God's sake? We had all tried to make him fit but twelve years between us did make a difference, it had to be faced, and I really didn't much care for him. I had to admit that. Slender, fair-haired, a bit arty-farty, always drawing something and painting large canvases with squares and circles and naming them *The Inner Angst* or *Resurrection* or something equally pretentious. Anyway, I thought so.

'I know what I was,' he once said to me. 'I was a sudden-turn-over-in-bed-one-sultry-night. Caught them both by surprise, didn't I? I wasn't wanted, or even intended; that's been made clear.'

He did well at art school – scholarship, modest exhibition, to which we all had to go, at some gallery in Bruton Street – then he just cleared off to France to paint, or 'live', as he called it, on a small allowance Father gave him. I got a couple of postcards from time to time, nothing much, out of the blue.

And we drifted apart. It didn't bother me at all. That was that.

Until the key.

'What was in your packet?' Helen, dressed, ready to take Annie to ballet school, a fish slice in her hand.

I told her briefly, without showing her the letter.

'What on earth for? What a crazy thing to do. Honestly, you Caldicotts. A rum bunch you are. What the hell do you want a cottage in wherever it is for? And what do you suppose *he's* done? Gone off to join the gypsies or something?'

'I've cleared the breakfast things. Mugs and so on.'

'You *are* kind. I'll be out for lunch. Maureen's meeting me at Fortnum's; there's cold ham, bully beef, salad, eggs, bread and so on, and a new chunk of Cheddar. I'll be back about fourish. Keep an eye on Giles, won't you; just liquids today, he's perfectly all right, no fever.'

She clattered away like a bickering magpie and I went up to the office to try and work out what to do next. I'd got enough on my plate for one morning.

Looked in on Giles, who was reading.

'You better?'

'Yup.'

'Mother's going out for lunch.'

'I know. She said.'

'I'll be in. Upstairs. We can have lunch together if you like.'

'She said only liquid stuff today. I'm ill.'

'Okay . . . well . . . if you want anything just yell out.'

'Yup.'

He went back to his book, indifferently. I went on up to my office and stood looking at the typewriter. A smell of stale cigarette smoke, balls of screwed up paper. I opened the windows and let in some fresh air, emptied the ashtray, sat down and wondered.

And wondered. Not that it did much good. That scene, downstairs just now, if I had written it, started a book, say, I'd have groaned and said, 'Oh, lor', not again! It's all familiar ground. Happens all the time. Start again.' The fact is, I suppose, that it happens to about 45 per cent of marriages, maybe 50 per cent . . . at least to marriages which are based primarily on sex, physical attraction. But it fades very often. As they say, it takes two to tango.

My parents, for example, adored each other from the very start. And when he died she just found no reason to live without him and followed on pretty quickly. I mean, that was real love. Lasting love, and it had been physical too . . . I know that: hand in hand, little kisses, a caress when they thought that perhaps we kids weren't looking. But we often were; we felt secure because of that love, it framed us tightly. We didn't say much to each other, but we sniggered, as kids do, covering our pleasure with vulgarity.

Elspeth was born first, I second. We were the perfectly planned little family, not too many, just enough not to strain bank balances or wreck that love. And then, of course, with bewildering surprise, we discovered that another one was on the way, more than a decade after we had all settled down snugly, complacently, together.

James. They called him James after King James the First: Dad was reading his letters at the time so James it was. He was unlike the rest of us. Elspeth and I were dark, with brown eyes, tallish; so were the parents. But James was blond, corn-blond, with wide grey eyes. Slender, small bones, almost pretty rather than actually handsome. People looked at him in the street in his pram. 'A lovely baby!' To everyone but Elpie (I called her Elpie) and me. I was, of course, very jealous. He became, had to become, the focus of the family. The 'ewe lamb', Mother said, and we had to be particularly loving towards him because he was a sort of 'changeling child'. That didn't make much difference to me, I might say, but Elpie was female, and slowly, after the shock had faded, became devoted to him, played with him like a doll, which he greatly resembled, discovered for the first time that he could use a pencil, or a crayon, with greater facility than we could, that perhaps he might be an artist. I suppose she really started him off, at least she encouraged him all the time, cooing and mooing over his scribbles. To the great relief of Mother; and, indeed, Father.

Father was headmaster at Dartwell, Mother wrote books. Successful books at that, historical 'romances' but not gushy or sickly – well researched, almost Jane Austenish. She did well, and it helped the budget.

Elpie and her husband, whom we all very much liked, were drowned in what the French call, rightly, a 'banal' little sailing accident off Chichester, and Dad never recovered. He'd retired by then, happy pottering about in his vegetable garden, or nailing things together in his little workshed. But Elpie's death hit him hard. Mother went to call him in for tea one afternoon and found him lying on his workshed floor. He went quickly and without fuss, and that was that. Mother didn't wait much longer, she just slowly died before our eyes, James's and mine . . . I was at home quite a lot now, to support her somehow. But that wasn't enough, so it was, all in all, a bloody year. James went back to France after everything was over: I got the house and contents, he got a legacy of some size, not much, but enough to keep him under a roof and in paints. And independent of me.

I sold the house at Faringdon for a fair price and moved up to London to work. There was no point in hanging about a place which had been so filled with love and emotions of various kinds, so I quit. Clean break, as they say.

I didn't get married; for some reason I was inhibited, I think. Inhibited by the destruction of our family, so although there were ladies about and often, it never came to more than 'long holidays', or little affairs which loitered on and finally fizzled out. I wasn't in the business for permanence.

And then I met Helen.

And here I was, presently, wondering what the hell had happened to us all, and how two families could fall apart, even in such very different ways, and end up so abysmally destroyed.

I'd married too late, that was certain; I had little patience really for the finer points of love and affection. The physical side was okay – managed that very well, I was often told – but, somehow, I didn't want responsibility.

Who was it who said, very vulgarly, 'Why buy a cow when the milk is so cheap?' I don't know. I deplore it, of course, but it made me laugh – once. Can't crack a smile up here today. But perhaps I'd have been better off – everyone would have been – if I had heeded the disgusting remark. Now there were Annie and Giles: responsibilities for life. Helen would manage, I was pretty certain about that. She wouldn't stay a divorced lady for long, not the type . . . but getting back into the wretched television business wouldn't be that easy. She had been right when she said that the 'bitches in *Harper's* and the *Tatler*' would have taken her place: she was not young enough now, her ideas had probably atrophied, she still possibly thought, and worked, as she had fourteen years ago. And fourteen years in commercial TV is a lifetime.

She'd marry some booze-sodden producer who would keep her in the manner to which she was not accustomed. My modest allowance, or separation-thing, would be a pittance in comparison. I'd have the children to keep, of course, had to face up to a responsibility at least once.

But what was there left? Apart from my work, which was still all right – better than all right, really – but there was nothing else. The kids, sure.

And the key.

James. What the hell did his letter mean? Suicide? Or just, as Helen had said, gone 'off with the gypsies'? He could do anything, end up in darkest Africa feeding the starving (*with what?* I wondered), or drift to America and join in the Lost Brigade, dope, drink, anything you want. Total disappearance.

The typical drop-out, join the huddled masses wrapped in cardboard, sleeping in the subway entrances on winter nights. People get mislaid like that easily. But, somehow, not James. I don't think it would have been James's way. He'd never get to America anyway; never get a visa, wouldn't know how. All his life, as far as I was aware, he'd had someone to take care of him, arrange things, set him up when he fell.

Of course, it was quite possible that he got married. Improbable but not impossible. He'd got the fey looks which some women go for: the lost little boy, the helpless child with the trembling smile. And with his painting, which some people pretended to understand, he might have hit it off with some rich American lady touring Provence, or the

Var, or wherever it was. Maybe she got him: overwhelmed by his mystery (what mystery? – plain silence and indolence in reality), she'd carted him to America like a package of goodies from Fortnum's or Fauchon.

I looked at his letter again, read it carefully, and knew that this was no letter of farewell-I'm-off-to-America. This was just farewell. Full stop.

'. . . don't come looking for me . . . not about any longer . . . drifted into the blue . . . leaving no trace . . . the road to sweet oblivion . . .'

Surely that was farewell? And three years to go on a rented house in a lost village miles away.

Where? Why? Everything 'seems to turn to dross, my work, my love, my life' . . . certainly a farewell.

The intercom buzzed. Helen said she was leaving, be back about four, to remember liquids for Giles, and that Annie was going over to the Merrows for tea so not to worry about her.

I sat and stared out of the window over slate roofs, tilting chimneys, a wispy poplar bending in the early spring wind.

A filtered London sun struck through the dusty glass, glittered on the key before me.

— CHAPTER 2 —

IN THE MICHELIN GUIDE, Bargemon-sur-Yves was indeed in the Var, some 900 kilometres from Paris. It had one small hotel, La Maison Blanche, with a rocking-chair indicating peaceful surroundings and no marks for cooking. It had eight rooms. There were two restaurants, Chez Titin and Le Sporting, a garage for Renault; the hotel and Chez Titin were closed from November until December. That was all.

As far as the guide was concerned, that is to say. But seeing the village in the warmer southern afternoon sun a few weeks later, I realized, in a way, why James had chosen the place. A small village strung neatly along the base of an immense line of jagged limestone cliffs, probably mountain high, certainly bare towards the tops, scrub and thorn at the base. The church stuck up like a warning finger, a shallow pointed roof, four rows of arches in the belfry. Around it lay the village; clustered tightly, chicks about a hen, it had spread to east and west as the years had gone by, but in general it was dominated by the huge cliffs behind and the tall, ochre brick and stone tower of the church.

La Maison Blanche was small, comfortable, unpretentious, and stood across the square from the church.

A little terrace, three concrete pots with laurel and a dusty cypress, a sagging, sun-faded blind, a scatter of battered tables and chairs, a wooden figure of a chef holding the day's menu, a drawing-pin through his pink, upheld hand. The paint had scabbed from his face, but the menu, in violet ink, immaculately written, was attractive, if simple.

Yes, there was a free room, not very much commerce so early in the year: late April was not a favourite time for tourists, the evenings were too cold yet at this height. A room over the square? Or perhaps at the back? It would be quieter.

From my window I looked down on to a small garden, a line of table napkins drying on a long line, fluttering like a ship dressed all over at a regatta. Two big lime trees breaking bud, a row of bushes, obviously fruit, and beyond a tidy vegetable garden with rows of things growing in perfect order. A tin shed in a corner with a wire enclosure and a scrabble of chickens. A solitary, proud cockerel standing on one leg on an upturned bucket. Beyond the garden, a cluster of roofs, red-tiled, at all angles, beyond them the high cliffs rising to the clear blue sky, shading into pale apricot as the afternoon began to fade.

My room itself was pretty bare: a huge Napoleon bed in mahogany, a small table in the window, a couple of straw-bottomed chairs, a wardrobe of immense size, one lithograph of Jesus baring his heart and looking heavenwards, a smaller picture of kittens with goldfish in a bowl.

There was a forty-watt bulb in the bedside lamp, and the lavatory was at the far end of the corridor. But there was a washbowl in a corner, and a shower with a plastic curtain, which was some sort of relief. One could always have a pee there without trailing down to the WC with a torch.

I unpacked the little I had, put it away in the two deep drawers of the wardrobe and went down to ask for a stronger lamp bulb.

'I am a writer. I have to work at nights sometimes and it's not possible with so small a wattage.'

'Ah.' The elderly woman in a black and white overall, looked worried. 'There is a good light in the bar . . . people sit there after dinner, not in their rooms.'

'I can't sit in the bar and correct a manuscript. You'll understand, Madame?'

She nodded in a rather distracted manner, muttered something which I couldn't hear and then screamed, 'Eugène! Eugène! Venez vite.'

Eugène, who seemed to be about thirty and was the waiter, probably the cook, and the luggage carrier as well, found a stronger bulb in a hideous lamp shaped like an elephant with a howdah. The bulb and the lamp, it would appear, went together; they did not come separately. But I thanked him and tipped him over-generously and he left smiling with a preoccupied expression. Maybe his soup was in danger of catching. He turned at the door suddenly.

'M'sieur is eating in the hotel?'

'I am. Certainly.'

'Then may I recommend the trout? Fresh this afternoon from the river below. And the veal is perfect, well hung, no hormones; from a man I know who farms at La Butte.'

'I shall have both. I'm hungry. A sandwich on the train last night, and only a croissant for breakfast.'

'You will eat well.'

'I expect to.'

He inclined his head gently, turned to leave again, turned back.

'You speak excellent French. Not many of our English guests can do that.'

'Two years at the Sorbonne, a year at Berlitz. But you knew that I was English, alas!'

'Ah yes! Perhaps the clothes M'sieur is wearing; perhaps just a lingering trace of . . . Albion?'

'I am rusty. The clothes are useful for travelling. Wasn't certain if it was tweed-weather or not.'

'Tweed-weather at this time of year. We have a fire in the evenings even. In the summer, of course, it is different, in the eighties in July.'

'Do you get very many English guests up here? Perhaps in summer?'

'Not so many, they prefer the coast. Some do come for the peace, it is a quiet place; one man even stayed here for a time, a painter.'

'Oh?'

'He went away. He was pleasant, very quiet, not rich, I think. Yes. He went away.'

'Ah. And never came back?'

Eugène was in the doorway.

'He came here sometimes. For a pastis or maybe some Gauloises cigarettes, not so often. He bought a little place. Dinner is at seven-thirty to nine, no orders after that.' He closed the door and left me standing under the lithograph of the Jesus looking heavenwards.

First clue. James had been there, naturally enough. So they'd be certain to know where the Pigeonnier was; someone might even know where and when he had gone.

In the hall, crossing it to the bar, the woman in the black and white overall suddenly called my name. She was behind the little desk; a calendar, a green china pot with browning-tipped fern, a ledger which I had signed earlier which did as a Visitors' Book.

'M'sieur Colcott. Your passport.' She handed me the thing. 'It is not necessary to fill in all the details, just your name. We like to have it in the book, for the next time, you see?'

I took the passport back, stuck it in my inner pocket.

'I believe that you had another Colcott here once, is that so? English? Do you remember him?' It was obvious that the 'aldi' part of my name, our name, was too difficult to pronounce, so I went along with Colcott.

She looked above my head vaguely.

'We have been colonized here, you know, by the Romans and the Greeks, the Celts . . . It is difficult to remember all the people who have been in Bargemon-sur-Yves . . . we are an ancient town, always full of visitors, I can't remember everyone.'

'This visitor wasn't here so long ago. A year about. He was called James Colcott. Does that make it any easier?'

She suddenly looked at me with clear, steady eyes.

'Ah yes: Jimmie, I remember. A painter . . . blond, very gentle. Oh yes, I remember. He was here.'

'But he's gone now?'

'Yes. Gone. He bought a little house.'

I took the key from my pocket, held it towards her in the dim light of the hall. 'This is the key. He sent it to me. I'm his brother.'

She looked at me with quick unease, plucked at the pocket on her overall.

'His brother?'

'There were twelve years between us.'

'Ah bon.'

'Where is his house, Le Pigeonnier, Madame? In the village or outside?'

She closed the ledger before her, pulled a few bits of brown from the fern, threw them into a basket under the desk, avoiding my look.

'It's not in the village, no. On the road to Saint-Basile, about two kilometres; I haven't been there, but I know that it is empty, no one is there now.'

I thanked her, put the key back in my pocket, went across to the bar. I knew that she was watching me, knew that she was standing perfectly still. Pondering.

The usual little hotel bar: long wooden counter with a

Formica top, pinball machine, poster for a local football match, green shiny walls, a TV set on a shelf jammed high into a corner, the sound off, the vision on; two elderly people talking at each other in sudden jumps and cuts. In the centre of the room a few tables and some chairs, a pot of plastic tulips; a door in one wall draped in lace curtains leading to the dining-room; another, across the room, leading to the WC, according to the hand-printed card above it.

People at the bar, all men, farmers from the look of them, talking, drinking, punching each other affectionately, laughing.

At one of the tables a couple of obvious tourists, he fat, bloated even, she thin with a face pinched by years of irritation. They were both reading, he a folded copy of some newspaper, she an old copy of *Figaro-Madame*.

I ordered a Scotch and Perrier from the pleasant barman. Two youths went over to the pinball machine. Lights flashed, bells rang, they were laughing, thumping the sides.

I took my drink and sat at a small table in a corner. Under the glass-covered top a small, stained map of the region, with the village dead centre in large letters, and 'delightful walks and excursions' radiating from it like the spokes of a wheel. Saint-Basile, I saw, was at the far edge of the map, to the west of the village, surrounded by woods, but not indicated as a 'delightful walk or excursion'.

I'd have to find that out for myself.

I had a couple of drinks, then went into the dining-room, tired, ready for a meal and for my bed. I'd been travelling all day, after all.

A comfortable, unfussy room. Tiled floor, large open fireplace with a log smouldering indolently; about eight tables. Round the walls, papered with large roses and trellis, the heads of various small horned beasts stuck on wooden plaques, dried corn cobs and gourds hanging in bunches. On the long mantelshelf a stuffed partridge in a glass case, a polished silver cup, won, perhaps, for the slaughter of so many horned beasts, or perhaps just the partridge? An ugly pottery jug with 'Annecy' written on it, grey with last year's lavender.

The meal, as Eugène had promised, and which he served swiftly and expertly, was very good, simple and fresh. There were about three other tables with people eating, and the couple from the bar arrived almost as I had finished my half-bottle of local wine, dressed for their dinner; it was just nine o'clock.

'From Paris,' said Eugène, clearing my fruit plate. 'They *always* arrive just as I think we have finished. Ha! The veal was good?'

'Excellent. Thank you. Saint-Basile . . .?'

He stopped, the plates balanced on his arm, a menu in one hand.

'Saint-Basile?'

'It is far from here?'

'Two, maybe three kilometres, not more.'

'There is a bus?'

'No bus, but Maurice in the bar has a taxi. If you ask him tonight he'll be almost sure to take you. It's the quiet season.'

He left, and went across to the couple from Paris and placed the menu before them on his way out to the kitchen.

The morning light was brilliant, sparkling on the chrome-work of Maurice's Citroën, dusting the poplars and plane trees along the road in soft greens and pinks. In the ditches, clusters of primroses, and a small blue flower I could not name. Perhaps borage?

'At Saint-Basile-les-Pins there is nothing but forest, you know?' said Maurice over his shoulder. 'Unless perhaps you go to see the little chapel? Saint-Basile's chapel: it is a ruin now, but the memorial to the Resistance is very fine.'

'A memorial?'

'The Nazis shot eight of our Resistance fighters there. One by one; the bullet marks are still in the door. Holes in the wood. You go to see that?'

'No. I don't actually want to go to Saint-Basile. I'm looking for a house called Le Pigeonnier. Madame Mazine said it was near Saint-Basile. Do you know it?'

Maurice, watching me in the driving-mirror, looked away when he caught my eye.

'I know it. It belongs to the Prideaux. Her father bought it years ago, gave it to her as her "dot". It was part of the estates of the Duc de Terrehaute . . . you know this? Destroyed in the Revolution and carved up for the people. The château is all ruins now. Only the pigeonnier still stands. But no one is there, it is empty.'

'It was rented by an Englishman, wasn't it? A Mr Colcott. You knew him?'

He coughed, or grunted. 'Went away.'

'He was my brother. My younger brother. He sent me the key – I have it here. Apparently he has paid the rent for the house for the next three years, so he said.'

'Your brother? My word! Yes, I knew him, he came sometimes into the village . . . walked all the way, or came on his cycle for provisions. In the bar he would have a petit rouge, or a pastis . . . cigarettes. He was pleasant enough. We knew him as Jimmie because his name was difficult for French people to say. So he said, "I am Jimmie, it is easier." He painted, but we didn't really see him very often. He was about. It takes a long time, even in a small village, to be, shall I say, "known". But he was all right. Spoke good French, caused no trouble, paid his bills . . .'

The Citroën began to slow down. On the right-hand side the beginning of a wall, tall weeds, bushes, a mossed stone pillar. Maurice turned right past the pillar up a dirt road.

'This was the entrance to the château. You can see,

nothing is left.' He stopped the car where a small track led away from the main one through an ancient orchard of unpruned apple trees. 'Le Pigeonnier is up that path. You'll have to walk – I'm sorry, the springs won't take the ruts. You want me to wait? No one is there, but of course you have the key, that's it. I wait?'

I told him to come back and pick me up in about an hour. He agreed, reversing the car down the main track to the road. He gave two blasts on his horn and drove off.

I stood at the edge of the little track, the warm spring sun filtering through the greening trees; an early bee swung past. Far across the orchard to my left it was possible to see, suddenly, one tall tower, roofless, windows gaping, a jagged length of wall, an enormous cedar of Lebanon. The remains, I supposed, of the château. Ahead, as the track wound through the trees, a low wall, behind the wall a round, fat tower with many small arches just big enough for a bird, or a bat, to enter. The pigeon-house. Next to it, but not joining, a small house: ochre walls, faded blue shutters tightly shut, a rippled tiled roof, a small trellis running along the front, entwined with the dark spirals of a vine, coming into bud.

There was an iron gate in the wall leading up to the house, a metal sign wired to the bars, the lettering peeling after years of sun and rain. Looking at it closely, the key already in my hand, I read the single word 'Jericho'. I pushed the gate open and walked towards James's house through ragged grass, past an abandoned potager, sere with some of last year's unharvested vegetables, beans on sticks, dried, curled, wind-torn; unpruned roses, a cluster of tall, dead sunflowers, their round faces empty of seeds long since thieved by birds; a torn rag fluttered forlornly on a bent cane, stuck in a row of dead cabbage stalks, writhen as old men's arms. A strange feeling of loss, of desolation, especially on the little raised terrace under the trellis. A broken broom, dead leaves from the vine had scurried into corners, a child's tricycle, rusted, tyreless. A large flowerpot cracked by frost lay fallen apart like the two halves of a split orange.

I opened the front door, letting sunlight stream into the shutter-darkened room like a searchlight, found a window, fumbled about with latches, opened the shutters and looked about James's room.

Pleasant, large, running, I supposed, the length of the house. Three windows in the south wall, none in the north. Beamed ceiling, canopied fireplace, tiled floor, rough white-washed walls. A battered settee before the fireplace, covered with a tartan rug and a number of sheets of newspaper. There was newspaper over almost everything in the room, presumably to keep off the dust. A losing battle already.

A small doorway led down two steps into a flagged stone kitchen. Good electric fittings, washing-machine, cooker and so on. Newspaper over them too. Walk-in larder with a few bottles of fruit, cucumbers, some kind of jam, a large bread-crock, empty. The usual paraphernalia of pots and pans and rolling-pins, all used, but all clean, neat, arranged perfectly.

Upstairs (the staircase led out of the sitting-room by the side of the big fireplace), bedrooms. A large one, double bed in heavy walnut, lace cover, lace curtains, a wardrobe and small dressing-table with a modern glass mirror, nothing else. Next door a smaller room with a bunk-bed surrounded by some form of grill-work, so that it very much resembled a cage. Blankets folded, newspapers as usual over everything. A small chair. On the seat a red and green rubber ball.

Beyond this room, a small bathroom, empty cupboards, newspapers in the bottom of the bath, a washbowl with a dried green stain where a tap had dripped a long time ago, a cork-topped stool, empty towel rail. Next to that a lavatory, seat closed, a tin of Harpic rusting on the floor. A third bedroom quite bare.

Nothing much to it – a simple house – but there was another floor above, up a small stairway by the lavatory. This also ran the length of the whole house, with a row of circular windows along the south wall and one enormous, new window in the north wall. There was a scent of turpentine and linseed oil, of varnish and paper, of size and glue. In the centre a tall easel, paint-splattered, heavy. Around the walls row upon row of canvases stacked; some, a few only, were hung. You could tell, instantly, that they were James's work . . . it hadn't changed very much over all the years.

Abstract, mostly. Vast circles and straight lines, jagged edges, like enormous teeth in a saw, colours of startling vibrancy: there was anger here, and fear, and fury.

Not very much to be found of the fair-haired, reserved, tremulous-lipped youth I had last seen some years ago. But, and it seemed to me strange, there appeared to be no suggestion, in the few canvases which I pulled out and examined, of the glory of the landscape in which they were painted. No suggestion that the sun, the air, the brilliant light, the great cliffs behind the house – for they dominated the place equally as firmly as they dominated the village four kilometres or so away – the old trees, the soft green of the grass under their shade, had had the least emotional effect on James at all. From the look of things he might just as well have been painting in prison – or Parsons Green. There was not the least impression of the land in which he had come to live.

I sat on a small wooden stool.

The thing, perhaps, which I found the most strange was the air of tidiness all over the house. James had never been a particularly tidy or neat person, I well remember: he was careless in his dress just as he was in his habits, eating rather coarsely at table, uncombed hair, a general air of deliberate, provoking casualness. But someone had done a very thorough job of clearing up the house after he went off to find his 'sweet oblivion', it seemed. Newspaper everywhere, blankets folded, the canvases perfectly stacked according to size. The kitchen and even the larder were not James at all. He would never have noticed muddle or mess. I was over-aware of things like that because, as I've said, I can't stand clutter, and James, on the other hand, seemed to live in clutter, especially in his later years at home. And then, too, there were other little things which sparked vague curiosity: the red and green rubber ball on the chair upstairs, the bunk-bed like a cage, the tricycle lying out on the terrace.

Walking round the studio there was hardly a sign of dust, unless you looked closely, not an empty tube of oil paint, papers scattered, old pots for oil and turps. Nothing. Brushes immaculately cleaned, standing in wide-mouthed jugs. Even his painting-rags, old bits of shirt or tablecloth, were perfectly folded, lying on the stool before the easel.

This was a dead museum rather than a working artist's studio.

Well, obviously someone had come in after he had left to clear up. Perhaps his landlady, Madame Prideaux? A feeling of – I don't know really what it was, unease will do at the moment – came over me, and to break my concern I pulled out a couple more canvases which were all the same size but in a different part of the room. They stood against the wall quite apart from the rest.

These were not abstract paintings: there were no jagged lines, no vicious curves, no triangles or disturbing cubes, lines upon lines, fading into an infinity of, as always in his works, darkness.

A young woman's face stared back at me, almost without expression except, perhaps, sadness. Not particularly beautiful; pleasant looking in a perfectly ordinary peasant way. A simple girl doing simple things in three-quarter length. I pulled out three or four more. The same girl. In all of them she was occupied with ordinary household things: stringing beans at a table, kneading bread, darning, holding a bunch of wild flowers. No change in the expression – a faint bewilderment, perhaps; certainly, to my mind anyway, the sadness.

I raked through the pile and took up the last one leaning hard against the white wall. The same girl, in a pink and white blouse, sleeves rolled up, pouring milk from a pitcher into a deep earthenware bowl, like Vermeer's milk-maid. But there was no 'feel' of Vermeer about the composition, no radiance, no love for the curve of an arm, the tilt of the head, no delicacy of line, brilliance of colour, no simplicity really, no sweetness and above all, perhaps, absolutely no sense of affection for either the subject or the task which she was performing. James had singularly failed to record the harmony of light or the subtlety or contrast in colour, the feeling of shadow, or reflections.

The paintings were unsigned and undated, so it was impossible to tell just when he had made this effort to alter his style and get away from the almost mathematical harshness of his cubes and jagged edges and vibrant colours. It was perfectly clear that he had made a valiant attempt, but he had missed, it would seem, even to my uncritical eye. Well, 'uncritical' in that I am not an expert.

These were as banal and without life, as unfeeling, or unfelt, and as barren of emotion as if he had painted them by numbers. They amounted to a series of dull statements about humdrum tasks performed by a humdrum creature. Quite without joy or life. They were the sort of things which could have been used as 'good taste' Christmas cards for stockbrokers. Nothing more.

I stacked them back against the wall, covered them with the newspaper, and brushed my hands on my trousers for, however tidy the place seemed to be to the naked eye, the dust *had* settled pretty thickly, indicating that the room had been abandoned for some time. A date on one of the pieces of newspaper stated that it was printed on the 19th of December, but proved nothing.

I groped my way down through the dim house. The light in the studio from the unshuttered roundel windows had been almost brilliant in comparison to the gloom below. I felt like a sightless man, and made for the front door, which had swung to, leaving only a thread of bright sunlight which streaked across the tiled floor of the sitting-room, like a laser beam.

The sun was warm, a chaffinch was chittering away. I felt a strange sense of . . . what was it? I tried to analyse it then even: a sort of release. Odd. I wandered round the house. It was completely surrounded by a wall, perhaps two metres high: rough stone blocks mixed with old brick . . . perhaps debris filched from the château ruins across the field?

There was a patch of coarse grass at the back crossed by a sagging clothes-line, pinched by one or two forgotten clothes pegs, stretched loosely between two cherry trees heavy with blossom.

Against the far wall, a low brick shed with a tin roof and a hen run. The door closed, the wire rusted, leaves stuck in the mesh like bits of cloth, relics of a winter storm. An enamel bowl, chipped and bashed, stood neatly on its end beside the door. The run, like the rest of the house, was swept clean, apart from a drift of leaves curled in a corner.

Beyond the wall an orchard, a small paddock through the trees which gradually gave up its tussocky grass to scattered clumps of thorn and scrub, marking the base of the great cliffs which rose high above the place.

Juniper, broom, myrtle, I guessed, studding the scree, climbing as high as they could over the craggy outcrops, until the sheer face of the cliff became too smooth and provided nothing more than narrow ledges on which ravens nested.

But here there was a curious, awe-inspiring sight, almost right behind the house itself. This great mass was split asunder, as if by some giant celestial axe, and a huge ravine tore the mountain open, wide at the top, narrow and dark at the base, tumbled with boulders and piles of shale, stunted pines and greening willow, through which a small stream wound lazily, spilling down in little falls as it swirled out from the throat of the ravine through the fields behind the house and, presumably, east towards the village.

Doubtless the Yves pulsing from the very bowels of the earth.

Romantic or fearsome? It very much depended on who you were and how you felt about such things. It was a spectacular landscape, and for some would be deeply romantic and savage; for others, including myself, it had a strangely sinister air, not really fearsome, simply a gash in a great mountain reminding one that nature was a far greater force to reckon with than even mankind. This was all clearly the result, many, many years ago, of some cataclysmic upheaval in the earth's centre. But I knew that in the dark of winter, with the roaring of a storm, or in the early days of spring when the first snows began to melt higher up and turned the gentle stream into a bullying, crashing, shouldering torrent, storming round the boulders, snapping at the dead branches which it had torn away in its violent journey, it could be indeed fearsome.

I could see what had attracted James to the place: the deceptively 'pretty' façade plus the angry background, the tremendous gash in the mountain, the wilderness of scrub and shale, the desolation of the dark gorge deep in the shadow at all times of the year, even high summer save for an hour or two, and the little house cowering beneath the great crags where only the raven, hawk and crow lazily wheeled high. Silent in the up-draught.

A painter's countryside, to be sure; probably a writer's one also. But not the sort of writer I was. I had no vestige of Edgar Allan Poe about me. Nor did I wish to have.

Turning to retrace my steps back to the front, and more congenial, part of the place (after all I had, it would appear, a three-year lease on the house, so I had to take it a little more seriously than a mere visit to my lost brother's paradise), I could see, shimmering through the trees on my right, the roofless tower, the ragged windowless line of wall on the ruined château, and the motionless, feather tips of the cedar tree. Still, silent, lost.

Romantic, all right. Gothic. Very Jane Eyre, very Rex Whistler.

Maurice was due at any moment, my hour was about up; but I had an urge to return to the house and make certain that James had left no other signs of his life in this place, other than his canvases in the studio. Surely there would be a dressing-gown? A pair of forgotten slippers? A jacket, some personal thing, even a toothbrush? But, just as I thought that, I remembered the Spartan barrenness of the little bathroom with its newspapers in the bath.

Back in the bedroom I opened the big wardrobe doors. Empty save for two or three coat-hangers swinging in the draught. Nothing in the cupboards at the bottom except an empty plastic moth-repellent packet and one horn button. Nothing either in any of the drawers of the little dressing-table with its cheap modern mirror.

Nothing remained, it would appear, of James, apart from his works in the room above and a few bottles of pickled cucumbers and preserves in the larder. To all intents and purposes he had gone away into his world of 'sweet oblivion' leaving little behind him, apart from the canvases.

Maurice sounded his horn three times loudly, a long pause between each blast, so that, wherever I was, I would be bound to hear.

I closed the front door, locked it, slid the key into my pocket and went down the path through the abandoned vegetable garden and the unpruned roses.

Standing at the iron gate, not attempting to enter the wilderness, stood a young woman in a thick woollen jacket, hair pulled back with a ribbon. We stood looking at each other for a moment from a distance of three yards. Pleasant eyes, grey; no concern.

'Bonjour,' I said.

She nodded, a slight inclination of head and neck.

'Bonjour. What is it that you want? Can I be of assistance?'

'No. No . . . I just came to see the house. My name is Col-cott, William Colcott. I am the brother of James Colcott who used, I believe, to live here? He sent me the key.'

'Ah,' she said, pressed her heel on an insect on the path.

'To London,' I said inanely.

'No.' She looked up at me, a slight frown. '*I* sent it. Not him.'

'Oh.'

'He told me to. I'm his wife.'

CHAPTER 3

'I SEE,' I SAID.

I didn't, of course, but could find no more intelligent phrase at that moment. She smiled, slightly, turned and began to walk down the narrow path to the main drive. I opened the gate and followed. She stopped suddenly, turned back.

She had those grey eyes which seem to be so particularly French, for some reason: dark with a darker circle round the cornea, an intensely black pupil. There was a dust of freckles round her neck and throat, and at the bridge of her nose, no make-up, otherwise a clear complexion, smooth, unlined. She was, I reckoned, about thirty, somewhere like that.

She pushed her hands into the pockets of her woollen jacket, hand-knitted, judging by the sag at the hem, but comfortable, and worn comfortably.

'You didn't, of course, know, I suppose? James would not have told you?'

'No. James didn't tell me. He hardly ever wrote anyway in the last few years, he just seemed to fade away in France. We were not, you will realize, very close.'

She nodded, scuffing the dusty path with her foot. 'I

realize that. But he always had a photograph of your family. You, I know – I recognize you now. And was it Elspeth? Your sister? You are all together sitting outside a tent – by the sea. I don't know where, or when. He was quite small, about ten perhaps?'

'Perhaps; it was at Dieppe, and he would be about ten.'

'You were much older.'

'Yes. He was the late arrival.'

She laughed again, not an amused laugh. 'I know! Oh I know. Poor James . . . You speak very good French.'

'Thank you. I try.'

'Very well. In the taxi –' She stopped suddenly. 'Maurice brought me here, you understand, he came to the house and said that he had taken an Englishman to Saint-Basile: news like this moves like a forest fire in a small village. I knew you had arrived last night. Madame Mazine from the hotel telephoned, most discreetly, you understand? Someone was asking questions about "Jimmie", she thought I must be informed. And this morning, when Maurice told me, in a great state of excitement, that he had brought you here, I decided to come back with him. And here I am.'

'I apologize for causing you any trouble.'

'Not at all. Not trouble. But when we are in the taxi I think it would be wise to speak in English; only my English is very, very dreadful! You will forgive me? But for the ears of Maurice it is best.'

She turned away and continued down the track, calling out to him, leaning against his car, plaiting a piece of grass. He opened the doors at the back and we got in almost together, one at each side. She had good legs, and pretty ankles.

'To Bargemon?' said Maurice.

'To Bargemon, to the hotel,' she said, taking charge quietly and firmly.

She sat upright, her hands on her thighs. Good, what they

call 'capable' hands, short nails, a wedding ring. These were hands which could very well scrub out a studio, string beans, knead bread, pour milk, cover everything in newspapers against the dust.

She sensed that I was looking at her, and that the silence was straining. She was, I felt, shy of starting a conversation in English, so I gave her the opening lines.

'You are the girl in the paintings? In the studio.'

'Girl! Alas, I am the woman! Not girl now. You like them?'

'No, truthfully, not very much. You are far prettier.'

She smiled, head on one side, shrugged lightly.

'He must have someone to paint, you see. So I do it.'

'When did he . . . when did he leave? I got a letter without a date in the packet which you sent me and I could not read the postmark.'

She looked lost for a moment, repeated the word. 'Post-mark? Is what?'

'Ah. The stamp, the date from the post office.'

'Si, si, I understand. In January. It was a bad time, cold, we had snow also, not so much, but snow. On the ten day of January he left a letter for me. I was in the village to make the food and things, you understand?'

'Shopping?'

'Perhaps? It is so difficult for me, English. When I come back there is a letter. It says he will go away to think. Alone. Maybe some weeks, many weeks. If he did not come home on the last day of March, the three one of March, then I must send the package to you and go away to forget him. He would not come back again. Not ever.'

'You have no idea where? He has not written to you?'

'I have no idea what?'

'Where he went to? No letter since?'

Again the short laugh without humour. 'No letter. Nothing. I do not know where. He tell me nothing. To go away is all.'

'I'm sorry.'

'It happens. He was not happy man, James, not happy with me, with the house, with work.'

'Did he not sell his work? He was quite successful, you know, in England.'

'Sell? Ah yes. Some work he sells. To an Argentinian man for his hotel he makes in Cannes. It is by the sea, you know? Cannes. Far away.'

'I know.'

'This Argentinian man, he sells many works to him for this hotel, maybe, oh . . . many. All in the studio are for this man when he makes his hotel finished.'

'For the apartments? The bedrooms? Do you mean that?'

'Is the Cannes Commodore Hotel, I know. They will be everywhere. It is modern hotel, you know. He is making it now nearly.'

A package deal of pictures for the hotel reception and rooms. A cheerful prospect for the guests, I couldn't help thinking, but he must have paid for them, so there should be some money. I didn't feel, at that moment, and in this rather stilted conversation, and in English, with which she was clearly not very familiar, that I should pursue any more personal questions until we were free of Maurice. So I just said something trivial about being almost at the village, and how pretty the day was and how big the cliffs behind the village were.

'Very high, yes,' she said. 'On the top, very much away, is a small place, we call it a "hameau" . . . I do not know in English.'

'Hamlet perhaps, a few houses, very small?'

'Very small. Not so many houses. Once there is a castle, but now not. It is called a funny name, Jericho. You know this place in the Bible?'

'I do . . . the walls of Jericho. I know that.'

'Is what they are called, the cliffs, the Jericho Walls,

because the invaders – you call them this? – the Arabs, the Romans, the Greeks, all kinds, could not get to the hameau, so it was safe. You understand me? I speak awful.'

'You speak very well. I understand perfectly. Le Pigeonnier has a sign on the gate: it is called "Jericho" also?'

'Ah yes. James made this. He called the house "Jericho" and he made all the walls to stop people coming. You know?'

'Le Pigeonnier is a much nicer name: why did he change it?'

She wrinkled her brow, concentrating on my words which I had tried to speak slowly.

'To change it? Why? Well . . . he said that it was Jericho because that was the first city the Jews had – what do you call it? – occupied in the Promised Land . . . he said it was because of this. His refuge, he had found his Promised Land, is it? And then we built the walls. Ouf! so difficult, all so many rocks and bricks.'

'And no one came. To disturb him?'

She looked at me quickly, looked away. 'No. No people came. Oh . . .' She shrugged in a hopeless way. 'Sometimes people did, people to buy his work, to look at it. The Mr Aronovich from Commodore Hotel in Cannes, people like that. Is all.'

Maurice turned into the square before the hotel. We got out and I paid his bill while the woman stood by the little pots on the terrace. I gave him a decent tip for waiting. He touched his forehead, smiled and said something to the woman I didn't hear because I was walking behind the car.

'Monsieur Maurice said he is back in good time. He must be in the bar by twelve o'clock so that Eugène can begin the lunch!' she said in French.

Maurice drove off, and left us standing by the terrace.

'I'm glad to speak in my own language again. I am so sorry for you!'

'Please don't be. Would you care for an aperitif? Coffee? It's only eleven-thirty.'

She shook her head, thanked me but refused. She had to prepare her own meal, but if I would care to, could I come to the house, her house, for some tea, about four? I accepted readily, there was still a lot to ask.

'I live at 11 rue Émile Zola, it's behind the church and down the hill.'

'I know the address. He put it in his letter, the one you sent me.'

'It is not really my house, it belongs to my mother. Madame Prideaux . . . I live with her. Jericho is too far away, too lonely, and too full of memories now.'

'I imagine it must be all those things.'

She turned to go, called over her shoulder, 'Four o'clock? Tea or, if you prefer, a drink?'

'Tea. Thank you.'

She had gone, and was walking briskly past the church; I went into the hotel. The bar was busy at this time in the morning. I took my pastis over to the little table in the corner. I felt, frankly, a bit weary and blurred, in a strange way, by too many thoughts. A confusion of questions tumbled in my head; perhaps the pastis would help me to steady them down and observe them calmly, one by one.

First of all, where was James? Had he really wandered off into the vast unknown, or was it suicide? How could one tell? The woman would have the clues, I supposed, and then, quite suddenly, I realized that I didn't even know her name except that, presumably, it was the same as mine. Caldicott . . . she was wearing his wedding ring. And she knew of us, Elspeth and me, which was, after all, only reasonable. He would have spoken of us certainly in the years they had been together. How many years was that? Rent in advance for three and all he had indicated in his letter was that he had been living in Jericho for 'the last few years'. Well, that could be two, three, five or as many as ten, couldn't it? 'A few years' was a measure of vague time, nothing more.

Had he been successful with his paintings generally? How had he lived otherwise? His allowance, or legacy, from Father was reasonably generous, but not enormous: he was no millionaire by any means. Perhaps he had done well in France – I'd never heard that he had, but then I had never heard anything of him anyway.

I supposed that he had become a French resident after so long. You are not able to stay in France for any length of time without registering somewhere, and having an identity card and so on. Let alone get married, I assumed.

And who was this woman I'd met? Not peasant stock as the paintings of her had rather led me to believe – she was finer boned than that, spoke too well, had a very distinct, brisk, sure air about her. In the portraits I'd seen there had been a look of bewilderment, I'd thought, and sadness. These, it would appear, had quite gone now. Marriage to James, I reckoned, can't have been much of a joy – a difficult haul – and then living as they did, and where they did, was hardly luxurious . . . quite all right, of course, acceptable, simple, an artist's place, but pretty hellish in the winter. Did they have a car, I wondered . . . someone – who? – had said he came to the village for his provisions on a bike. But perhaps he used a bike just for the exercise. Maybe she drove. It wasn't important anyway.

But what was important was the next move. Tea at four o'clock. I'd really have to ask her her name. Forgetful fellow, I am.

A typical French house. Square as a box, three storeys, shuttered windows, tiled roof, trim, neat; not at all unfriendly, merely reserved, standing back from the street behind a low wall, iron railings and a lilac hedge. On either side of the gate there were two tall lilac bushes, a white and a purple, the number in blue and white enamel, No. 11. A perfectly raked, wide gravel path led towards the small flight of steps to the white front door. In the centre, a circular bed of grass, fenced about with scallop shells long since bleached by the weather, and, thrusting upwards with feathery grace, a rather fine acacia spread its branches across the shuttered façade.

At one side of the house, sticking to it like a limpet, but looking very much like half an upturned boat, the prow sticking into the garden and a thicket of laurels, was a conservatory. White, pristine, rattan blinds lowered against the warm April sunshine.

I was admitted to the house by an unsmiling, dark-haired woman in her late fifties who obviously expected me: asked me to follow her, assured me that I was not late – could I not hear the church bell ringing the hour of four? – but that Madame was a little delayed.

The hall was almost dark; faint light gleamed on a heavy carved banister rail, a brass rod on the staircase. There was a coat rack with various coats and woollen scarves hanging like striped banners, an umbrella stand in the form of a stork in bulrushes; beside it, a pair of children's blue wellingtons . . . one had fallen on its side. The wallpaper was dark, embossed. The woman pushed aside a thick velvet curtain and ushered me into the conservatory.

Brilliant, clear, no shadows here. Save for bars of sunlight slatting through the rattan blinds, which the dark woman was raising by cords, in a far corner.

Pots of plants, a tall banana tree in a ceramic bowl, cane chairs painted white, gay with chintz cushions, little tables scattered here and there, a small tank of goldfish, Japanese fans, a bronze figure of a heron, a brass tray on ugly carved legs, an Arabian, or Tunisian, or anyway Arab coffee pot burnished like gold, its small cups hanging around it on hooks like kittens around a nursing cat.

The woman left with a nod of her head, drew the curtain, and closed me into this glittering world which had little if anything to do with the dark, solid, bourgeois house beyond.

I sat in one of the rattan chairs under a bulbous Tunisian birdcage, containing a yellow paper canary on a perch, as if I was sitting in a dentist's waiting-room, except that here were no tattered magazines, and no smell of antiseptic, only green, damp earth. I was pleased when the curtain was pulled back and my hostess arrived, looking slightly out of breath, still buttoning the cuff of her shirt.

She looked very different from the woman of the morning out at Jericho. Hair neatly brushed, a cream silk shirt, blue skirt, bare feet in leather sandals. She smiled, put out a hand to stop me moving, for I was attempting to get to my feet.

'Don't move! Please! I am a little late . . . a rush today; it irritates me to be late. The sun is not too bright for you?'

'I love the sun, it is very pleasant here.'

'It is more cheerful here than in, what do you call it in English, the parlour, I think?'

'Very probably.'

'And the banana tree. You admire the banana tree? You must! My mother tends it with intense care. She lived much of her life in Algeria, you see, so she became attached to the things and insisted that she would have one in mainland France. My father was in the army. A colonel.'

'My father was a schoolmaster, that is to say a headmaster.'

'Oh I know. James told me of him. He spoke very little of his family. But now and then he would begin to remember things. I think he was not a very happy child, would that be so?'

'Well, it depends. He had no reason *not* to be happy. He was adored by my mother and sister . . .'

'Perhaps not by you?' Her head on one side, the light smile on her lips, the grey eyes steady, inquiring.

'I hardly saw him. You know? School, university and so on . . . there was a difference in our ages after all.'

She had taken a chair directly opposite mine, and was sitting forward, hands lightly clasped on her knee.

'I will play a game with you,' she said suddenly. 'You will play?'

'Certainly. What game?'

'The photograph of you all at the sea, outside a tent? Remember, we spoke of it this morning?'

'Very well.'

'James is holding something in his hand, in his fingers really . . . he is not, I think, very pleased with it. Do you remember what it was?'

I laughed at her suddenly, her smile faded, the eyes clouded. She was playing a game all right. This was a test of proof. Proof, of course, that I was indeed his long-lost brother and not some imposter. No fool here.

'I could have brought my passport over, had you asked, you know. All my details are there, date of birth, place, everything . . . it would have given you all the information which you seek.'

'I did not mean to be impolite. But one has to be sure in life.'

'If I remember correctly, after some twenty-five or so years, I think it was some kind of fish, or a crab; maybe a starfish? He was holding it up by one leg, it was dead and a bit smelly. A *crab*, I feel sure.'

She clapped her hands lightly. 'Bravo!'

'My memory amazes me! But that photograph was, I think, the one which my mother had enlarged. It stood on her writing-desk. His look of distaste amused her, I think.

That's why I have remembered the thing. Could it be *that* photograph?'

'Perhaps. It was in a small wooden frame, about this size.' She measured a space in the air, ten by eight.

'You would not recognize me, of course,' I said. 'After all that time I have grown gaunt and old.'

'No, no!' She brushed her hands in the air as if she was swatting flies. 'No, not at *all*. But time is, after all, time . . . and twenty doesn't last, does it?'

'No. Alas. But I remember the photograph so well, now that you have reminded me, in my mother's study, at Faringdon. The little ewe lamb with his first crab.'

She rose and pressed a bell somewhere behind a pot of geraniums. 'She called him that? Ewe lamb?'

'I'm afraid so. He was the centre of her universe, after my Papa that is. *He* came first of all, every time.'

She sat down again, twisted her wedding ring. 'The ewe lamb. That was his name?'

'That was his name. Behind his back of course. What is yours? Your name? Do I call you Madame Colcott? I suppose that I do.'

'My name is Florence . . .'

'Mine is William.'

'That I knew.'

'It would be all right to be as familiar?'

'Perfectly. Why not? After all, we are related. By marriage?'

'You will see how distant I am from James. I never thought of that.'

The dark woman pulled back the velvet curtain and wheeled in a sort of trolley with a tray, cups and saucers, a box of Twinings teabags, a kettle steaming gently over a small burner. There was a plate of neatly cut fruit cake, a bowl of brown sugar, milk.

The woman set the trolley in front of Florence and then left.

'We are not very used to English tea, you will notice. But Annette has made a valiant effort. Scotch cake for tea. We call it that. But I know that you will hate teabags: they are not at all correct. However . . .'

She was expert with her cups and saucers. I took my cup and piece of cake, which I didn't really want, and sat back in the rattan chair.

'I have James's letter with me. Perhaps you'd care to read it? It's his Will, if you follow me. His testament. Apparently I am now the lessee of Jericho, for three years at least. Would that be so, do you think?'

She stirred her tea carefully, removed the teabag and dumped it on a saucer.

'Possibly. I know that he paid the rent for three years just before Christmas. He was paid quite a lot by Mr Aronovich for the paintings, you see, so he put it all to the house. My mother will know, it belongs to her. Her house, not really mine.'

'But perhaps it could be mine for a little?'

'You would like it?'

'I don't know. It's difficult to tell just at the moment.'

She took a sip of her tea, set the cup down. 'Are you married?'

'I'm in the process of being un-married. My wife and I are separating after ten weary years. I have two children. So nothing is absolutely clear in my mind. I just came here out of curiosity, to find James if possible, to see the house, to rest.'

'I'm sorry.'

'It's an amicable separation, we just don't care for each other any longer, which may seem rather a callous way of stating the fact. But that's what it amounts to, and it will be better for the children in the long run: it is no pleasure for them to live with quarrelling and sulky parents. Creates a bad atmosphere all round.'

She looked out through the large conservatory windows, across the gravel, to the lilac hedge.

'One must consider children,' she said, and then addressing me, but avoiding my eyes by taking another teabag from the box and pouring water on it, she continued, 'I have a letter also from James. You realize. The one he left for me, telling me to send the key to you. There is also a packet of papers, bank statements, contracts for paintings, like the one from Mr Aronovich, a birth certificate even, stuff like that. Perhaps you would like to see all this?'

'Perhaps. When you have time.'

I handed her James's letter, which she read very slowly, not altogether understanding written English, but with a bit of translating here and there ('What is "runt"?' she asked at one point, and when I explained as best I could in my French she nodded and simply said, 'Ah, yes, of course') she managed to understand enough, and then handed it back to me.

'And we have no idea where he has gone, or what has happened to him,' I said.

She shook her head, ignoring her fresh cup of tea. 'None. Only one thing I know is that he took his bicycle with him, it was the only thing that I could find which he did take. That, his wallet, his raincoat and a cap – it was in January, you see, and very cold as I told you – and just a little bag. Otherwise, he left or burned everything.'

'His passport too?'

She looked startled. 'I suppose so. I don't know . . . perhaps.'

She took my empty cup – I had refused a second – and began to stack the tray ready to be removed. 'I think that James is dead. I don't think that he is anywhere else . . . I am *certain* of it,' she said, getting up and pressing the bell behind the geraniums again.

'I'm sorry. I mean sorry for you. It's a hopeless remark; words are so inadequate.'

She stood looking out of the windows, a good figure, arms folded across her breasts, still, very upright: of course, an army child.

'I loved him so much. So very much. When we first met I thought that I had pushed open the gates of heaven, it was so wonderful; beyond any dreams I had ever had. It happens, doesn't it? An instant, a look, and suddenly one knows.'

'An instant. I understand that well.'

'But heaven turns to hell sometimes, doesn't it? Anyway . . .' She came and sat down again as the dark woman hurried in and pushed the trolley out of the place and was on the point of closing the door when another figure pushed it open with a thud.

A tall woman, grey hair held back with a metal slide, a tweed skirt, woollen cardigan over a knitted jersey, a brooch at the throat, a small plastic watering-can in one hand. She was, I'd imagine, about seventy, a sprightly seventy, eyes bright, hand outstretched towards me.

'Don't rise. Please don't let me disturb you, but it is my watering time, you understand what I mean? I have my plants to do every second day; I'll just continue while you talk. I know who *you* are, but you don't know that I'm the mother of Florence. I am Sidonie Prideaux, this is my house and you are welcome to be here.' She turned her back and, humming lightly under her breath, went to a tap in the wall and began to fill her little watering-can.

It did not make for very relaxed conversation between Florence and me, and Madame Prideaux probably knew this perfectly well: it was obviously a delicate hint that my time was up.

Florence said suddenly, 'I'll go and get the papers and that letter, and you may take them to the hotel and study them in peace. Will you wait a few moments?'

When she had left, Madame Prideaux stopped humming

and busied herself with her plants, topping up the goldfish tank and generally being as disturbing as she could.

'What do you say to my banana tree? Eh?' she said. 'I brought it through the most awful winter with just one small gas heater in here.'

'A great achievement, Madame. It is very fine.'

'Six years old. Can you believe it? Your brother James was very handsome, and had certain attractions, but he made my child's life hell on earth with his moods and his sullenness. My other child, Raymond, was killed, you know, a few years ago. He was the elder, and my husband was killed in Algeria, so I am the widow and I am cared for by Florence now that she has, at last, come home from that house. *My* house. Left to me by my father, who bought it for me, which was very kind, don't you think?'

'Very.'

She refilled her can. 'There is little enough kindness in this world, Mr Colco, believe me. Little enough. I am a widow now and Florence is an old maid. And we *know*.'

I looked up at her, I confess, startled. I'd been looking vaguely at the bronze heron and thinking how hideous it really was, hardly listening to her ceaseless chattering and her pushing and shoving about of the potted plants. She caught my sudden look instantly, continued watering.

'But she is married? She married James?'

Madame Prideaux dribbled the last contents of her little can over a fern.

'In one way perhaps. Wedded by mutual consent, without benefit of priest or church, a wedding ring exchanged, and a mutual agreement to love, honour and even, I think, to obey or something – one was not there to hold the candle, you see? Under a tree in the full moon on some beach on Porquerolles. Such foolishness.'

I sat in silence. I felt that to interrupt would be unwise; let her continue, if she would. And she did.

'They went away for a month together, a little holiday of love and adoration, all nonsense of course! The marriage . . . But when they returned it suited the village very well to believe that all was as it should be, and so she moved into the house with him. Voilà! Everything was normal and natural. But they have no deeds, and no marriage. In the law my child is unmarried. She is only married in her own mind.'

'Did you know, Madame?'

She laughed dryly. Refilled the watering-can, straightened her cardigan which had risen up over her broad backside. 'For a little time, no. But . . .'

She now attacked some wispy plant with striped leaves, tut-tutting with anger. 'White-fly! They are impossible. I get them on my pelargoniums and that's the end of them. They are almost impossible to eradicate.'

'You were saying that for a time you believed that James and Florence were really married?'

'So I was. Yes, I did. For a little time. But you can't conceal a terrible lie so easily. Oh, romantic, I agree – they always wanted to get married but disliked the idea of churches and all the tra-la-la which goes with weddings normally, so they did it their way. Foolish children. They were caught out in their sin . . .'

At that instant Florence returned with a large battered envelope. She appeared not to have overheard anything which her mother had said, and when she handed it to me Madame Prideaux was still humming away under her breath and scolding, quietly, various plants to which she was attending.

'Here are the papers, and a diary. Only a part, I fear. He was not a regular diary-keeper, I'm afraid: he was either busy in the studio or else working on the walls of Jericho, as he called them. It took us a long time . . . but this is all that is left of his stuff. He burned almost everything he had, except the canvases.'

I thanked her, took the packet, and prepared to leave.

'I would like to have them back, when you have read them.'

'I'll bring them to you as soon as I can. Is there any day which is not a suitable one for you?'

Madame Prideaux suddenly said, 'One likes notice. The house becomes disturbed by sudden arrivals, and it vexes Annette greatly, and that *cannot* be allowed.'

Florence touched my arm gently.

'You can leave them, with a note if you wish, on the front doorstep, if no one answers your ring. The mornings are busy here. I work, but about this time, your English tea-time, is usually . . .' – she hesitated for a moment, looked at her mother's back among the ferns and geraniums – '. . . safe,' she said. 'But half-past two is better. She rests then.'

I said goodbye to Madame Prideaux, who merely waved her unoccupied hand in the air without turning her head, and Florence showed me into the hall.

'I hope that Mama was not too fierce? She frightens people sometimes. Very much the colonel's wife . . . widow . . . but she has a kind heart under the brusque exterior.'

'I'm certain she has. No. She was most interesting. Very cross with her white-flies.'

Florence had her hand on the open front door. She laughed softly, thanked me for coming and began to close the door. As I stepped out into the garden and turned back to promise to bring the papers back as soon as possible, I noticed that, on the floor behind her, the little blue wellington boots were no longer there.

CHAPTER 4

THE FOLLOWING DAY, to my vague surprise, was the 1st of May, a holiday, and suddenly cool and cloudy. April had gone. I stayed in my small room overlooking the hotel vegetable garden for the day, sorting out the scattered relics of James's past which I had been given, and venturing out only for a short walk to clear my head, to get some air, and have a beer and a meal at Chez Titin, which made a change from the hotel.

I discovered that it was a holiday when I got down to the hall and narrowly avoided a collision with Eugène, hurrying through with a wooden box filled with little pots of lily-of-the-valley.

'First of May!' he said. 'We give all our friends a little brin of muguet; these are for my tables.'

'I'll not be in for lunch, Eugène.'

'Ah! Then I can have your table, excellent.'

'I will eat Chez Titin.'

'You have booked?'

'No. Need I?'

Eugène rolled eyes heavenwards. 'A holiday! She'll be like us, complet.'

Madame Mazine picked up the telephone behind her

counter and said she would 'have a little word, just one person?' I thanked her, Eugène hurried on, and I went into the square.

A full market seemed to be taking place. Stalls packed with little clay pots of muguet, bowls and 'arrangements', fearsome things covered in nylon bows, moss and cellophane speckled with hearts. The muguet almost smothered in the kitsch.

But everywhere flowers: sprays of cherry, almond and japonica, glass jars full of wild sweet-peas in clouds of gypsophila, wallflowers, sweet william, fat bunches of white and yellow daisies. All these, stuck in rusting tins among the vegetables, the broad beans, early peas, tiny bunches of wild asparagus bound with string, made the dullish day gloriously festive. The bar in Chez Titin was crammed, the room a fog of Gitanes smoke, the air sweet with the aniseed scent of Ricard, the sourness of cheap red, the pungency of strong coffee.

Through the arch, in comparative peace, the restaurant. Six or seven tables, a tank of angel fish, plastic nasturtiums, ivy-leaved wallpaper.

I had been given a small table in a far corner, a sprig of muguet set in a mustard glass, picholines de Provence in a saucer and the menu.

Titin, plump, sweating slightly, recommended the estouffade Provençale – beef, onions, a 'soupçon' of orange – accepted my order, and promised I'd be well satisfied.

I was, and made my way back to the hotel to face the chore which was before me up in my attic room.

Trying to make any kind of sense of the odd pieces of paper, bills, the half-diary, a few photographs, mostly unannotated, including the one of us all on the beach at Dieppe, plus the farewell letter which he left Florence, was almost impossible. There simply were no clues: he had been thorough in the destruction of his papers, that was clear. Sometimes I thought I had a clue, but it was never followed up, the half-diary was fragmented, days and whole months even were not filled, some seemed to have been deliberately ripped out.

In general, from these scraps, he seemed to write mainly about his painting, and about building his wall with the aid of Florence and a couple of local men. He felt that the house was now his refuge, his promised land, after the years of wandering about Europe as he seemed to have done in the years since he had left home. The clues from this period amounted to very little indeed, practically all trivia. Things like hotel bills in Brussels, catalogues of his paintings or his exhibitions (which were more frequent than I had thought, frankly): two shows in Paris, another in Nice, Nîmes, Arles and one in Berlin. There was a laundry bill from some pensione in Milan, an unposted card from Ghent. Nothing at all of any value to me, except that it did prove that he had moved about for some time, and the letters from solicitors in London, or bank statements, all higgledy piggledy as Mama used to say, and transfers of monies from here to there, gave the movements some form of truth. I'd have to deal with that aspect of his life when I returned to London.

The half-diary, a scuffed blue book with 'Agenda' stamped on it in faded gold, was probably the first, or only, one he kept, and provided the most information, very inadequately.

It would seem that he had reached Bargemon-sur-Yves at the beginning of a warm June. He notes that 'Paris and all the other hell-hole cities simply stifle any creative urge or interest, I absolutely had to get away, and quickly, before rotting.' Apparently a fellow artist had suggested the simplicity and calm of Bargemon, and assured him that he would find it both healing and constructive to go there.

He arrived and stayed, as I had done myself, at the hotel.

Simple, clean, friendly, above all glorious peace. Silence apart from the church bell and the sound at night of the distant river. No tourists staying; two Germans with rucksacks left the day I arrived. It is all mine!

He had a sketch book which did not, apparently, survive.

Went out with my book and small paintbox to study these amazing cliffs. Mountains, whatever you choose to call them. Their sheer immensity, majesty, silence, power, overwhelm me. I fill page after page with colour notes and with the shapes of wondrous crags, pinnacles, sheer faces, cringing little trees which struggle in the fissures to survive. Like myself! I try to grab every shade on the amazing palette of colours with which every glowing hour of the day provides me. A hopeless task. The cliffs seem sometimes to smile, even beam at one, in the brilliance of noonday sun, and then scowl and threaten at sunset! The colours bewilder one: crimson, vermilion, cobalt, magenta through to deep violet. How to get these on to canvas? They change so swiftly. How did Turner paint his skies? Would that I knew the secret! I will take note after note and study this phenomenon of the light, I must *catch it and set it down.*

In the first flush of happiness in the village he filled a number of pages in this manner, but they were repetitive and provided nothing more than the ordinary joys, frustrations, excitements and sometimes mild triumphs of any painter. However, one entry a few weeks later provided firm information.

To Saint-Basile. A fair walk in brilliant sunshine. Nothing but woods and fallen stones. Ruined château very romantic, only the pigeonnier and a small house seem to have remained intact. Deserted, I thought, until I heard someone clanking a bucket about in the forlorn bit of ragged garden of the little house. Young woman, very good looking, cleaning windows. We spoke French, she very shy, but very pleasing, good eyes, well set, lithe figure. Said there was nowhere I could get a drink or meal nearer than back in the village. Had small car parked in the track but made no offer to give me a lift. So walked back, after making some rough sketches of the château tower and a curious length of crumbling walls, plus quite fantastic ravine splitting through the massif which looked as if the mountain had been cleft asunder, a small stream meandering, almost loitering, through great falls of rock and scree: very Salvatore Rosa, Italian Gothic. Attractive but in some way almost sinister. Am captivated and will go back again, but it is not my sort of landscape really. Perhaps I can adapt the strata and the brutality of this magnificent scar! No sign of the woman when I left, or her car. Got to the village about 2.30 p.m., too late for a meal but ate a hard-boiled egg and drank beer in the frowsty little bar.

His first meeting with Florence Prideaux, I assume. There were a few more pages dealing with colour and light and what he had or had not eaten and drunk. A very strong feeling of happiness and contentment which led, in the Agenda, to a long blank stretch.

Late August:

I can rent the pigeonnier at Saint-Basile from the Prideaux family. They very warm and pleasant. Rent reasonable, they delighted to get it off their hands, hard to let because too lonely, small and no telephone. Suggest a year to start with and then to make further negotiations. This agreed. F. agrees to help me clear out hay loft for studio and they all *agree to me installing a north-light, which I will have done by Monsieur Simon in the village. F.* [obviously now Florence] *more and more curious and interested in my work, and makes sensible, intelligent comments. We spend a lot of time together. She is lonely, only child (soldier brother dead last year in motorcycle crash), stuck with widow mother, pleasant, tough, army-type, but a good heart, I imagine. F. drives me over to pigeonnier whenever her domestic duties allow. Take picnics of bread, cheese, ham, fruit, wine. Agreeable indeed. I feel twenty all over again, and she makes me laugh. I begin to think that I could put down my roots here, but it is late at night as I write this and I have taken my wine . . . however, I have not felt so settled, so happy, so secure for years. This is my little 'promised land' and I think, think, think, I have found my refuge after all the years of rootlessness. I will be prudent naturally. The cliffs fill me with wonder, I shall never tire of painting them, or trying to capture their magnificence. Oh God! Could this really be the gates of paradise? I wonder?* I'm pissed!

And there it ends. It is not picked up again until late October, but at least we do have the first introduction to Florence here; she's now in the story. But what *is* the story, I wondered?

I had not seen, when I looked, any of the cliff pictures about which he writes with such joy and delight. But then I had hardly really looked at any of the canvases stacked up in the studio, apart from those of the obviously-not-peasant Florence. The ones hanging on the wall might have been his abstracts of the cliffs – I'm not clever enough to know, frankly. I dislike that sort of wild painting, restless and, as far as I can see, only ever in the eye of the artist himself, not the eye of the beholder. Surely, like a writer, a painter must get across to his audience? He didn't to me. But as Helen had often said, I'm pretty dense sometimes. Sometimes. Dense, successful *and* cheap. She said that too.

In late October there is a sudden flurry of writing. But it doesn't last long.

Sworn to F. that I will keep this Agenda going. But have been occupied all season with our wall, not easy. I never built a wall before, but Georges and Marc give expert help, especially with the stones; too heavy for me. F. covered in cement and dust and loving our 'security' as she calls it. I will call the house Jericho because there is a little hamlet high on the top of the cliffs which survived all the attackers through the centuries, from the Saracens to the Germans, I gather. F. says I am crazy, that the walls of Jericho were brought down to rubble just by the blowing of a trumpet! I reckon a bulldozer couldn't touch our effort here. Cherry trees brown, leaves spiralling down in the still of noon, the fig all spotty-yellow, mists start in the mornings. The swallows are leaving . . . have gone! B. M., and etc., leave for Paris. No grief.

And that was that. He never wrote again, at least in this Agenda, save for one final entry just before Christmas which I nearly overlooked.

Bitter today. Can't paint for some reason. Can't write either. Restless, cold, hands and feet frozen, light gone in the studio, shadows fall across the wooden floor, the cliffs scowl, mists drift like ragged strips of muslin. I must get away to a milder, a kinder place, the coast perhaps? F. says that she will come with me wherever I go. I think that I am deeply in love now, and only that fact keeps me from crushing despair. Her lips and arms, her sweetness, her gentleness. The house is lonely. I wander from room to little room, all inspiration gone. If I could only hear her singing in the kitchen, banging a tray, clattering spoons, calling my name. If we were married she could be here and do all those things and give me joy: but we are not married and the bloody village would be shocked! Bugger the village and the narrow bourgeois minds. Because of them she must leave here before dusk. As if one only lay together after dusk!

Does a marriage last? Shall we try? Can I ask her? Would she come away with me? Would I grow bored once I got her? *The light has almost gone, grey as an alley cat, the mists drip off the windows in little beads. And what of D.? I'll close this wretched book.*

The end of the Agenda.

Who is 'D.'? and who are 'B. M., and etc.', who leave for Paris, causing no grief? Curious indeed.

The few photographs told me nothing at all. There was the family group at Dieppe. Faded rather, but still five cheerful people, Mother, Father, Elpie and me, with a slightly self-conscious smile holding a pipe. I must have been twenty-ish. James, his face screwed up in distaste, about ten, something like that. Difficult to date exactly. The rest were all standard, dull snapshots in not very good colour. Florence and James smiling, covered in plaster or cement or some form of dust, building their wall. A blurred photograph probably taken by one of the two helpers: Florence sitting under a tree, shadow-dappled, smiling, holding up a shirt which she was apparently mending, James naked except for a pair of very brief swimming-trunks posing self-consciously on a log, like a muscle-builder. Which he most certainly was not, although his figure was slender and in good form – he'd certainly kept that intact. They were a pretty couple, one had to admit that. Perfectly matched one could say, right ages, right shapes.

His heavy fall of blond hair, her wide-set eyes, laughter lurking on her lips. One picture of them standing together, arms round each other, against a background of scrub and pine trees, bare feet in wet sand, and the long shadow of the photographer thrusting across the bottom of the photograph, camera and arms making a bold blur of its head. Whose shadow? Some unknown friend they met on their escape to the coast? For on the back of the photograph, in

James's flowing calligraphy, were the words: 'Porquerolles. March 24th. Joy-Day!'

The day of the false wedding, I felt certain.

And that was just about all the envelope contained, except, almost forgotten at the very bottom, a scatter of black and white photographs: a hand, muscular, hard, curled against a piece of tartan cloth, two feet . . . not particularly attractive . . . the curve of a thigh and a knee raised, obviously photographic details for some portrait he was painting. These were annotated on the back, in the familiar handwriting, 'Daniel. No. 1' and so on through to No. 7.

Who *was* Daniel? What had happened anyway to the glowing happiness of Porquerolles? What had gone wrong, what had happened to destroy the soft delight in the eyes of Florence, which now, or rather in the portraits in the studio, held only sadness and shadowed bewilderment.

I slid everything back into the envelope, except for the family group at Dieppe. It was, after all, the only photograph of us all together that I had. I'd have it copied, one day, and then return it. Then I put the envelope in a drawer of the wardrobe and wandered across to the window overlooking the vegetable garden and the hen run.

A young girl, taking down some tablecloths from the line, looking anxiously at the darkening sky.

I lit my hideous elephant-lamp and sat on the edge of the bed with Florence's blue envelope in my hands, which was the farewell letter she had received from James and which I had not yet read.

It was undated, and like the notes in the Agenda I copied it out in long-hand that day, aware that Florence had asked for them back. It began without any greeting.

I am going away. This will perhaps not surprise you, it may even give you some relief. The taut line which has stretched between us during the last few years has stretched too far and now has finally snapped. Or perhaps only I have snapped? I have reached the breaking-point, men are not as strong as women, I know, and you are braver than I. But I can no longer work, as you are aware. I no longer see the colours, the light, the forms, or feel the inspiration. They have gone, and I am barren. I shall go away now alone. To think, to try and cleanse my mind of the miseries and sadness which have dulled my sensibilities. Don't inform the police, they won't find me, and it would be foolish to plaster my disappearance over the local paper. Let it rest, let me rest. *Go away from the house, go back to your own house. Begin a new life if you possibly can.*

We are not married in law, only in our own, foolish, childish minds.

The money from Aronovich is all for you and my 'punishment'. The rent has been paid, as you are aware, to your mother for three more years. That has practically cleared me out at the bank, there is almost nothing left now, but I shall not need much. If anything at all.

If, by miracle, I should find a method of survival, should clear my head of the agonies and despairs which crowd about it like evil bats, I'll contact you before the last day of March. The 31st exactly. *If you do not hear from me by that time, send off the enclosed package (it is the front-door key – there is your spare one presently in your basket, I imagine) to my brother William, the address is written in block capitals on the packet. All you need to do is fix a stamp on it and there is nothing to declare to the Customs.* Remember, *if I am not back, if I have not contacted you,* by noon at the latest *on the 31st, mail it off and go away. I do not care much for William, nor he for me, but he is the last remaining member of my family.*

I know I am running away, a cowardly thing to do, but perhaps I shall find courage eventually? Or perhaps find eternal peace at last? I do not try to apologize in this letter. I have tried to do that already, words are inadequate and hurt more than they heal sometimes. I have hurt you brutally, this I also know, and it is mostly because of that fact that I now have cracked. I can't bear *the sad eyes, the uncomplaining love, the bewilderment. They haunt me and taunt me to the point of madness. Forgive me, if you can, and remember that I did love you most desperately. The error which we made, or I made, scars one for life.*

I am sorry.
Goodbye.

It was simply signed with the initial 'J.'

A sad, weak, ill-written letter. How now to face Florence? The confession that there was no marriage, 'only in our own, foolish, childish minds', posed no great problem. I was pretty certain that her vigorous mother would have told her already that I had been informed, but what did he mean by 'my "punishment"'? What was that? What punishment did they merit, these two cooing doves, these foolish and childish creatures, which was so severe that it had, apparently, ruined their lives?

The room had grown dark. I folded the blue paper and replaced it in its envelope, sat on the edge of my high, bumpy bed, looked through the window at the clouding sky and wondered why on earth he should have taken the trouble, and such infinite care, to involve me in this unhappy history.

There was really no need: we had never been close, and had he just faded into his 'sweet oblivion', as he called it in my letter, I doubt I'd ever have given it a thought. People *do* just melt away, it happens all the time. It wouldn't have mattered a tinker's gob to me.

But by mailing me the key to his house he had deliberately implicated me in the ashes and residuals of his wretched life, and I'd obviously fallen for the bait and swallowed the hook.

Curiosity kills the cat.

I really had no wish to rake about in the debris of his life, at this moment. I had enough on my own plate without scraping up his leavings. All my own fault, of course. What does one do when one is sent the key to someone's front door?

The first spatters of rain hit the dark window, hard, tat-tatting against the glass like a handful of dried peas. The sky was plum-blue-black, the room shadowed and depressing in the shrill light cast by the single bulb in the elephant-lamp. A sudden fearsome feeling of loneliness, hopelessness and indecision swamped me. I am not an easily depressed person: I usually manage to stick things which hit me hard on what you call the back-boiler and let them simmer away quietly until I am ready to deal with them. Helen called this my 'ostrich attitude'.

But now I felt lost: no good sticking all this on the back-boiler. I would have to face up to things, and quite soon. I could not, and in fact realized in that shadowed room with the kittens and goldfish and the Jesus baring his heart that I *would* not ditch the situation, would not.

Because of Florence.

I got off my bed, stuck the blue envelope back with the other papers and considered that it was time to go and have a stiff drink, which very often helps me to get the 'story line' in proportion, when the telephone by the bed started ringing.

'Allô? William?'

I knew her voice instantly. Her English accent obviously being used deliberately to evade the curious ears.

'William here. Are you all right?'

'Very good. You would like to make a little promenade with me? Tomorrow? In my car? About, maybe, two o'clock you could be here?'

'I could. Yes of course. I will bring the envelope, if you wish.'

'I do wish. Thank you. Two o'clock tomorrow. I tell you tomorrow everything.'

She rang off.

I metaphorically removed my pot from the back-boiler and went down to the bar for a drink. It would not, I knew, help me to get much into proportion, but it might just steady my nerves in order to prepare the questions I would have to ask, and consider the answers which I might then receive.

She had an out-of-date small green Renault, which she said was useful for parking: she worked five days a week, every morning, as a dentist's receptionist, and the village could be very hard to park in; and it was far worse when she went into the local town of Sainte-Brigitte for the weekly shopping.

This was all idle chatter as we drove out of the village and turned out on to the road to Saint-Basile. She was looking neat and attractive, perfectly composed, and drove well.

'We shall go to Jericho. We can sit there and talk, if that is all right with you?' We were back to French again.

'Perfectly. I thought that you were rather trapped, I mean at home? I didn't expect to see you for a few days really.'

'Oh, it was most fortunate. Friends of Mama telephoned yesterday. They have arrived from Paris for a spring holiday and taken her off for the afternoon. It was a very big relief! She never goes out now. She just stays at home and does her garden and her tapestry and so on.'

'So we are free?'

'For a little while. I must be back by five.'

Driving the short distance to Jericho we spoke only of the

weather, how pleasant the air smelled after last night's rain, how green the land was looking, how happy she was that spring had arrived and the winter had gone. I made polite comments and then we turned up past the mossy pillar and she parked the car where Maurice had parked his, on the main track. We walked up the little path towards the walls of the house, through the iron gate, to the little terrace, past the broken broom, the rusted tricycle and the fat pot split like an orange. At the door she turned towards me, a faint smile on her lips, a key, the same as the one I had been sent, in her hand.

Together we opened the shutters in the main room and let the sunlight stream across the neglected, newspaper-covered furniture. With the full light of day it looked sadder even than it had looked the first time I had seen it; there was an odour of damp and mustiness.

Standing in the centre of the room she ran her hand through her hair, stood still.

'Maybe', she said suddenly, 'we should sit outside. This is sad, I think.'

I followed her into the wreckage of the garden and we found two battered little tin chairs, the paint peeling, the rust bleeding, tipped side by side like rubbish in a ransacked tomb. She trailed hers across the ragged grass into a patch of sunlight and I followed, with the envelope.

'You have read everything, I suppose? Did you have time?'

'I spent all of yesterday reading, trying to put it all together. There is not a lot, I can't fill in all the picture.'

She shrugged slightly, twisted the wedding ring, looked up at me suddenly. 'You know now that this is not real? This ring? Mama told me that she had told you the truth anyway, she cannot bear the lie . . . I'm sorry. You would have found out from his letter. I'm not Mrs Colcott at all.'

'I'm sorry. I'm sorry for you.'

'Oh no! I am not. I *feel* that I am anyway. Legality is not so important until you come to legal things, is it? Do not fear. I have no claims on your family!'

'Let me remind you that I am all that remains, I presume at least, of my family. So what you really mean is that you have no claims on me. Is that it?'

She laughed, sat back in the little chair, relaxed, smoothed her skirt, shook her head as if awakening, nodded. 'I suppose so. That's what I mean. James had a hatred of anything legal, of being tied down, as he called it, of not being "a free spirit", left to do as he wished and not be forced by a set of man-made rules. At that time I didn't care – I was a free spirit myself, at least in my *mind* – but I was trapped by the triviality and monotony of my life, perfectly pleasant, comfortable, but, oh God!, so dull. So I agreed with him, agreed with everything that he suggested. I was so certain, after a little time, that he was mine for always, that nothing could ever change. How mad women are! I had not the least hesitation in accepting to live with him as man and wife with a ring, which we bought in Sainte-Brigitte, pushed on to my finger under a great pine tree by the sea, our wrists cut, just a little, little bit, so that our blood could mingle, a certain sign, to us, then anyway, that we were betrothed for ever. The ring,' she said wryly, 'was the only "legal" symbol we allowed, to reassure the village people here and, of course, my horrified mother, who would have, even though she liked James, made every effort to prevent a "real" marriage between us. He a foreigner, a Protestant, I the only help she had, and the only comfort since my brother had been killed. We returned as a fait accompli. There was not much that she could do about anything. And so I was free, and as you know he rented this little house, and we moved in together. With a cheap ring from Sainte-Brigitte on my finger. I beg you in all humility to forgive my deceit.'

'Of *course* I forgive you. There is nothing to forgive.'

'Lies need forgiving. One is always found out anyway.' She picked up a piece of stick from the ragged grass and threw it in a curving arc against the blue sky. 'And I was punished, you see.'

'What was that punishment? He writes about it in the letter to you? What does he mean by that?'

She got up quickly, started to walk down the path away from me towards the remains of the vegetable garden, and the tall clump of dried sunflowers. I followed at a careful distance, not wishing to crowd her, not wishing to make her feel that I was pursuing her.

'One is always punished for too much happiness,' she said over her shoulder. 'We were so radiantly happy, two idiotic children who had never really been happy before suddenly finding such joy that we – what is the word? – we were *satiated* with laughter, pleasure and delight of each other.'

There was a blaze of marigolds running along the path, humming with bees. We had reached the front gate, the little tin sign on which 'Jericho' was painted.

'All rust,' she said, pushing it open a little with one finger. 'All rust . . . the garden a ruin and deserted. How we worked here! Like two peasants. Really, from dawn until dusk. And I was so sure it would be for ever. Ha!'

'The wall still stands firm,' I said. 'The wall you built.'

She looked down at the stone blocks, the little brick pillars which supported the gate. 'Not really,' she said and turned quickly away, walking slowly towards the house. 'It fell.'

It was perfectly clear to me then that she was deliberately being evasive: her sudden, swift movements, avoidance of face to face confrontation, when I had asked about the 'punishment' were obvious.

She was restless; the false marriage didn't worry her so

much for she knew that I had read James's letter and also knew that her mother had told me the truth so there was no point in ducking the issue. That part was simple. What might follow was not.

I stood for a few moments by the marigolds and then walked up to the little terrace where she was occupied in clearing away the broom, the broken pot and the rusted tricycle. She pushed them all to the far end of the tiled floor, and sat down on the raised step, chin in her hand, looking towards me.

I decided on direct tactics: a sudden change of thought might catch her off the guard behind which she was hiding so deliberately.

'Who was Daniel?' I called.

'Daniel?' She looked genuinely surprised, her brow furrowed with a crease of incomprehension.

'There are some photographs here, in the envelope at the bottom. I found them after all the rest of the stuff; a head, feet. Numbers one to seven. Obviously photographic studies a painter might make of a model. Was Daniel one?'

Her brow cleared suddenly. 'Daniel Jacquet. Daniel . . . ah yes. There are photographs of him? I forgot –' She looked away quickly.

I had reached her side by this time and sat on the step a little distance from her.

'But you did know him?'

'Yes, I knew him, and Martin and of someone called Jojo. Yes, I knew them, boys from Sainte-Brigitte . . . not from the village, James was too cautious for that, of course. They posed for him. Yes, you could call them "models", I suppose. He was trying to alter his style at that time. I had sat for him many times – well, you have seen them – but he grew bored with the same face, and I was not very good at posing. I had other things to do anyway: the house, cooking . . .' She waved a hand vaguely towards the garden before us. 'And all this. He gave this up. After a time, when the glory and the dream began to fade.'

'And did it fade?'

'You know from his letter that it faded. Of course it faded. He was bereft.'

'And Daniel and Martin and whatever his name was . . .'

'Jojo,' she said quietly, her head down, picking with one finger the skin round her thumb-nail in a preoccupied manner.

'They helped him? They posed for him? I found no portraits up there – did he sell them?'

'They posed. He sold them all to an American man who has a large house in the forest on the edge of Saint-Basile, L'Hermitage. Sold them well. He was very occupied for some time with his "nudes".' She looked directly at me for the first time. 'He made a good deal of money. The American found his models for him, paid them a modest sum, enough to keep them in petrol for their motorcycles, you see . . . and hash, or gifts for their girls. They didn't mind, it was all just for money. The American, you see, liked young men. So he made James paint pictures.'

'Did he enjoy doing that?'

She looked away again, down across the land towards the gate, picking still at the skin round her thumb-nail. It had started to bleed.

'If you continue doing that,' I said, 'you'll have a very sore hand. Stop.'

'I'm sorry.' She stopped, put her thumb in her mouth, sucked it, spat. 'I didn't know I was doing it. How silly!'

'James . . .'

'He enjoyed that. Yes. A little bit, not too much, I think. He found it difficult in many ways, but it was good money. He never showed me anything he painted, so I was certain that he felt I would not, shall I say, care for the works. They were all for the American man. He even suggested the poses sometimes.'

'He was here? The American?'

'Oh no. Never! He drew little scribbles on paper and sent them by post. I found some in the studio when I was clearing it for Mr Aronovich from Cannes, you recall? The man who bought all the canvases for his hotel.'

'And?'

She looked at me again, the eyes clear, almost defiant. 'And? I destroyed them all, of course. They were not absolutely comme il faut, if you understand what I mean.'

'I do. And James?'

She leant against one of the iron supports of the vine over the terrace. 'James. You ask always about James.'

'I'm trying to discover what *happened* to him. Why did, as you said, the glory and the dream fade, what went wrong? Something cataclysmic, surely.'

She moved her head against the iron support, rubbing it like a calf against a tree, easing her neck and back, her eyes searching the garden and the sky.

'I think that the youths ... I think that he was quite excited when he was painting them. They would do anything for a little money, for the drugs, you know, for the petrol, for a new leather jacket ... *anything*. They were all in the studio. I never went there, I don't know what happened, but I can imagine. I can imagine a lot of things.'

'I'm sorry.' I felt invention was starting to creep into her story.

She shrugged, sat forward slowly, hands clasped on her knee. 'No need. Really no need. To be sorry, I mean. We had not been lovers for, oh, for some time. I cooked and washed and even posed for him sometimes. He had such terrible feelings of guilt and depression, he tried hard to come back, do you follow? But he could not ... I did the garden, picked the fruit, I made the jam, I did all the things a good wife should do. Except sleep with him. We never did again, you know? I shared his bed – we had only one as you have seen, surely? But I never shared his body, and he never took mine, after the first two years.'

I remembered the sadness and bewilderment in the portraits which I had seen in the studio and compared them with the calm, almost casual woman now at my side, her back against a pillar.

'But why on earth did you hang on, stay with him when you must have realized that everything was finished and done?'

'Because, foolish as it may seem to you, I loved him with all my heart. He was my life, there was no other life without him. As long as he needed me, even as a servant, sharing a barren bed with him, I would stay. It was impossible for me to leave him. I am certain that you will find that difficult to understand?'

'Not difficult, really. But foolish perhaps. However, finally you did go . . . so . . .'

She pushed her hand through her hair roughly, keeping the torn thumb clear of the fringe that fell about her forehead.

'Yes. Finally I did go. When I found the letter on the table, saw the ashes in the stove, the smashed palette in his studio, the mess and confusion there . . . I realized that he had gone for good, escaped, and that I had to accept my fate. Life, anyway, had become as worn and threadbare as an old slipper, we hardly spoke to each other, except perhaps for simple things like "The supper is ready" or "Do you want salad?" Nothing else.'

'But why! Why!'

She suddenly got to her feet, looked at her watch, straightened the belt of her cotton skirt. Briskly. 'We must go. I shall be late. You know all that I can tell you now.'

I remained seated on the step.

'Florence, I don't believe a word that you have told me. Oh, some, certainly, of your love – of *course* I believe that –

but the rest? No. I can't believe all that stuff about "models", as you call them. I knew James pretty well. Not closely, as you know, for we seldom saw each other, but I have known him since his birth – he was not the kind of man who could become "excited" by a few callow youths in the nude. I do not dispute that he painted a few pictures for some perverted American gentleman, but that would be for money, for no *other* reason – it was simply not in his character to be like that. Whatever had happened between you and himself, he would never in a million light years have become infatuated with a man or boy. Nothing could be further from possibility, whatever the circumstances.'

She stood looking down at me on my step, her eyes hard with anger, the grey iris in each beautiful eye hiding anxiety. When she spoke her voice was low. 'Sex', she said, 'has an odour.' She turned and crossed the terrace, entered the house.

I sat still for a moment, knowing, perfectly well, that she was still evading me, still dodging the true fact, embroidering the little clue which I had thrown her about the photographs of the wretched Daniel. I was equally certain that she was aware that I knew this, that she was frightened I'd pursue the conversation: things were to be left as they presently were as far as she was concerned. I would be told no more.

From the house I heard her calling me to come and help her with the shutters and in silence we closed the house, locked the door, and walked down the track to the car.

We drove back to the village in more or less polite, but extremely strained, silence, speaking only now and again about the beauty of the light, the traffic, and the fact that clouds were gathering above the cliffs. We avoided looking at each other.

We were both uneasy, uncomfortable. I because I felt certain that she had, somewhere along the line, started inventing things to deflect me from the truth, and she because, quite clearly, she knew that she had and that I was aware. The poor story of a possible change of sexual interest in James simply did not wash with me: for all his carelessness, his loucheness as a young man, for all his faults, and there were quite a number, that was not, and never could be, one of them. He would have been nauseated by such a thing. And even allowing for the fact that he was no longer a very young man, and could conceivably be going through some sort of traumatic experience with Florence, that is one direction which he would never have taken.

To leave, destroying everything, wrecking his life, disappearing into the air without any sense of responsibility, that indeed was easily understood because it was quite typical of James. But the rest, her story, was rubbish.

We got into Bargemon about four-thirty. I remember that the church bell struck the half-hour with its tinny tongue as she dropped me off at the hotel.

'I would ask you back, you know . . . but perhaps Mama is already there, they may have returned from the trip, it would be difficult . . .,' Florence said lamely, not looking at me, and I agreed, thanked her, and watched her drive round the square to 11 rue Émile Zola.

I went across the hotel terrace, past the painted menu-holder with the pink hands, and then discovered that I was still holding the envelope which I had promised to return.

Her green Renault was parked outside the house. The front door was shut – she had clearly been in a hurry to return. I opened the gate and crunched up the gravel path, rang the front-door bell, heard it clanging somewhere inside, and stood looking at the house opposite, private, shuttered, aloof like her own.

She opened the door suddenly; she must have only just entered the house. 'Yes? What is it?' Her voice was hurried, eyes anxious. There was a sound behind her which clearly distracted her attention; she held the door only half open.

I proffered the envelope. 'I forgot this. I'm sorry. You wanted it back.'

She reached out to take it, a word of murmured thanks forming on her lips when Annette's voice – I assumed it was Annette for I could not see her at that point – cried, 'Madame! Madame! Quick, quickly –'

Florence turned instantly, the envelope fell to the floor, and a small figure burst into the dim light of the banistered hallway. The door swung wide open as she bent down and swiftly grabbed the flailing, staggering creature, hoisted it up, held it hard against her on one hip.

She looked at me, a mixture of fear and defiance.

The child, for child it was, stuck pudgy little arms towards me. Its mongoloid head, flattened eyes, snub nose, mouthed odd sounds which sounded, in a spurt of bubbles, like 'Ppppf . . . Ppppf.' It struggled and wrestled for release, the head nodding, stubby arms and legs kicking, waving in one small clubbed fist a tin red and silver trumpet.

CHAPTER 5

I DODGED THE flailing trumpet, reached out for the child, took him from Florence and held him tightly to me. His broad face suddenly hooped in a huge smile, like a demented Hoti, a laughing Buddha, head nodding and swaying, little bubbles of mirth splattering into my face, the trumpet hitting my ear. He was suffused with joy, crowing with a wild high cry, spurting little cries of 'Pppf . . . Pfpppf'. Saliva dribbled down his chin and I wiped it with my hand.

'What's his name?'

'Thomas.'

She was stiff as a rod. Ashen. Behind her, frozen in a tableau, stood Annette and, halfway down the wide staircase, one hand on the banister, the other at her throat, Madame Prideaux.

'Thomas,' I said. 'I am your Uncle William.' And kissed him.

I handed him back to Florence. He struggled violently, banged wildly about with the trumpet, screamed in a high strangulated pitch, his face contorted with fury, and then mercifully, because Florence was finding him difficult to hold, Annette swooped into the battle like a small hawk and with an agonized look at me grabbed him up and carried his screaming, spluttering, jerking body off into the dark beyond the staircase.

Madame Prideaux moved down into the hall, touched Florence lightly on a shoulder, inclined her head gently to me.

'Shall we go and see my banana tree?'

In the conservatory she and Florence raised the rattan blinds and the spring sun flooded in. I remember all this as if it had happened in slow motion, like one of those films about natural history. Beans or sunflower seeds unfolding into life. The conservatory was obviously only used occasionally. For watering time.

Somewhere in the house the angry cries of Thomas were cut off with the firm shutting of a door and Madame Prideaux gestured vaguely to the scattered chairs. We all sat, rather as if we were attending the reading of a will. I felt slightly silly. Florence looked at her feet, hands clasped loosely in her lap, shoulders like a bottle. Resigned.

I began to try and apologize for my clumsy return to the house. Madame Prideaux cut in without waiting for me to finish.

'You were not to know. How, possibly? It was not right that you should know, but now that you do . . . well . . . you do. So, there is nothing to be done. The only fortunate thing is that children who are born with this condition do not often survive for long. Nature is finally merciful.'

Florence shook her head, pushed her hair about, smoothed the skirt over her thighs.

'It is not sure, Mama. Not certain.'

'Nothing is sure or certain in this life. You saw, Mr Colco, that he recognized you as his father? The trousers. Not a woman in skirts with whom he is surrounded all his life. He misses his father very much. All the more because his father rejected him. Children are like small animals: if you push a cat away it will always try to come to you. It's true.'

Florence looked up, smiled a wan smile.

'I'm glad that you know. I dislike, very much, being evasive, lying. It is a form of lying, isn't it? Everyone else knows, now you do too.'

'Yes. Now I know. I'm –'

She raised a hand gently. 'Don't try to be sympathetic. To apologize or something.'

'I really wasn't going to. I mean I am a parent. I can't pretend to know how you feel because it has never happened to me, but I can say how bitterly I am aware of your grief.'

She shook her head. 'Boff,' she said with an air of dismissal. 'Boff.'

Madame Prideaux rose heavily, stood with her hands on her hips looking across the conservatory through the windows, her eyes quite unfocused.

Florence said suddenly, 'That was rude of me. I apologize. But he's mine. I made him, I love him. So, there you are.'

Madame Prideaux slowly pulled her woollen cardigan down over her hips. 'One has to be firm with him, of course. He is very determined, stubborn, a terrible temper. Terrible!' She turned to look at Florence. 'True, my child? Eh? But wonderfully loving. When he feels like it. They all are, those children. Rage and love!'

The church clock struck five. Madame Prideaux lifted one hand and counted the hours off on her fingers with deliberation.

'Five o'clock. You would like a beer? We have some beer. Or perhaps tea. It is a perfect time for tea.' She was smiling at me suddenly. Head to one side, a kind, gentle, weary smile. Almost apologetic, strain draining away.

She left the conservatory after I had assured her that I wished for neither tea nor beer, and when the door closed Florence looked up at me.

'So,' she said. 'She has suffered, for me, more than I have suffered for myself. Her army training with my father sometimes forces her to deny her goodness, her fallibility. But . . .' She got up and wandered over to the aquarium, rippled the water with a finger. The fish swung about, rose to the surface, sped away. 'I tease them. Poor fish. Poor James. This was the situation which broke him finally. Broke him like a saucer shattered on a brick floor, a thousand fragments. What is the English nursery rhyme? "And all the king's horses, all the king's men . . ."?'

'"Couldn't put Humpty together again."'

'That's it. That was it.'

'And we don't know where any of those fragments are, do we, even if we could put them together again?'

She crossed her arms over her chest, a containing, very feminine gesture. Shook her head.

'No. Not at all. Gone.'

'I suppose, looking at things clearly, that Thomas is a fragment? Would you say that?'

'Yes. A fragment. And I know where it is.'

'Do you think that Thomas is the "punishment" he writes of in his last letter to you?'

She was instantly evasive again, pulled at a plant, turned a pot about in its saucer, small gestures to give her time to think. Or consider – there is, after all, a difference. And once she had decided on what to say she turned back to me.

'It's possible. I don't know.'

'For what? I mean why would he be punished? What did he do?'

'Perhaps, I don't know, for being too happy? He said that often – "I am too happy" – when we were working at Jericho, at the wall, or sitting by the fire in the evenings. Silly things. Happiness is composed of trivia, don't you think?'

'It can be. Yes.'

'You are married. You don't know?'

'It is not the happiest of marriages. I told you, we are separating.'

'And the children?'

I know that I laughed. I remember the flash of shock, I suppose, on her face. So I readjusted *my* face. It seemed a bit cracked. I mean the grin had to clear. It did.

'They really don't care much for me. I am at fault, not them. I write. I lock myself away, read, type, I get irritated. I suppose I am a bit unpredictable. Children hate that. They need security in a person; I don't give them that. Helen, my wife, does. She has sacrificed a career, as she so often tells me, for the family. I don't. I mean, haven't. I continue as I was. It really isn't fair. I see that now. Bad luck all round.'

She nodded absently, half listening, half elsewhere.

'I'm sorry. I mean for you all!' She laughed. 'Fragments everywhere in this life!' She made a definite, casual-seeming, yet quite determined, move towards the door. The interview, if that is what it had been, was at an end. I put out my hand to halt her.

'What I don't follow is this. Why was James the one to be "punished"? Why did he concern himself with his own punishment only? Not you? After all, you were together, so radiantly happy, the house, the land, the wall and all that tra-la-la. Yet he apparently has taken total blame on himself? Is that fair?'

She had almost reached the door but turned suddenly, her arms stiff beside her, fists clenched, face white, eyes blazing, her throat corded with anger.

'He was convinced, if you insist on this, he was convinced that it was physically his fault. Not mine. *He* was the father, *ergo*, he was the one responsible for the terrible deformity in his child. *His* genes were the cause. He was absolutely convinced that he had sown a malign seed within my body. Nothing would alter this fact. *He* was guilty. *That* is why he blamed himself.'

I stood perfectly still, shocked by her vehemence, the outrage in her voice, the tears which had sprung suddenly to her eyes.

'Forgive me. But, Florence, surely that is not medically so? Is it proven, does anyone really know?'

'Proven! Oh God! If anyone could tell me! If anyone would! My fault, his fault, the mama or the papa, who, *who* is culpable? No one knows for sure, no one will say for certain.' She wiped her cheek, her nose. The tears had spilled.

She opened the door and stood aside to let me pass first. In the hall a dumpy little woman in an apron seemed to appear from the darkness behind the stairs wiping her hands on a cloth. It was almost as if she had been summonsed. She bobbed lightly, opened the front door.

Late sunlight glanced and glinted on glass and brass, on the polished banister, faded Persian rugs. A tall plume of pampas grass trembled in the draught.

Florence stood leaning against the door-jamb, arms folded, looking out into the quiet street, avoiding me.

'In any case,' she said, 'what does it matter whose fault it was? His or mine. The child was made. I kept him, I love him, and James is dead.'

'There is one small thing,' I said.

She looked at me, face quite drained, tears dried.

'What?'

'Is he dead? Are you certain? Do we know?'

She turned away, shrugged lightly. 'I know,' she said, 'and that is all that matters. In my heart I know.'

'But there is no proof, Florence. No proof, is there?'

She stood upright and moved back into the hall, one hand on the door. 'No proof. No. Goodbye. There is nothing more to say.'

I felt profoundly miserable walking back to the hotel. All that I had managed to do by my error in returning the envelope in haste, and without having the tact to merely shove it through the letter box, was to cause infinite distress in this small fortress which had so long sought to keep the invader at bay. I had assaulted the sanctity of a family's private grief.

I remembered the grey eyes full of pain, the welling tears, and knew that I had been responsible. But, I reasoned, after all, it was my family as well. James, even if we were not particularly close, was my brother. My blood was at stake here if he was responsible. Did the 'monstrousness' course in all our bodies? Imponderable. But I was not a complete outsider, married or not. Thomas was a Caldicott whatever name they chose to attach to him.

She had said, 'There is nothing more to say.' She was right.

For the time being.

Madame Mazine handed me my key, and a postcard, when I got back to the hotel. Her face was perhaps a little less disinterested than usual and she asked me, with civility, how long I intended to stay. Did I know yet? There was absolutely no urgency, it was just a matter of bookings made ahead and I remembered, she supposed, that May had already begun?

'I think two or three weeks. Would that be possible? The last week of May?'

'Perfectly.' She scribbled something on a paper before her. 'After the 26th of May I would have to move you. An old client always comes then; he has your room. He walks a great deal, and he likes the peace in that room.'

'I understand perfectly. Let us say until the 26th?'

'It is noted. Thank you. You will dine in the hotel tonight?'

'That is so, Madame.'

The postcard was of Milton's Cottage – from the children. They were both having a lovely time. Hoped I was well. There was a scribbled line from Helen. Sleeping and eating. Utter bliss. No love. Just signed 'H'.

There was no reason to suppose that she would have sent love. She had made it perfectly clear that she had none to offer. So why, sitting in my really fairly wretched, if perfectly adequate, little room, did I suddenly feel the need of comforting? Why did I feel a very small pinch – not a stab, that would be far too strong a word – but a pinch of regret?

The evening light waned in the sky. Small clouds, a swoop of starlings, the napkins on the line below in the garden flapping in a breeze I could neither feel nor hear. It was rather as if I was being 'kept in' after school. A perfectly ridiculous feeling of being, as it were, penalized for some misdemeanour. Alone in the classroom. Five hundred lines to write in copperplate. A chunk of Wordsworth. Adding and subtracting, long division, LCD. School stuff. I hadn't felt like it before. Irrational.

Perhaps it came about because we had been talking of family, blood, marriage, fragments, time lost and, it would seem, little gained. A lonely sensation. And then this postcard. 'Having a lovely time with Gran.' 'Utter bliss!' No one needed me.

I lay on the Napoleon bed, hands behind my head, staring at the kittens and goldfish.

Just remember: the kids had sent *you* that card. Not the other way round. I hadn't sent a thought their way. They were my responsibility just as much as they were Helen's. Only, it would appear, that she loved them rather more than I did. Well, give or take a friendly cuff, an absent-minded goodnight kiss, I'd never shown them any form of paternal love, never been what you might call a ball of fire on the holidays we had. I mean, I didn't go in for the sandcastle bit, or exploring walks in woods or over rocks. I don't remember that I ever even took them shrimping, or to sail a boat, or to look for crabs in rockpools.

James had once been part of a family which went looking for crabs in rockpools.

There was a photograph to prove it.

I couldn't really think exactly where I had gone wrong, or why. Just that I had. And that today, and the day before today, had rather cleared off the varnish, so to speak. I suddenly saw the real portrait of me under the layers of dusty indifference. I *did* care, of course I did, but in an abstract way. One had children, the mother brought them up and that was that. I had thought.

But just supposing that one of the children – Annie, Giles – had been born like Thomas. What then? Unbearable to contemplate. But quite possible, if James's theory that the fault lay in his genes, his chromosomes, was right. It could be in the Caldicott strain, I could have been responsible myself.

It was strange, in a way, how Thomas had so deliberately reached out towards me and how easily I responded. He needed, and recognized, a father-figure. Obviously. Madame Prideaux had said that he had been rejected by James. Disabled or not he was perfectly capable of recognizing the image he wanted, and he wanted a father. A boy needs a father. They always say so. A boy needs a father every bit as much as he needs a mother. It is the normal, natural, perfect balance.

Had I ever needed? Or Elspeth?

Never. We were both idolized to the edge of over-indulgence by two adoring parents who had planned the Perfect Family. Until James arrived it worked. But by that time I was no longer dependent on paternal love.

So here I presently was, stuck in a small hotel room in some remote village in France I'd never even heard of, coming to terms with, and accepting the affection of, my brother's rejected child Thomas. And what about my own flesh and blood? Giles? Had *he* reached out to me, metaphorically, and found rejection? I didn't think so. He was a happy child, loved in a vague sister way by Annie, loved by his mother. Whatever one said about Helen she was not a bad mother. Amazingly, considering her own past, she was a devoted, caring, firm and loving mother. I suppose it was me who did the neglecting. Admit that. My job, however, was not a nine till five deal. Certainly, one sat at a desk for hours until the capricious muse decided to arrive, but research means reading a damn library of stuff, trailing about to talk to people, see places, taking notes. Like a detective. You get stuck in a room with a typewriter, books and papers. The gestation period is hell, the working period worse. Surfacing for meals, for example, I was usually preoccupied. Thinking. Half my mind was wandering about somewhere else. I was, during that time, intolerant of noise. Banging doors, laughter, dogs barking, shouts of pleasure, the Rolling Stones, beat music or anything at all on television.

A sod to live with, Helen said. Helen was right. I admit that. Why, if I appeared uncaring of my own children, was I apparently so good with other people's? I had a splendid reputation for my avuncular benevolence. 'The children adore it when William is here!' This, with reason, usually drew a look of smouldering resentment from Helen. Why great with other people's kids and not the home-grown variety? Why? Lack of responsibility? Showing off? Guilt? Possible. Helen, in time, had erected a subtle barrier between herself, the kids and me. With true concern at first: *'Don't make so much row, darling. Think of Daddy, he's having a difficult day.'* Later the admonishments grew terser, colder, irritable. *'Don't bang about, for God's sake!'* Gradually I felt the coolness of her icy disdain as it grew, frankly, into dislike. *'Your father is not just sitting in a heap. Not sulking. Thinking. He says.'*

That was slung around pretty often, so I kept out of the way. And then the children pulled away. Why not? I'm not a bit proud of the fact. It just happened. I state this in all humility so that you will remember what I have said later. Annie was all right. She and Helen were like sisters. Whispering, giggling, having secrets. I didn't figure in her life. Giles? He was a very contented child. Read a great deal, nose in a book all the time, scribbled a bit too. He had his mice, rats, tree-frogs, lizards, and so on. Contented, I'd say. Helen filled any gap I might have caused. Unwittingly. Giles had never asked to be born. He was a desperate attempt to save a failing marriage.

Poor Giles. Perhaps *he* made me feel guilty? I was far more at ease with Thomas than my own child. An uncomfortable feeling. Odd.

Well, well. Great, old boy. But too bloody late now to reassess your life and misdemeanours.

My two families – that is to say, that one which I came with and the one which I made all-by-myself-no-hands – were really a couple of self-destruct units.

Consider: on the one hand, Ma and Pa, Elpie and James and me. On the other, me, followed by Helen, followed by a gloriously impetuous surge of lust which produced, in time, Annie, and followed, a bit later when the brasses began to tarnish, by the poor old bicycle patch, the effort at a 'quick mend', Giles.

And Bob's your uncle.

The light, as light does, had begun to fade. The room was growing dark. A thin red line, like a skein of scarlet silk, crept across the blush in the sky of the after-light. The day died as I watched.

A saffron sky, one star bright and hard above the branches of a tree, like a mourning frame, frilled with motionless ebony leaves.

I was here, I reminded myself, not to wallow in self, but for one quite simple reason. To find James, if possible, and to restore him to his wife.

Florence.

Just you remember that. I said it aloud to confirm determination.

Florence . . .

CHAPTER 6

THE BAR WAS fairly quiet, it was still early and the men had not come in from the fields or wherever they worked. The same gaggle of youths were banging about at the pinball table, laughing, jostling. A couple of men at the bar. The television flickering on its shelf, the sound off – a cartoon, a mouse chased by a cat.

I took my Scotch across to the corner table. The tourist couple from Paris were either not down yet or had left.

Under the glass tabletop the map looked tattier than it had yesterday, and Saint-Basile still fell off the edge. The man behind the bar, bald, shirt sleeves, cigarette butt stuck at the corner of his mouth, made some remark which caused a laugh, lifted the flap of his counter and came across to turn up the volume on the TV.

'The news,' he said.

A sudden howling crash of cymbals and trumpets, a station logo, and a woman speaking, with crimson lips.

No one paid any attention, then one of the men at the bar half turned and I saw that it was Maurice from the taxi. His companion looked vaguely over his shoulder and away again; the world could explode as far as he, and the youths at the pinball table, were concerned.

The barman stood beside me, looking up, a dirty cloth in his hand, the cigarette butt switching thoughtfully from side to side of his mouth.

A cow and cud.

Then the sports news and a shout from the youths, the room was silent and attentive. Famine could reap its harvest, guns recoil, students leap barricades, flames roar from high windows and the only thing which held anyone's attention was the sight of one thickhead kicking a ball at another thickhead. They cheered, pounded their fists in the air, embraced each other.

A final jingle of music and a météo summary for the region and the barman switched off the sound.

'Lille won. Three nil.'

I followed him over to the bar, ordered another drink and nodded to Maurice. I asked him as we stood drinking if he could tell me where to rent a car for a few weeks.

'A few weeks? How many?'

'Two or three. I'd like to drive around, have a look at the land.'

He shrugged. Sipped his Ricard, suggested, politely, that this was not Nice or Cannes. There was no Hertz or Avis in Bargemon.

He pushed his cap to the back of his head with a thumb.

'A Simca Brake?' He suddenly made a suggestion. 'My brother-in-law has one. He's in the clinic for a time. Perhaps he would rent it? Last year's model, good condition.'

'You think that he would?'

'I can ask him. You have a licence, of course.'

'Of course.'

'In France it is not permitted for a foreigner to drive someone's car.'

'Ah. I see.'

He shrugged. 'We can fix that. You see. A week or two?'

'Maybe three. Just to use in the area; not to drive to the coast or miles away.'

'Where you go is not my concern if I don't see you. Eh? You would like to do a deal?'

'When you ask your brother-in-law.'

'He'll agree. Money in the hand is worth more than a Simca in the garage.'

We made a deal; I handed over a week's rental in advance, ordered drinks, the atmosphere became convivial. Maurice said that I could come to his house – he gave me the address – after noon the next day.

'The car must be cleaned up. Dusty. The seats. I'll fill her up for you.'

His brother-in-law had been in the clinic for two weeks, no one knew what was wrong. But the car needed a good cleaning, the tyres were new this season. I'd need them if I wanted to go to Saint-Baume to see the cave of Mary Magdalene.

I wasn't absolutely dead set on seeing Mary Magdalene's cave, but knew it was wiser to show interest.

'Ah yes.' Maurice was beginning to enjoy himself. 'She went to this cave to rid herself of her sins. Thirty-three years she was there! Hey! It is a very holy place, the roads are winding about like a mad serpent. But there is a fine view. You must visit the grotto.'

I suggested that all this area must be a very holy one; full of many strange things. The land was savage, secret. One could get lost here for ever.

Maurice's companion agreed cheerfully. He explained that the road was not only zig-zagging but was dangerous. Seven hundred metres high! People could fall from that height! They could die from exposure! Easy.

I said that I would start off doing little trips, local ones so that I would not get lost or climb too high. I wanted to see the forest at Saint-Basile-les-Pins. That was not so far?

Maurice finished his drink, but I did not offer another, and he agreed that it wasn't far, twenty kilometres about, but there was nothing to see there unless one liked trees.

After dinner among the roses and the trellis, and the heads of the small beasts, I wrote Florence a note on a postcard of the hotel, asking her if she could meet me the next afternoon at Jericho, about four. I said it was extremely urgent, that I'd wait until dusk there for her.

Later, before a last drink in the bar, I walked down to her house and put the card, in an envelope, through the letterbox. I did not expect her to come at such short notice, perhaps not to come anyway, notice or not. But nothing ventured, nothing gained. I had questions to ask which only she could answer.

If so she chose.

I found Saint-Basile-les-Pins in the green Michelin tourist guide which Madame Mazine loaned me with a pleasant smile. It was, as Maurice had said, about twenty kilometres away. A camping-site and extensive views, three pointed little trees indicated woodland near by. There was a ruined chapel, sixteenth-century, in the park of L'Hermitage. A Resistance memorial, 1940–44. No visit.

I had a final Scotch in the bar, which was almost empty by this time, returned the Michelin to Madame Mazine and said that I would not be in for luncheon the next day.

Florence was less timid than Maurice had been. She forced her green Renault up the track almost to the gate of the house and jerked to a stop in a rather lop-sided fashion. It was half-past three, earlier than I had suggested. Annette got out first, then Florence and, from the back, the dumpy young woman I'd seen in the hall, holding Thomas.

I was on the terrace, sitting on one of the little tin chairs as they came up towards me, Thomas wobbling, pointing, lolling his head about in apparent delight. The dumpy woman held him fast. Florence waved; a slight gesture as if she had brushed aside a bee.

'We are early, I did not think you would be here yet. I brought Thomas, you see? He loves the garden.' She took his other hand and, with the dumpy woman, came up through the abandoned garden, past the dead cabbage stalks.

A bird suddenly spiralled up from the tumbled grasses and Thomas screamed with excitement. When he saw me, which he did as soon as he had got to the terrace under the thrusting vine, he tugged at the hands which held him, and as I went towards him Florence let him go and he and I and the dumpy woman collided lightly. His arms went round my legs and held me tightly; he had wrenched himself away from restraint.

Florence said, 'This is Céleste. She looks after Thomas.'

Céleste nodded towards me, and started to prise Thomas away from my legs, so I lifted him up, and held him. He was spitting and laughing and crying, 'Pfffp!', which appeared to be his short-hand word for Papa.

Annette was standing a little way off. Watching. Polite, anxious. There if needed. I called a greeting, and she raised a hand in salute.

Florence took the second little chair, asked me to release Thomas and let him go back to Céleste and Annette, and told them to go and see the garden.

'I wanted you to come because I have things to ask you,' I said.

'What things?'

'Oh. Many. I have rented a car. From Maurice. His brother-in-law.'

Florence laughed softly. 'The Mayor's car! Goodness . . . he's ill.'

'Correct. I went over to Saint-Basile-les-Pins, to find L'Hermitage.'

She looked at me without curiosity. 'Why?'

'I thought that perhaps the American you spoke of, who

lives there, might have an idea where James has gone to. Or even why perhaps? You know . . .?'

She shook her head slowly. 'No. Why? Because he commissioned some ugly paintings?'

'You never saw them, you said. *Were* they ugly?'

'I don't know. I just . . .' She picked up a dead leaf and began to shred it carefully. 'Just had an idea they would be.'

'How did James come to know the American?'

'He was working for Aronovich, the hotel owner in Cannes, and he introduced them, I think. James didn't really tell me much. I *think* it was like that.'

'When will Aronovich collect all those canvases upstairs? Does he know they are ready?'

She sighed, screwed the pieces of leaf into a tiny ball and dropped them. 'Yes. He knows. But the hotel is not ready. The pictures are but the walls are not. I think there is a problem with money. The usual thing.'

'Does he know that you have moved away, the house is empty?'

'I have written. All the mail that came here, and there never was much anyway, is redirected to rue Émile Zola. You know? Bank statements, things like that. But the bank knows anyway. James made everything over to me for Thomas. You knew that?'

'I know that. How did James meet Aronovich? Can you tell me?'

Florence shook her head in disbelief, a small smile on her lips. 'You are Mister Maigret! So many questions.'

'There are so many questions, Florence. If I can try to trace James, I will. I'll have to talk to the people he knew and you did not. You see?'

'I see. He met Aronovich years ago. When he was living in Paris. Before here. Before me. Before Jericho.'

I could see Annette and Céleste, Thomas pulling hard

between them, coming slowly towards us through the little orchard.

Florence sat up, shielding her eyes from the westering sun. 'Did you find L'Hermitage?'

'Eventually. It's very isolated. Do you know it?'

'No. I never knew it. I think I have to take Thomas home. He'll tire.'

'The next time I go, I'll call at the lodge; there is a little house inside the gates. Very impressive. Locked with a chain. And there were dogs . . .'

Florence got up and started to walk towards the straining child and his guardians. 'Did you also see Snow White perhaps?' She was smiling, so I knew it was not a rebuff. For the moment.

'Not Snow White,' I called, 'but a very odd person. Perhaps the witch, she had an eye-patch.'

'And wore a tall black hat? Eh?' She stooped, said something to the two women, lifted Thomas and walked back towards me. His arms were outstretched imploringly.

'You have made a conquest,' she said.

I took Thomas from her and sat him firmly on my knee. He switched round and stared up at me, the smile, like a melon-slice, cut across his wide, bland face, and then he settled himself hard against my chest, stuck his thumb in his mouth, swung a leg idly.

Florence sat in the little chair again. 'You see. A conquest.'

Annette and Céleste stood at the edge of the terrace smiling a little uncertainly. I smiled back, doing my best to dispel their anxiety.

'A conquest,' I said, rather foolishly.

'It's so strange. Never with James, you know. He never did that with James. James disliked any form of . . . ugliness? I can use that word? He wouldn't touch a dead bird. Sometimes the hunters maimed one – you know? – in the autumn.

But he would never touch it. Or a dead frog or lizard, nothing dead.'

'Thomas wasn't dead. Very much alive.'

'But ugly. You would say? Deformed. Imperfect. James disliked that.'

'I never knew, but then I never knew him.'

'In that photograph. Remember, the one on the beach, with the crab? He looked so funny, but really he disliked it very much. The crab. It was dead. He only cared for life; and beauty was life.'

'He told you that?'

Florence sat forward, chin in her hands, a slight smile on her lips. 'Yes. Often.' She put out her hand and touched the child sitting on my knee. 'Poor Thomas. What a shock you were. What a terrible blow! He is so calm. I have never seen him sit with anyone like this before . . . well, Annette from time to time, sometimes Céleste. You must have the touch!'

'I was thinking, not so long ago, just how bloody I have been to my two. I'm pretty awful with children: I don't like them much. I felt swamped with guilt the other evening. Perhaps this is making amends? You think so?'

'I don't know. I do know you are making him happy. He has spent much of his short life being rejected. I can only imagine that he wanted this security. He gets it from us, of course, the women, but you are the first stranger to offer him . . . love, I suppose?'

'Yes. That'll do.'

She rose, began to brush her skirt full of crumpled leaf, called to the two women, who had settled like a pair of frogs on a fallen log. Thomas started to wrestle and cry out when she reached, firmly, for him, and it took all our combined strengths, Annette's and mine, to shove him into the car. His howls made further conversation impossible, but I managed to yell to Florence that I had decided to move into the house.

She heard me clearly, for she looked startled, turned on the ignition, and called out, 'Jericho? Here? You are crazy.'

'Thought it out. Carefully. This afternoon.'

She was reversing the car slowly and badly, hit the wall lightly, swung round to face down the track. I walked beside the car, my hand on her door.

'It's impossible.'

'James paid up for three years? Right?'

'You talk to Mama, it's nothing to do with me.'

And she began to bump slowly away, the furious cries from Thomas growing fainter.

I walked back to the terrace. Over in the orchard a pear tree had broken into white blossom. The buds on the vine were fat and bursting into leaf; it had not been pruned for a season. I snapped off a twig and the sap began to bleed. There would be a lot to do. I had better, I thought, make a start.

Before her a tray of little brass things, a bell, a fish, some small ashtrays, an inkwell. Madame Prideaux was doing what she called the monthly cleaning.

'I don't know why I bother. These things are never used, they are things my husband bought in North Africa. And I hate dull brass, don't you?' She was buffing away with an old toothbrush; her hair, normally very severely caught up in a sort of loaf on the top of her head, had begun to fall in grey wisps with the efforts of her work.

'It is true that James has paid for three more years, equally true that the money is necessary. For Thomas, for this and that. But it would appear to me a capricious thing to do, to reopen the house. Why? A whim? You have a family, a house of your own elsewhere? Why come here? It is hopeless with no telephone, it has been empty for months.'

'I will manage. I will take all the responsibility, if you will permit me to take on my brother's lease.'

Madame Prideaux took up a yellow duster and started polishing, quite unnecessarily hard. 'I have no objections. The house is mine, yes, but I think you should perhaps ask Florence.'

'She told me to ask you.'

'She thinks you are mad. You know that?'

'I know that. I know too that I am starting divorce proceedings with my wife, amicably, that I shall sell up my house in London, that I am a writer and that writers can write almost anywhere. As long as there is peace. Silence.'

She looked at the inkwell critically, fiddled with its lid. 'If you wish. It is for you to decide. But I will not be responsible for anything.'

'Anything? What kind of anything?'

She set the inkwell down, picked up the bell.

'Oh. The drains, damp, electricity, woodworm . . . I will not be your landlord. It is entirely your responsibility. Florence has the documents, she will show you everything. If she agrees, that is.'

Florence agreed. We sat for a time together in the conservatory and talked it out carefully. I could see a stirring of interest and a desire to help behind her natural caution. I explained that all it meant was that I would take over James's responsibilities, as they applied to the house, set it to rights, get the garden into shape, that she could come at any time with Thomas, and remove anything from the place that she wished. After a little thought she said, very simply, that she thought the bed should be removed. Nothing else had any value, but the bed, valueless, held intense unhappiness. She'd remove that.

I took that suggestion to mean that she had agreed to my occupation of Jericho.

I think that the thing which finally swayed her to agree to my rather impetuous idea was that I had pointed out, quietly and firmly, that the very best place from which to start operations to find out what had happened to James, or where he had gone, was to be in the centre of it all. I would be able to move about the countryside, speak to people, talk to, for example, Mr Aronovich, or go over to L'Hermitage and try to find out if anyone there had any knowledge which could be useful. To be sure, people did just disappear; it was very much a commonplace situation, people just dropped out, and it would seem that James had reasons. Anyway, as far as he was concerned.

Talking together like this, she seemed to grow stronger: there was a surge of interest in her which I had not seen before, and when she saw me to the front door her eyes had a light they had lacked in the past. There was a sort of complicity between us. I could feel it – I know that she did – and when we heard Madame Prideaux calling from some far region of the house, she was not startled, but smiled, and placed a hand on mine and told me that I was completely idiotic. But we could make it work.

Of course I knew then exactly how much I had bitten off. I was not absolutely certain that I would be able to chew it, as they say, but at least I knew what could be, not definitely, not for certain, but what could be ahead. Helen had to be talked to; the children . . . They now seemed to be a little more important than they had been to me before, and the Parsons Green three-floors had to be dumped as soon as possible. The sooner I got the place sold, the sooner my family had no roof over their heads, the sooner they got used to the idea that I had gone, if you like, for ever, then the better. At forty-seven I could see a new life ahead for myself. Uncluttered, calm. I could start out again.

One doesn't get second chances all that often. Cross out the pages, turn them, start again under a new heading. I had three years ahead at Jericho, perhaps more, who could tell? I suddenly felt twenty, not forty-seven. I knew perfectly well that what had been done had been done and would remain for good, for the rest of my life. Annie and Giles, Helen, I would not be able to quite escape them. I was responsible after all. Even if unloved. I would behave absolutely honourably. Do all in my power to help them. Apart from living their lives with them. That was out.

It is, I admit, quite difficult to burn down your bridges with one box of matches; but no harm in trying. Burnt fingers for sure, but take the risk anyway.

What I did not tell Florence was that at L'Hermitage I did, indeed, see a rather odd lady with an eye-patch, an American lady. The accent was chop-able, not cut-able. And she called through the locked gates, 'Bugger off. Mr Millar never sees his fans. Would you please go.'

I got back into the car and, just as I did so, a half-naked young man, wearing wellingtons and a pair of indecently short shorts, came round the side of the little lodge. He had a mass of dark curly hair, a rake over his shoulder. The woman said something to him and he turned to me, legs apart, thighs like tree trunks, and waved the rake in anger.

I waved back; the woman stopped, picked up a handful of gravel, threw it with force through the gate. The dark boy laughed, shook the rake again.

I knew that he was Daniel.

CHAPTER 7

THE DINING-ROOM was busier that evening. The Season, so it would seem, was upon us. There were two hefty Dutch people at one table, blond, fat, in sensible clothes, gobbling – not so much the food as words, poring at a map. Beside them a solitary man, probably a traveller in agricultural products, reading a paper slanted against his Evian bottle, wearily crumbling bread crumbs. And the couple from Paris were back again, silently eating, slowly, precisely, looking towards each other now and again for approbation, rather as if they were making a mosaic or laying out a jigsaw puzzle. Their intense concentration on a fairly tough guinea-fowl in a thick red wine sauce irritated me. Quite unreasonably. But I was, I remember very well, in an unreasonable frame of mind.

I felt odd. Jagged, fragmented, restless. Strange for me. I don't lose my marbles easily. Rather too tame sometimes. Reasonable usually. Dull. Helen said. Probably rightly.

Eugène had suggested what I should eat and I had agreed and asked him to bring me a suitable wine. He did. I drank half, more than half actually, of the bottle but still felt grotty.

I thought that a decent claret would soothe, or set at ease, my restlessness, but it did not. So I went off to the bar and had a large brandy; that made it worse. Or made me worse. I rather think it stimulated more than soothed. I still felt uneasy, un-tired. Wretched. Of course, what I was doing really was trying to delay the moment when I would have to go up to my little room with its bleeding heart Jesus and the kittens and the lumpy bed. I would be stuck in there and forced to think things out. The best way to think things out would be to walk.

That is what I did. The little town was dead. No one moved. There were shaded lights here and there slitting through shutters, a cat ran across my path, a thin shadow. There was a light, fresh, clear wind. The fresh air of height, not low-lying air.

Now, where was I? I had been sent a key. Correct. I was presently in the deserted streets of a small French village. I had decided to take over the lease of my brother's house. For three years. My *missing* brother. Whom I had determined to try and find. Somehow.

So far those facts were clear.

My life in London, fixed permanently I'd always thought, was now at an end. I was facing a new start. Hence my irritation, my imbalance, my ragged feeling.

I found myself at the top of rue Émile Zola, the end nearest the square and the church which, at that exact moment, struck the half-hour. Ten-thirty. Across the square the signboard of the hotel suddenly went black as the lights were switched off. I stood alone on the cobbles, a little breeze riffled past, caught a paper wrapping on the street, danced it into a spiral, let it fall.

Down the street, beyond the lilac hedge of No. 11, a light glowed through the white lace curtains at an upper window.

It could have been her window.

Or Madame Prideaux's. Or the child's.

A gathering of folds suggested birds and leaves.

Would she have a room facing on to the street? I didn't know.

But, quite suddenly, I was calm and collected. Clear-headed. It was as if a sudden violent temperature had dropped away. I felt perfectly fine, high-hearted, ready for anything ahead, no confusions, no restlessness. I would cope perfectly well.

After all, in my dull way, I always had. Never spectacular, just safe. It is amazing how swiftly, how suddenly indeed, one can alter; it seemed to me that there were no problems at all.

And I suddenly knew (with only very slight misgivings) that I was in love.

Simple. Could it be? It could. And it was so. What *she* thought of the idea was, of course, not for me even to guess about. But for the moment I knew what *I* thought about things and I liked what I thought very much.

But, those things, looking up at a lamp-lit window and being in love, don't happen like that. Ah! But they do. Love of that kind, the sudden, swiping, heart-stopping joy of it all, does happen. Like instant coffee.

I wandered back to the hotel, making the glorious moment of discovery last as long as I could. It was such a towering feeling, exalted. Idiotic. Hands in my pockets, scuffing the cobbles, almost whistling, like a just-released schoolboy, I went across the little terrace of the hotel, past the potted laurels and the pink-faced chef, his pinned-on menu flapping and twisting in the slight breeze, and to delay my rendezvous with the bleeding-heart Jesus and the kittens I went to the bar for a final drink.

There were two slightly drunken men leaning on the bar prodding through their wallets for something. The barman poured me a generous brandy. I looked across the smoked room.

The Dutch were at a table folding up a map, still gobbling,

the Paris couple were leaving, he checking his pockets vaguely for glasses, she pulling down the jacket of her tweed suit. They nodded goodnight to the barman who, at that moment, switched off the neon strip light, leaving one hanging lamp to blare coldly from the ceiling.

I asked him, cupping my glass in my hands, if he had ever heard of a Monsieur Millar living at L'Hermitage in Saint-Basile. He corrected me politely as he wiped down his Formica-topped bar with a dirty cloth and said that Saint-Basile-les-Pins was where I meant; he knew of a Millar at L'Hermitage but had never seen him. He said that there was a woman called Millar who sometimes came into the village on Thursdays – market day – but they were really not known in Bargemon. They belonged across the valley in the forest area.

I took my key from Madame Mazine. The Dutch had caught me up. I said I'd be out for lunch the next day, and asked for my coffee at seven-thirty.

The light from the elephant-lamp was over-bright, but I felt extremely happy, undressed, washed my face and did my teeth, had a pee in the swirling water, and got into bed; wriggled about in the lumps and in a moment or so found a small valley and settled down to sleep.

Which, of course, I did not.

I suppose that I might have gone off into a deep sleep for about half an hour, not more, and then shatteringly, blindingly, I was wide awake again. Alert, filled with fear, a sort of creeping terror which slid into my veins and suffused my entire being.

I switched on the elephant-lamp and lay staring up at the damp-marks on the blotchy ceiling.

I felt like a child at a pantomime who, while contentedly watching the fairy grotto behind the rose-petalled gauze, suddenly sees it ripped to shreds and blown into ragged tatters before his very eyes to have revealed before him a hideous black landscape of writhen trees, towering crags and wheeling ravens.

The land of the wizards and witches lay before me. Sulphur trailed in the air, silent lightning forked into the dark chasms. There was no thunder. Silence, fear.

The reason for this? Reason a-plenty, for no wizard, no witch, stood dead centre in this evil scene. Glowing, with the force of atomic light, stood a white and gold creature, so brilliant, so dazzling, that a great aura of light trembled all about it, giving the impression that the figure was imprisoned in a gigantic white and gold sea anemone, a surging, pulsing, weaving halo of evil.

It was James.

Love had not awakened me; but fear had. I knew, I suppose for the very first time, that something which I had suppressed all my life had quite suddenly broken through my years of restraint and reserve. As certainly as I knew that I had fallen in love with Florence, I knew that I hated – and always had done – James. The years of envy, of jealousy, of simple dislike and mistrust, had, like the flesh of the oyster, absorbed the grain of sand, the symbol in my case for hate, and had turned it into the pearl of indifference, casualness, apparent brotherly love. Uninterested, remote, but agreeable when called upon to be so.

The lace-curtained window had suddenly released demons in me, had given me strength, the strength to take from him that which had been his. That which he had so cruelly used. I could, and I would, make up to Florence for the brutality of his malign seed. By taking over his shirked responsibility, the monstrous lolling head, the bewilderment of a deserted, not-even-married woman who had loved unheeded. He had gone of his own volition, so let it rest there. Let him go. Why bother to search for him? To question and to look? In time, for time will heal, he will be a memory, and I would do all I could do to redress the pain and the distress.

Why had it taken so long to come to terms with this fact? I suppose that up until now I had occupied myself with forging a life for myself. Helen, children, my writing – he had not been a part of that life of mine. We only came into contact in our early youth at home. From the moment that James was born it was clear that he had taken his place centre stage and I was edged gently, with perfect kindness, to the side. Elpie worshipped the creature of gold, with grey eyes, my mother basked in the amazement of this late gift from God. Or, as she sometimes was heard to say in a voice which always made me ill with dislike of her, this 'gift from the fairies'.

Well, there he was. The centre of an academic middle-class family which had thought that the life forged for it was suitable, comfortable and placid. Suddenly a golden glory had arrived, and everything changed.

Just as Helen had decided that enough was enough, that love had finally rotted past repair, so I fled the smugness of a family worshipping its golden calf. I was free.

I swung myself out of the lumpy bed, sat on the edge, legs swinging.

Nightmares. Brought on by heavy wine, heavier guinea-fowl, cheese and more brandy than was wise.

But even so, the fact of hatred could not be dismissed. Nor, indeed, could the fact of love. The two things together were naturally indigestible. It was so absurdly late to discover either of these in my usually stable self.

Was it a physical love for Florence? Hardly. She was not sexually a very exciting proposition. Calm, clear-eyed, loyal, but not sexually attractive. Perfectly all right. And I was in love. The very thought of her brought me intense pleasure. The remembrance of the soft down on her bare forearm, the gentle greyness of her eyes, the sudden gleam of joy which could light them like a candle flame in an abandoned room, the laugh, half mocking, half delighted: wholly intriguing.

She was altogether intriguing. That she was hiding secrets was pretty evident; that she knew a good deal more than she was letting on I was quite certain. James would never have lost his head over a perfectly ordinary country-army-provincial-town girl. She would have to have had a bit more going for her to attract him. He was an odd fish. Savage, swift, sleek, secret. What then had attracted him? The same quality, I could only suppose, which had attracted me to her.

But – and I had to get up and start wandering about the small room to sort this out – the sudden realization that I actually was capable of hatred, and hatred of my own brother, rather winded me. The strange dream, vision, what you will, of the golden figure standing among the blackness and the storm disturbed me greatly. For the first time in my life I had become aware of the darkness which was a part of that carefree, golden, adored creature.

All was not as I had imagined. My resentment started from the moment that I had, at the age of – what? – twelve, thereabouts, first seen Elpie coming towards me carrying this raw, crumpled creature, fists flailing, mouth wide in toothless fury, silent, wobbling head supported by her hand.

Watching Elpie, my late beloved sister, cradling and cooing over the ewe lamb made me weak with anger. But hate? I was never remotely aware. I always considered myself to be a reasonable, sensible, evenly balanced person. It shattered me to discover that I had been growing a tumour unawares, and that now the poison had made itself manifest, and it was out in the open.

A relief in fact. I felt stronger for the knowledge that I could be positive. For if anything else, hate is a positive reaction, and one that I had never considered before.

Standing at the window, looking down into the night, over the backyard, across the drying-line to the shadowed cliffs, I realized that I had at last come of age. All the emotions were mine now. I had gone through life like an unfinished crossword. Perfectly all right, almost complete, until you took a good look and saw the blank. Only four letters.

Hate.

I just thought you should know that.

I did, eventually, get some sleep, awakened only, at first light, by the cockerel in the yard. Nightmares, as you probably know, have a very happy tendency to dissolve almost on waking. For a moment one lies in shaking horror, and then, with almost a cry of relief, one realizes that it was 'only a dream'. Well, mine had faded a good deal. Almost nothing remained of chasms, ravens and towering crags. But the strange vision of James, glowing like phosphorescent amoeba in the wake of a ship, standing naked and golden in the centre of pulsating glory! – *that* remained. The rest had gone. Hands were dry, brow unwrinkled. I lay for a bit in the pale morning, the cockerel crying. Somewhere in the house a tap running, a lavatory chain pulled. Day had started.

Before my coffee even arrived, punctually at seven-thirty, I was washed, shaved and dressed, and had written a card to the children and another to Helen simply to tell her that I was working away at finding the lost ewe lamb and would, probably, be returning by the end of the month. It might give her a slight nudge, I hoped, to get herself, and the kids, together.

I then wrote a short note to Mr Millar explaining who I was and why I was in the place, and that I was desperately anxious to try and find any possible clues which might help me to locate James, or at least try and discover where he was, and if possible why he had left so precipitately. I added that I would be at the Maison Blanche until I had managed to get a lead to James's discovery. It was a very polite note, begging his pardon, and saying that I would be happy to meet him anywhere he suggested which would be convenient to him.

I left the hotel on a brilliant morning. The air was light, clear, invigorating after the stuffiness of my little room and the writhing distress of nightmares. Birds were singing in the little copses and the trees already, in early May, filigreed in jade. Here and there, in the fields, great sheets of tiny golden narcissi lay on the slopes exactly like laundry spread out to dry. The heavy scent of the miniature yellow flowers filled the air. They – or rather, I suppose, it – made me almost forget the word hate. Far too strong, I realized in the bright light of morning, to harbour in my mind. Nonetheless it stuck.

Stuck quietly at the back all the way into Saint-Basile-les-Pins, and to the rusting gates of L'Hermitage. Screwed to the gates a green-painted mailbox. No sign of life. The long track led away up from the lodge into the gloom of the trees. I slid the note into the box, reversed, and drove away. No sign of anyone or anything living.

All quite still.

At Jericho I saw, for the first time, that the garden was not quite as desolate as at first I had thought. I was, I admit, seeing it in a very different light. Brilliant sun, a cerulean sky, sparkling air.

And I was, or liked to think that I was, in love; middle-aged love, but nonetheless love. It coloured everything. One behaved like a youth. To be sure there were the rows of withered sunflowers, seedless and pale; there were dead cabbage stalks, the arms of old men sticking out of the dry earth; last year's leaves had blown around from the giant cherry tree, and come to rest in rusty piles in furrows and corners; there were clumps of dusty grey lavender here and there, and one solitary rose swinging a bud, frosted and brown, on a skinny unpruned stalk, timid.

I don't know why I had not noticed the cherry tree before. It had very clearly been there for half a century and now was an explosion of white blossom, a gigantic gone-to-seed cauliflower, leaning against the prevailing winds shadowing what might have been, once upon a time, a patch of grassy lawn. The feeling was, I suppose because of the cherry tree and the desolate house, a bit Chekhovian.

But. Among the rusty piles of leaves, the grey dust of the dead lavender, fat clumps of primroses, daffodils and a white tumult of narcissi speared up through the matted grass, and here and there, in tight cushions, long neglected, blue and purple aubretia spilled wantonly along the rutted path. Under the fig tree the new grass was hazed with violets.

None of this, it would appear, had I noticed when I had first arrived at the house, or when Florence and I, and indeed Thomas, had spent the afternoon together. I suppose that I was so preoccupied with a good many other things I had not taken in the simple pleasures which now I could see surrounded me. But it was perfectly obvious that life was resurging again: the long winter of sadness and neglect was over, the amazing miracle of spring had suddenly hit this forgotten piece of land and the cycle was beginning again. I felt the surge myself, and as if to endorse that feeling, just as I began to move on up towards the house and the terrace I saw the toad.

Fat, heavy with promise, golden eyes blazing, she lumbered slowly up the path on a route which she obviously knew from years before and from animal instinct. She was on her way to her destiny, and her destiny lay in the little stream which bickered and whispered through the boulders beyond the little orchard. Toads, I knew, always return to the place where they were born. Nothing could deflect them from the instinctive route. She would slop into the stream and wait there until a mate, or a number of mates, would find her, and then the ugly waltz of copulation would take place. In time, if she survived, she'd weave a lattice of glossy black pearls in ropes among the reeds and grasses, and new generations would one day emerge. I felt extremely comforted by the sight of her lurching along on her way to her mates. She was now *my* toad; she inhabited my land, I would follow her rules, not touch her, let her go where she wanted.

It was an exceedingly pleasant feeling to think that I was now on my own territory. Without even entering the house, I had already banished James. He had never existed. I had been given an amazing chance to kick-start my own life again and I was determined to make the best of it. Come what may.

I walked up the path, stepped over the ambling toad, who froze as my shadow crossed her and then, when I had passed, continued on her determined way.

The terrace, with its two little rusty chairs, lay in the freckled shadow of the unpruned vine, whose plump little fans of leaf looked more like green hands reaching up towards the sun and the brilliant sky, speckled with scudding white clouds. There would be no pruning this year – far too late, the vine would bleed away – so summer would mean a heavy canopy of green and no grapes. Next year I'd do it.

The big oak door groaned on its hinges when I pushed it open rather as if I had awakened it from a comfortable sleep. I opened all the shutters, light streamed into the room, dust danced like platinum confetti in the sun, shadows fell crookedly across the tiled floor, the old newspapers covering the furniture flapped idly in the sudden draught, lifting and fluttering like the wings of a cruising skate, silently, rhythmically. I opened up all the rooms, throwing wide the winter-sealed windows, cobwebs trembled and bellied, a dead butterfly, dry as a corn husk, spun about on a window sill.

I'd get rid of everything this house contained. The atmosphere of James, the walnut bed, the caged cot, the bottles of cucumbers and yellow gooseberries. I'd repaint everything, every wall, every piece of wood. I'd change the bath and the lavatory. Nothing which had once been familiar to Florence, apart from the walls and the ceilings, would remain to remind her that once upon a time, in the haze of memory perhaps, she had known this little house before.

The only room I didn't go into was the studio: that would have to stay as it was until such time as I could get Aronovich to come and remove his canvases. I wanted them out of the house as much, even more so, as I wanted the walnut bed to go.

Coming down the stone-flagged staircase, I heard the sudden urgent sound of a car horn summonsing me. My car. From the terrace I looked down the length of the garden to the track, where I had parked the Simca. Standing beside it, an arm thrust through the window jamming angrily at the steering-wheel, was Madame Prideaux.

I waved, hurried down to meet her. 'Good afternoon! How did you find me?'

'It was a lovely day, I thought I'd come out to the house, to see if there are any narcissi I could pick. It's the time I always come.' She looked very slightly flushed, a length of her hair had started to fall in a loop, as it had done when she was cleaning the brasses.

'Yes. There are plenty. A mass. Come along.' I led her up the path.

'I've parked rather badly. Not really my fault. I am a poor driver, as Florence has no doubt told you. Not safe to drive, she will say. I find reversing difficult, and you have parked where I normally turn round. You see? While I take some flowers – your flowers, I suppose – would you be so kind as to help me by turning me around? Get the car pointing in the right direction? Towards Bargemon? It's the reversing, you see.'

I reversed the car, an elderly Renault, the back and the front filled with a jumble sale of old maps, candy wrappers, half-empty packets of biscuits and plastic bags mixed up with a tattered Algerian rug. Turned it round and got it facing the track and the way down to the main road.

Walking back up the path to the house a sudden squall of wind sent scurries of blossom from the cherry tree across the stooping figure of my landlady. She had gathered a decent armful of white narcissi. She stood upright, brushed her skirt, hooked the loop of hair roughly behind her ear.

'I didn't think you would be here, but I recognized your car. I was lunching with friends. You were most kind to help me. Perhaps the next time you park you could leave the turning-point free . . .? A thought. We are always used to it. In the past anyway . . .'

'I'm sorry. Not certain of the rules yet. This is really my first day at Jericho to work out my . . . moves, I suppose.'

'I suppose so. The car goes, doesn't it? Mine?'

'It goes. It needs a coat of paint. And a little oil might be a good idea.'

She moved her quite large bunch from one arm to the other. 'I'm quite hopeless with cars. They go or they *don't* go. I don't know any more, except for petrol. I do know about that. Ah yes.' She started off down the path and I followed her.

'What a pretty day,' she called over her shoulder. 'We'll have a frost tonight. You are quite right. I do need a coat of paint, but it is so expensive. Look at that dent in the mud-guard. I hit the pillar on the corner just now. As you can see. A silly old woman, but a taxi costs too much for one lunch with friends, and I did once drive extremely well . . .' She nodded her thanks as I held the door open for her.

I watched her try to start three or four times, succeed, and with a quick flap of her hand inch down the track, weaving a little from side to side, turn into the road, and, after a prudent halt, turn left and become lost to sight.

She'd hit the stone pillar at some time. The front mudguard was deeply scored, but it was an old scar, rusty. Nothing recent.

CHAPTER 8

I SPENT THE next couple of days just mucking about, really, over at Jericho. There was no point in my making any definite effort to trace James until I had heard something, if I ever would, from the people at L'Hermitage. I'd give it a couple of days or so, I thought, and get down to thinking out my new property.

The weather was kind. I found my way about Saint-Basile-les-Pins in a short twenty minutes. It was a developers' village; the only original part of it was a small chapel at a crossroads in the pine woods and a battered little bar-tabac called La Source. It had a single-meal menu, a zinc, six tables and a blaring radio. The people who ran it, a young man and his dispirited wife, were civil and almost welcoming. I ate in the restaurant obviously what they were having themselves that day. She didn't seem to me to be the kind of woman who was about to cook two meals. There were children banging about, and the atmosphere was casual, friendly, incurious. I gathered, by the second day, that they had just bought the place, were not locals, had moved down from Arras in the north and were, as he said ruefully, more foreign there than I was.

'They don't like us from the north. Don't like the accent.

But my wife has a kind of consumption, and the dry air here is better for her breathing than up there. Too damp. The fogs in winter . . .' He cleared my plates and said that there was cheese if I wanted it. I declined and finished my demi-carafe of not very good local wine.

All around La Source and its mournful little chapel, closed as it so happened because there was rot in the roof timbers, the pine woods were stuck about with hideous little Paris-rustic villas, each with a small fishpool, an arch, a flying buttress, roman-tiled roofs and chain-link fences. They sat like Disney-dainties in tiny plots of land, pottery cigalas on every wall, wreathed in an agony of wrought-iron gates and shutters. They were almost all summer rentals; a few pinched-looking aged people moved about slowly, wrapped in thick sweaters, anoraks and plastic hats. It was altogether very depressing: I couldn't imagine, even in the heat of summer, that there was any joy or pleasure, laughter or music, in this sad, still, damp pine wood. I had a feeling that Madame at La Source might have been better off in Arras. At least there was air in the north. Down here, in this silent no-place, there was almost no air and no view. Hemmed in by tall trees, dark in winter, shaded gloom in summer, Saint-Basile-les-Pins had been developed by some bright spark because there was absolutely nothing else to be done with it.

So, after my usually greasy meal, a cut of meat, beans, a salad and, as offered, a bit of cheese, I'd go off back to Jericho and open up the house, make lists, pull up the bamboo wig-wams, the dead sunflowers, and walk my boundaries. Beyond the wall which surrounded the property, obviously a safety barrier for Thomas if nothing else, there was the orchard and the little rough-grass paddock, yellow now with great swaths of cowslips mixed in with the wild white narcissi, and then that petered out into tussocky grass, boulders, shale, bushes of camphor and myrtle and the little stream, winding like a silver chain, between whippy crimson dogwood and clumps of marsh marigolds.

I was extremely pleased with myself that I, a city fellow if there ever was one, could place all these pleasures with accuracy because I had known them all, years and years before, as a child with Elpie in the fields and meadows between Faringdon and Lechlade. The days before James. The happy decade.

Up by the stream there was a little pond which the waters had carved out of the scrubby land, a kind of lung of stillness in which the old toad of yesterday gyrated slowly, grasped tightly by her lovers. Trust her to know the best place for mating. Never in running water, only ever in still. I was immensely pleased with myself for remembering all this. I'd bring Thomas up one day . . . perhaps. And, certainly, fence it off. Just in case.

I walked back to the house well pleased with myself and in the big room wrote to my editor telling him of my plans, but to write to me in Parsons Green until I returned to England.

The light was starting to fade as I walked back up to the little shed by the far wall, carrying a pioche, a fork and a battered rake which I had found there. Neatly stacked. Clean.

An agriculturalist. I felt amazingly free almost to the point of being a bit light-headed. Closing up the shed, I heard myself whistling, tunelessly. A sound which came from a contented heart.

I drove back to Madame Mazine, the kittens and goldfish, and the haven of the Maison Blanche, singing, very loudly, 'Oh What a Beautiful Morning!' Apart from getting the time of day wrong, I got the mood absolutely right.

In the bar Maurice was, as usual, installed at the far corner by the wall telephone. He had no telephone at his house so clients called the bar for his taxi. An extremely useful idea on his part, although his red face and raspberry nose might have deterred some. Especially with the kinks and bends in the local roads. The barman, whom I now knew as Claude, gave me my large Scotch and I took it to the table in the corner by the Dutch, who, mercifully, had walked themselves to silence and, with assorted haversacks scattered around them, were writing cards home to Deventer or Haarlem or wherever.

It was a comfortable feeling of belonging. Belonging without any kind of responsibility. Now and again, Florence drifted into my mind, was there, drifted out again. I had deliberately kept away from rue Émile Zola, feeling it wiser to get on with my jobs, leaving her to contact me. If she wanted to. All too obviously Madame Prideaux was keeping an eye on me and would, doubtless, report on my activities. That was all right: at least Florence would know that I was making a start on Jericho. Even if it was a limited one.

Eugène arrived, white napkin over his arm, menu in his hand. Gigot with haricots verts or, and this was extra, petit poussin 'Eugène'.

'Is what?' I said.

'Is in a small casserole, with chipolata, pearl onions, mushrooms and a touch of cognac. It would be wise to order now.'

I settled for a gigot. One nightmare was quite enough. I had no desire, after a day of such pleasure, to be haunted again by the pulsing hate which had made me so wretched two nights before.

I slept well in my feather valley, and slept well the next night. The daily drive out into the clear morning air, my work in the garden, opening up the house to sweep it clear of dust and odours, my solitary meals at La Source with my dispirited host, my evening bath and my meal in Eugène's dining-room relaxed me to an almost zombie-like state. I hardly even read *Var-Matin*. The world could get on with itself without any assistance, or interference, from me.

On the fourth morning, just as I had finished my croissant and coffee and was about to get ready for Jericho, the telephone rang. Madame Mazine was cautious. A person was in the hall and wished to see me; a Madame Millar.

I took the car keys, my wallet, loose change, pulled on my jacket and went down to the hall.

She was a tall woman, taller than I had remembered her to be when she had slung gravel at me. Fair-white hair dragged back on each side of a good forehead by two cheap plastic combs, a bush jacket, slacks, boots. No eye patch. Instead a red, shiny scar round a milky eyeball.

She came towards me – she had been looking at a copy of some magazine lying on the counter – hand outstretched.

'Martha Millar. Martha as in "Washington". And you are which Caldicott? I forget.'

'William.'

'Excuse me. Head like a sieve. But it doesn't even retain the important stuff. It's Thursday. I come into the market sometimes. Shall we sit down somewhere? A coffee?'

'Perhaps not here. They usually wash down the bar at this hour.'

She eased the strap of a bulging sling-bag over her shoulder. 'Boring. I'm from L'Hermitage, but I guess you already know that? Do you know the Sporting? Just across the square. It'll be busy, market day, but I reckon we'll get in.'

She led me briskly across the square, filled now with trestle tables, sagging shade-umbrellas, boxes and sacks, bewildered chickens, tied by their legs, rabbits hunched in cages, fruit and vegetables in spilling mounds, eggs in large crocks, people shouting, laughing, weighing, selling.

Pushing into the Sporting, she said, 'Very Bruegel. Nothing changes.'

The place was crowded but she found a table at the back between the end of the bar-counter and the WC. Bentwood chairs, plastic-covered tables, poppies and cornflowers, a small bottle of Maggi sauce, salt and pepper.

She dumped her bag among these, calling out above the noise to a girl behind the counter, who seemed to know her, for two coffees.

'Coffee? It's just to play with while we talk. Okay? This bag has every goddamned thing of mine in it. Except perhaps my soul. And I lost that years ago somewhere. Mislaid it.'

We sat opposite each other under an advertisement for someone's ice cream.

'You gather that your letter got to Mr Millar? He's my brother. I live in the little lodge. He suggested I come visit you.'

'That was civil.'

'He can be. On occasion.' She adjusted the plastic combs in her hair. 'Do you know Brent Millar? A name with which you are familiar?'

'He writes? You *do* mean the writer?'

'I do mean the writer. He'd be ill with rage if you did not. Brent Millar has an elevated opinion of himself. *Elevated*. He's hardly known in England, which infuriates him.'

'I thought, I don't know why, that he lived in Paris.'

'He does. Île Saint-Louis, but he prefers it here when he's writing. Less hassle.'

The coffee arrived on a tin tray. She set out the cups. 'Don't you write? I think that your brother told Brent that you do?' So. James had been discussed at L'Hermitage. We begin.

'Nothing alarming. I mean intellectual. I write the kind of books that people leave behind on airplanes.'

She milked the coffee heavily, having first removed the wrinkled skin with a degree of distaste, dumping it on the tray. 'Mock modesty is not a beguiling quality.'

'Well. I suppose I mean that I am not in your brother's league.'

She pushed the wrapped sugar towards me. 'God knows what league he's in. He has his own opinion, of course, and he sells. I just know his books take a hell of a long time to write and you can almost not get them on to a plane, let alone leave one behind. They are brick-thick. I suppose I was excessively rude that time you came to the house.'

'A handful of gravel and a threatening rake can hardly be considered as signs of a pleasurable reception.'

'That kind of behaviour frightens away the blue-rinses from Tulsa and Portland, Oregon, as well as those god-awful Japanese-camera-freaks. We get them all summer. If Brent Millar ain't so well known in France, he sure as hell is in the US of America and Japan.'

'Where do they come from?'

'Oh, they rent those little buses, you know? Drive up from Sanary and Toulon, sometimes as far as Marseilles. I think half the concierges in the area have L'Hermitage on the counter at Reception.'

She shrugged, stirred her coffee, one steady blue eye staring me out. 'No eye patch, you are saying to yourself? No. I wear it when I am working in the garden. Dust, or twigs, stuff like that. Otherwise I face the world thus. People get used to it.'

'I really wasn't wondering.'

There was a sudden spark of amusement in the bright blue eye. 'Shame on you! You must: I like telling people.'

'Okay. Then I wonder.'

'Well, I wear the patch for Best. At suppers and with company. One does try not to offend. But I don't bother here, marketing, in the village, and I hate to drive with the thing. I find it restricting.'

'I'm still waiting to be told something. Wondering.'

'I was a news photographer. For WWP, the agency, you know them? My last assignment, surprise, surprise, was Beirut. I got this there. Splinter from a mortar. That put paid to my activities quite a bit. You can't shoot with one eye, for God's sake.'

'I'm sorry. Lame. But I am.'

'Be sorry for the other guys with me. *I* walked away.'

'You live here permanently now?'

'Semi. Brent was supportive. The lodge was empty. I needed peace for a while. He gave it me. In exchange for throwing gravel at tourists and taking in the mail and so on. I make myself useful. Try to.'

'You look very daunting.'

'I didn't know your brother. I saw him often enough; I have, among other things, to open the gates. He was very blond. Slender. You are not the least alike.'

'Not alike in anything, I'm afraid. A twelve-year difference between us. He was what you might call the changeling in the family.'

'The cuckoo in the nest?'

'In one. We were not in the least close.'

'Then why the search? Maybe he just wanted to drop out? People do.'

'I know. But I have a tidy mind. And there is a wife. And a child.'

She looked down at the cornflowers and poppies, fiddled with a spoon.

'I see. And you think my brother can help you?'

'Well, he might be able to give me a line. A clue. James destroyed nearly all his papers, but I do know that he knew L'Hermitage, someone called Aronovich and another, Daniel Jacquet. The one with you at the gate, I think? Right?'

'Right. Dumb but a good worker. He's a pépiniériste. Nurseryman. He does the trees and so on for my brother.'

She looked away across the crowded bar, pushed her hair vaguely about her head.

'I don't know an Aronovich. I learned a long time ago to

keep my nose out of some things which don't concern me. I lost an eye that way.'

'Would your brother see me? Anywhere, at any time, at his convenience? I have to make some kind of effort. Not for myself – I frankly don't give a tinker's gob what happened to James. Or what *happens* to him. But you can't just let someone fall off the earth without making a token gesture and trying to find out why and where. He sent me the key to his house here, a note to say don't try to find me, that he was off to "oblivion". But I must be certain of one thing.'

'Which is what? As if I didn't know.'

'I must be certain that he's dead. Or that he's alive. It's difficult for things to settle otherwise. Difficult for me, impossible for his wife. That's reasonable, surely?'

She began to stack the coffee cups slowly. '*Thus unlamented let me die, steal from the world, and not a stone tell where I lie.*' She looked directly at me, a slight smile, head to one side. 'Pope. I think? Remember it?'

'If I have heard it, I've forgotten. But I'm here to ask a few stones some questions. That's all.'

She took up the heavy bag, pulled it over her shoulder.

'Brent said to tell you that he will see you. For a short time. A drink at about six-thirty. When he's through proof-correcting, you know?'

'That's perfect. Will you thank him. When – I mean, what day?'

She got up, brushing her jacket.

'Saturday. Saturday's a quietish day. Okay?'

'Fine, thank you.'

She rummaged about in the shoulder bag for money, pushed a ten-franc piece under the saucer, waved away my fumbling offer to pay.

'I really wouldn't thank me, you know? Frankly, I think it would be so much wiser if you stayed away from

L'Hermitage-and-all-who-sail-in-her. Leave the stones unquestioned, for God's sake. Be abashed, Mr Caldicott. Look what happened to me when I intruded into other people's affairs.'

She turned abruptly and I followed her tall, arrogant figure as she pushed and edged her way through laughing and gesticulating people. At the door, she stopped, her hand on the brass latch. A sign swung gently against the net curtains: 'FERMÉ'.

'Don't meddle. Remember that a key opens more than just a door, and on this trip you won't find that you are opening a can of sardines, Buster. Think about it.'

I thought about it all right. She was not the sort of woman one can afford to ignore. Her words were weighed before delivery and were meant to be valued. But, consider, why else was I in Bargemon unless it was, indeed, to meddle? After all, if you suddenly get a whacking great key sent to you out of the blue, if it falls on the breakfast table before you, a note attached suggesting suicide, or at best a case of dropping out, you don't just ignore it all. If the expediter happens at the same time to be your long-forgotten, almost, little brother, it increases the curiosity. You have to make the trip. Try and find out why the wretched man should mount his bike and just piss off into the snow without a backward look, seeking oblivion.

And, to be frank, since I had been in the village, I had started to pick up little shreds and shards of his life. Nothing much, not enough to make the proverbial pot, but just enough to whet my appetite for more. And, too, there was Florence. A bonus if ever there was one, a turning upside down of one's life, standards, beliefs, expectations of the future. There was Thomas, a darker shadow than I had remotely thought of in the spring sunlight of her presence.

There was her mother, the house beneath the cliffs, Martha Millar with her good head and voice like the gravel which she chucked at me. And Daniel Jacquet.

Now what about Mister Jacquet?

The only fish that is known to swim backwards is the conger eel and I was in too far to try to swim backwards.

Consider Miss Millar (I assumed she was a Miss). I liked her very much, liked her hands. I go a lot on hands. They give a good deal away about a person. Hers had square-tipped fingers, blunt, no nonsense, she had the knuckles of a manual worker: obviously she could saw logs, hem a skirt, change a plug, fire a gun as easily as she could plant out a bed of pâquerettes as, indeed, she had been doing the first time that I saw her.

Florence had slender hands. I had seen them for the first time in a portrait, kneading bread; there was something maternal, eternal, gentle, healing about them, small, firm, strong, unfastidious. I liked that very much.

At one time, light years ago now, I had been greatly attracted to Helen's hands. They were extremely capable, slender-fingered, long nails – talons to be exact: scarlet, unchipped, gleaming, predatory, smooth, unblemished. Those hands had never loaded film, sewn on a button, used a hoe, peeled a potato, but they *had* held a glass with extreme grace, and the scarlet nails bit excitingly into one's shoulders, to leave red crescents in satiated flesh. They were suggestive, beckoning, quite unpractical and so damned pampered that rubber gloves were worn to wash a salt spoon.

But they had excited me.

Thinking of all this, I nearly drove past La Source and missed my lunch.

Madame Yvonne set a deep bowl of cassoulet (clearly tinned) before me, a basket of yesterday's bread and a carafe of the red. She had a cold, and tripped over a Donald Duck on wheels as she returned to the kitchen. She shouted at someone, and slammed the door.

At Jericho, parked neatly beside the track under the apple trees, the out-of-date green Renault. My heart did a sudden leap, resettled.

She was sitting on the edge of the terrace, a bundle of narcissi and cowslips scattered beside her, sorting them into separate bunches with care. She looked up as I came towards her, a sudden smile, she waved a handful in the air.

'I am a thief! Stealing your flowers.'

'Yours really.'

I sat beside her. 'Sorting things out. Who for?'

'Some for Céleste, some for me; Mama got all her loot the last time she was here. She always came at this time of year.'

'There are enough. Do you know how to make cowslip-balls?'

She looked at me with mock indignation. 'A joke?'

'No. Really. Children, in my village, used to make them. Balls. Very pretty indeed. There is a special art in making them. Only the blossoms.'

'You can show me?'

'No. I don't know how to. I only know they were made. I was told so.'

'I haven't seen you for a long time, I wanted just to tell you that I will give up my work with Monsieur Colin. The dentist. On Monday I am free. Ouf!'

'But why?'

'Thomas is almost three years old now. He is rather difficult for just Céleste to handle.'

'Will you miss it?'

'Miss the rinsing? The forgotten appointments? The swirling water? The bad tempers? The filthy mouths? The whimpering cries? No. Not at all. I *will* miss the extra money. It was not much but it was useful. Little things: an extra bunch of flowers, which is why I am stealing today, English tea, *Elle*, just silly little things like that. I enjoyed my *Elle*. Simple pleasures.'

'So from Monday you'll be trapped?'

'No! Not trapped. I am just sharing a larger part of the burden: it is my affair after all. And anyway . . .' She gathered up the two separate bunches, wrapped them round with some old raffia she had found. 'Anyway, I am here this afternoon, am I not? I am not trapped, you see.'

The sky was a brilliant egg-green, almost blue. Like a blackbird's egg. The sun slanted through the trees, blossom scattered from the big cherry tree. I got up suddenly. I had never touched her, and the desire to do so overwhelmed me. Just to touch her; to put my hand on her arm, to feel her warmth.

'Would you take me up to Jericho?'

She looked at me in surprise, the flowers in either hand.

'This *is* Jericho.'

'No. The hamlet. Jericho up there. On the cliff. I've never been. We can take your car? Leave mine. Would you?'

She got up, looking rather helpless, then down at her two bunches.

'These'll die. Without water. It's quite a long drive.'

I took the key from my pocket and opened the front door.

'Stick them in the sink, until we get back. Okay?'

She drove well, carefully and in silence. About two minutes along the road to Bargemon-sur-Yves there was a left turn on to a track which began to climb gently through olive orchards, stands of walnut and, here and there, cane breaks and the tall admonishing fingers of dark cypress.

'Maybe it is closed, you know? The road. If you hear the roar of the cannons you'll *know* it is closed.'

'Cannons?'

She turned towards me patiently, a smile, eyes alight.

'Dear Englishman, you are approaching the enemy camp of the French. We are headed for the Zone Militaire. You know what that means?'

'No. What?'

'Army training-ground. All the area up here is a range for tanks and heavy weapons. Jericho, dear Mister Englishman, is abandoned. It is not a target, because of its history, but no one can live there, it is quite fenced off and deserted. You will only hear the birds and goats; unless you hear the roar of cannons.'

'Why didn't you tell me, you idiot child?'

'Because you didn't ask me. You just demanded to be taken there, and after three years with a demanding child, I know the only thing to do is to hit it, or . . .', and then she touched my hand, 'humour it! So I humour you. For a long time Mama and three old ladies used to be allowed to come up here on Christmas Day and New Year and at Easter. Just to put flowers in the church. But the old ladies died one after the other and Mama lost heart, and *she* got old. Now no one comes; except the soldiers.'

We were getting higher; the plain fell away below in a great pattern of dark-green and light-green squares. In the far distance, the towers of some town, which might have been Sainte-Brigitte; and nearer, the dark mass of the forest and Saint-Basile; and far to the east, like the blade of a knife, a sliver of steel light which could have been the sea.

The track became rougher, churned up by tank tracks and carriers; a metal sign, bullet-scarred, stated clearly, in large letters, 'ATTENTION! INTERDIT! ZONE MILITAIRE! DÉFENSE DES MINES!'

Florence changed down, we drove slowly, easing over the ruts and holes in the track.

'You see?' she said happily. 'We are *not* welcome.'

'It would appear so.'

'Can you hear the cannons roar?'

'No. Nothing. Larks.'

'Do you see a red flag flying anywhere? Look carefully all round.'

'Not a sign. Nothing. Barbed wire, a fence, a skull-and-crossbones.'

'Ah. That is a danger sign. The wire is to keep the soldiers in and us out. The village is not actually *in* the range, but . . .' She shrugged, and drove slowly on.

'What happens if we hit a mine?'

'What do you think will happen? Boum! Boum! After all,' she said reasonably, 'we have been warned.'

On the left of the track, which had once been a minor road, the land was close-cropped by hares, rabbits and feral goats until it spilled over the edge of the cliff which fell some hundreds of metres to the plain below. Ahead, and to the right, the tower of a small church and the broken roofs of some houses huddled together as if they cowered in fear. There was a sun-faded painted sign for 'BYRRH' and another on the side of a crushed building for 'DUBONNET'. The last three letters of the name were splattered by a shell blast. The metal sign announcing that we had reached 'JERICHO 0 KM' was twisted, rusted, colandered with bullet holes.

She stopped the car, wound down her window, and we sat in the strange, echoing silence. Then a bird started to sing, a goat bleated for its kid. We watched it skitter away across the fallen stones of the village.

Where the land fell steeply away to the plains below, a flurry of ravens planed and soared, wheeling high in the draughts, black and hard against the ache of blue-green sky. A wind, a continual wind at this height, wuthered and whiffled through stunted clumps of thyme, myrtle and cropped thorn. It seemed, from where we sat, that we were on the rim of the world; apart from larks, the anxious bleating of the goat, the cries and cackles of the ravens, there was no other sound. Wind and birds. Certainly no cannon.

I said, fairly abruptly, 'I met Millar's sister, from L'Hermitage, this morning. I am to go and see him on Saturday.'

She didn't speak. I fiddled with the handle of the door, polishing it between forefinger and thumb.

'To see if I can discover any kind of clue about James. Where he might have gone. Why. I can't sit about doing nothing. It's my duty really.'

She hugged her body tightly with both arms folded hard against her breasts. She looked away far up the road to the crumbling church spire.

'I wish you would not. Please don't. Don't go.'

'They may know something. He knew them all, didn't he?'

'He knew them all. Yes. But you won't find out anything that I don't know myself. He went there often, in the last two years, since Thomas, he was very often there. Painting. He said. I knew of Jacquet. He came to the house, and I knew Jojo. He came to the house also. He came to our silly "wedding". Jojo came there. You will find nothing in that house which will give you release.'

'Was Jojo the one who took your photograph? On what James called Joy-Day? At Porquerolles? On the rocks? There is a long shadow of someone who took the picture.'

'Jojo. James is dead, William. I am certain of that. I loved him so deeply. He was the first man, the only man I have ever loved. If he was still about, if he was alive, I would sense it. I know that. I am certain. But he *is* dead. He has gone. Please leave all alone. Leave it now. Please.'

'I can't do that. I must be absolutely certain for myself.'

'Very well. I can only ask. I cannot stop you.' She laughed, a caught little sound, more sigh than laugh. 'Poor James. Even in death he will not find peace. He never found it in life. Oh, he tried. He thought, for a little time, that he had found it, but . . . Look about you here. He only saw this as grief, in agony. He translated this beauty into madness. You have seen the canvases in the studio? How could a mind find such torture, such pain, in so much glory? There was no sense, no security, no love in his work. Madness and despair. That's all. And that is all that you will find at L'Hermitage.'

'I just might find the reason?'

She switched on the ignition, began to reverse slowly down the torn track.

'Never,' she said. 'Not the reason. The result of madness, but not the reason.'

CHAPTER 9

THE SUN WAS blindingly bright as I drove over to L'Hermitage. The amazing thing about spring in Provence is that it arrives all of a sudden in a flurry and fluster of bud and blossom and then, just as suddenly, before one has even become adjusted to the splendours, it is instantly summer. There is no pause, no gradual slide into boskiness: the bloom is on the olives, the plum trees froth with white blossom, the grasses are all at once lush and green as if aware that, within a very few months, two to be exact, they will have become sere and brown under the relentless sun. Summer in Provence is fairly harsh. Burning, bold, prodigal. Spring, that evening, was already fading: summer was impatient.

The high gates were closed when I arrived precisely at 6.25 and sounded the horn. Martha Millar appeared garden-gloved, eye-patched, in a faded shirt, battered trousers and scuffed boots. Perversely, she wore a bright red scarf knotted frivolously into her hair, dragged back tightly from her good face. She waved a small hand fork at me, shouted at a dog which I could only hear, and pulled the gates wide.

'Salut!' she said. 'Would you come right in and park just beyond the lodge? Cars are not encouraged up the drive. You'll see why when you get to the house.'

I drove in just as an extremely large, glittering motorbike came roaring down towards us, scattering gravel, bouncing high on the ridges purposely constructed, it would appear, to cause any kind of vehicle to slow down and take care. But not, apparently, Daniel Jacquet, for he it was nakedly astride this huge Kawasaki who roared to a halt and adjusted his helmet. He was grinning. Miss Millar stood mutely, hands on her hips, the small fork sticking out like a metal hand.

'You are a real bastard. You know that? Tomorrow you will rake all that shitty gravel back again. Why the hell do you have to show off every damn time you see someone in a car, for God's sake? Killer instinct?'

He had fixed his helmet, that is to say he was wearing it now, without buckling the strap under his chin. He pulled down his visor, making himself instantly unrecognizable, and with a wave of one gauntleted fist swung into action and roared off towards Saint-Basile-les-Pins.

'My brother was out of his skull to finance the bastard with that method of transport. Originally it was a modest affair, a village boy's bike. He sulked for something bigger. He got it. Now he tears through the countryside like a naked Goth. One day,' she started to close the gates, 'one day, one really *fine* day, they'll find him splattered all over a wall and that'll be just great by me. Really neat.'

I had parked beyond the lodge on a paved area obviously intended as the Visitors' Parking Area. There was a small shed beyond, with her own car neatly lodged.

'And now that you are here I'll call the house. And you walk. Right? It's no great deal. A gentle slope only. You won't even be breathless when you arrive. *Leaving*, however, *may* find you distinctly short of breath. I myself seldom make the trip. Okay?' She went into the lodge and I began my walk.

It was not a 'big deal', as she said. The air was soft,

warm. Sunlight danced under the trees on drifts of narcissi and scatters of scarlet anemones which studded the brilliant new grass like gouts of blood. All along the verges, thick and tall (hedges almost), something very like Queen Anne's lace frilled and tossed, and bees and bugs droned, drifting languorously through the evening air.

What I had thought to be gloomy, dark trees the first time I had seen them turned out to be giant olives, their dark-green leaves, silvered on the underside, stuck about all over with tight bunches of cream blossom which, as I walked, were scattering petals like wedding confetti.

Suddenly, almost as a surprise, the house was before me, set behind a long balustrade, a terrace, pepper-pot towers at each corner, high mournful windows, a wide flight of steps leading up from a surprisingly trim sloping lawn.

It was an Edwardian monster, not, as I had for some reason imagined, a Provençal building, rough stone walls and sun-baked tiles on the roof. The drive did a kind of left turn and went off behind the terrace to be lost somewhere behind the house. The towers had ugly pencil-pointed roofs, crowned with rusty iron letters. In this case S and W. Probably the other towers, for there had to be four, one at each corner, would be N and E. They were tiled with ugly blue and yellow glazed tiles set in stripes. In the centre of the building, high on the roof, a huge clock stared blindly down over the landscape. It stood in an agonized riot of rusted iron vegetation, the filigreed hands pointing out, for all the world to see, that time had been abandoned at twelve-twenty exactly. The elegant Roman numerals bled rust down the cracked enamel face.

On the terrace, some chairs, the cheap slatted metal ones you find in public parks. They stood around like waiting, or abandoned, insects, and gave me the impression that no form of conversation or discussion had ever taken place there among them. Generally there was a distinct air of neglect, of carelessness, of impermanence. I don't know why I was surprised by this. Perhaps because I knew that the owner was exceedingly rich, one of the most successful writers of the day, and must therefore, in my Parsons Green blinkered mind, be rolling in riches and deep luxury. Perhaps he *was* vastly rich, perhaps he had wealth which was uncountable, but none of this drifted out on to his terrace. No jolly sun-umbrellas, no fat, wheeled, cushioned chairs for lying in the sun and sipping chinking glasses of wine or whisky. All was tidy, that was clear, well tended; the lawns, gently sloping to the bend in the drive, were mown like velvet, the gravel, the scattered stones I had just seen flying, were here immaculately raked. All was serene. Daniel?

Perhaps, in this house, it was all work and no play? A writer who dealt with books thicker than bricks probably had not the time for any form of slothfulness like sitting about on terraces sipping champagne.

Turning and looking back at the top of the steps, down over the trim lawns and the curving drive up which I had just walked, comfortably, I caught my breath. The view was, it had to be confessed, extraordinary. Beyond the drive, and the little lodge looking like a cuckoo clock set in the valley below, there was an infinity of green. Olives and cork, after them row upon row of vines stretching as far as vision, until everything softened into a lavender blue, a haze of distance and, rising serene, shimmering in the late-afternoon sunlight, a great range of mountains, the Pre-Alps, their jagged edges tipped and fringed with scars of snow, pink now in the late sun.

A breathtaking view. Perfectly simple, nothing of immense grandeur, merely nature normal, unbrutalized by house or even spire, pylon or chimney. Silent. Still. Eternal. So one wished and prayed; a strange contrast to the ugly Edwardian château and the deserted, unwelcoming terrace. With all this beauty, did no one ever look at it?

'It's inspiring, isn't it? I mean, truly inspiring. It is God's work, and doesn't it make you believe in Him? Don't you want to shout Glory Hallelujah! Don't you *just*?'

She was standing close behind me. Short, very thin, thin as a plucked wren. Her hair was just dun coloured, cut in a fringe, held by a fillet, or an Alice band as we had known them. She had thick rimless glasses, wore a grey tracksuit and scuffed sneakers. A large metal watch hung on one wrist, the other carried a clatter of varicoloured plastic bangles. Wide, like Nancy Cunard. She rattled them at me, shook them in the air and let them clatter down her skinny arm to a knobbled elbow, thrust out her hand. She was in her late forties perhaps.

'Welcome! I should have said that before, shouldn't I? But that view always gets to me. And I forget. I could see it had got to you too.'

'Yes. It's got to me.'

'Well, that's exactly why I didn't say, right away, welcome! like I should. But anyway, welcome. I'm Mrs Millar. I'm your hostess and you are a Mr Caldicott. Right? That's what I was told anyway. And you have come to visit with my husband. Is that all correct? I do hope it is. I get so muddled. It's new. Being muddled. I used to be very . . .' She looked round her vaguely as if she had lost a dog or a cat somewhere. 'I don't remember. Unmuddled. But my sister-in-law just buzzed through and said you were on your way up. And you were. And here you are! And so . . . well, welcome!'

We shook hands solemnly. I had been holding her thin hand in mine like a closed fan for all this time.

'I'm William Caldicott. You got that right. And I am amazed by the view.'

'Oh! That's great! It is nice to see you. Do you write?'

'I do. Yes.'

'Books? Or just for newspapers. I mean a journalist? But that's silly of me because if you were a journalist you would not be standing on this terrace. Not at all. Oh dear no. So it's books?'

'It's books. Yes.'

She adjusted the Alice band, her bangles clattering with her nerves. 'My husband is very famous. Did you know that? He's more famous in America than in England. But he's famous anyway. Do you know his book on Catullus? You know that? They made a *huge* movie from it, it was huge because it was a huge book. But they screwed it up.' She laughed, looked at her watch. 'It was a huge book, you see. I know. I typed it. Goodness me, yes.'

'I know your husband. I mean I know his work. I hope that I'm not late for him? I was told six-thirty.'

Mrs Millar shook her head worriedly. 'No. You aren't late. They'll buzz – or come when he has finished. Proofs. You know about proofs?'

'I do indeed.'

'I am sorry I'm not dressed properly to meet you. I mean, a tracksuit for heaven's sake! But I have my swim about this time, well, about five o'clock. Every day. I do twenty lengths, morning and evening. I have a funny back. It helps.'

'A funny back?'

'Yes. I reckon it's all the years I have sat typing in the wrong kind of chair, don't you? It can be dangerous. But swimming helps. Do you swim?'

'I do. Yes. In warm weather.'

'Oh. We have a pool indoors. It's always warm. The boys like it. They fool about there, but not at my times. I have priority. Isn't that nice?' She turned without waiting for an answer and, beckoning lightly with her bangled hand, motioned me to follow her. 'Now you know why they are called french windows? Right? Because they open all the way down like, well, like glass doors. Right? And this is the Big Room. We call it that because it *is* big. It is the whole length of the house. And what would you like to drink?'

The Big Room was as hideous as the house. Brown varnished wood, a vast turkey carpet, at either end enormous marble fireplaces stuffed with dried flowers. Around the panelled walls, amber old masters – that is to say, forgotten people peering through years of cracking varnish, cows crossing black rivers, cottages in sepia lanes, simpering children holding wilting bouquets, a donkey panniered with flowers.

I asked for, and was given, a Scotch. I stipulated Scotch because I had a feeling that Mrs Millar might think that whisky was just anyone's old whisky. She poured herself a Diet Coke. The bar was in a corner cupboard full of bottles and glasses; on the top a stuffed badger in a glass case. There was a sadness of unpolished brass dishes and dusty Chinese jars everywhere.

'We never really come in here. It's hardly used. My husband bought the house fully furnished, you see. He lives up on the top, and I have a cute little flat in the south tower. It's very nice. I'm really lucky. When the buzzer goes – it's right here in my pocket – I'll take you to the hall and the elevator. So we just wait a while. Okay?'

We sat, uncomfortably, on a pair of scuffed red-leather chairs, the backs of which appeared to consist of interwoven deer antlers, precluding any form of relaxation or ease. Bracelets clattered. Mrs Millar hunched forward eagerly and ready with a platitude to cover the period of waiting. It came easily enough. Did I know this part of France very well? I confessed not, but that I was touring about finding my way. My, she said, that's interesting. Did I ever get to New York? I said no, not very often, and she confided, as if it were secret, that she had once had an apartment, very small, on East 38th Street and that she missed it very much from time to time. She was saddened that you couldn't see the kind of view from her windows on East 38th Street that you could, for instance, from the terrace of L'Hermitage. But, and she laughed nervously as if she had made a worrying confession, home is where the heart is, didn't I agree? And before I could reply there was a sudden and urgent bleeping from the region of Mrs Millar's own heart.

She sprang to her feet, set her glass down on a Benares brass tabletop, with the speed of light took mine, and hurried me towards a towering pair of double doors.

'They are finished. The proofs. So you just take the elevator up to the third floor. Right this way.'

The hall was vaulted. An uneasy mix of the Sistine Chapel and a Scouts' hut in Chobham. Acres of dark varnished wood, panels, beams, a ceiling far above apparently covered with scenes from the Chase. It was difficult to see from the point of view of height, dirt, gloom and damp rings. A hefty staircase led upwards, stuck about with carved heraldic beasts; the panels were cluttered with more dark oil paintings in cracked gilt frames, and in a far corner, glaring at this desolation, an upright stuffed bear from whose outstretched paws hung, in the one, a hammer, in the other, a tarnished brass gong.

In the centre of the room a huge pietra-dura topped table big enough to seat the Last Supper; beyond it, glittering in steel and glass, an elevator thrust upwards to the top gallery.

'Here it is,' said Mrs Millar unnecessarily as the grilled cage descended softly in a whisper. 'Off you go now.' She rattled open the cage and pushed me inside. 'Press No. 3. I'm off to my jogging! I do hope we might meet again one day. Look at the view together? It's been great to see you.'

As I was carried heavenwards I could hear her thick rubber soles squealing hurriedly across the parquet below. The elevator stopped silently at a metal door with a large Gothic figure three painted on it in gold. Before I could open the gate, it slammed back and I was in a different world. Light, steel gleaming, glass flashing, white and yellow all about me, a heavy white marble figure on a tall plinth and a smiling black man with extended hand.

'Welcome! I'm Joseph. Late, I'm afraid. Our error. You are Mr Caldicott, and Mr Millar will be right with us and what will you drink? Did Mrs Millar offer you something? She usually forgets. Millie is a little vague with guests.'

By this time we were into the flat, for that is what it was, and my host, or my host's assistant, was leading me to a chair. He was tall, at least six foot four (the shadow in Florence's photograph?), with exceptionally fine features, slender build, very tight jeans, no shirt, and about, I guessed, in his mid-thirties.

'Sit anywhere. No matter. Be comfortable. A Scotch? Malt? Bourbon? You ask, we got.'

It was a very pleasing room after the Edwardian gloom of the lower floors. White carpet, white and yellow walls, glass tanks filled with white flowers, Bauhaus chairs covered in zebra and pony skins, glass-topped tables, a Derain on one wall, a Miró on another. The room of a man with money. And taste.

'Your Scotch,' he said. 'You don't look like your brother. Not one teensy bit. But I guess you are bored with that remark?' He settled himself into a zebra skin opposite me, a glass in his hand.

'I get a bit bored, yes. Did you know him well?'

He waved his glass vaguely before him, prodded the ice with a long finger. 'Here and there. Now and then. He was very blond and you *so* dark. I guess it's genes, right?'

'I guess. You are very tall. What? Over six foot four? I feel crushed sitting here.'

He laughed. Even white teeth. Humourless eyes, no laughter there. 'Don't be, man. I think I'm an Abyssinian. Y' know? Talk of genes. That or Ethiopian . . . something! Else my daddy was very, very tall. But I am not skinny, right? And I don't have those fat lips, right? Mr Millar said I am a "patrician". That feels good. Do *you* speak French?'

'I do. And you?'

'Enough. For what I need.'

'When did you last see James?'

'When? Oh, I don't rightly recall. Not right off. A while back.' He brushed his hand across his naked chest, smiled again, white teeth. 'Time I went to fetch Mr Millar. He said to give him a moment just so he could freshen up. You be all right?' He uncoiled himself, crossed the white carpet soundlessly, as smoothly as an oiled snake, pressed a button somewhere and Mozart, very softly, drifted in among the flowers, chairs and glass-topped tables. 'I'll be a second. See you.'

Sunlight faded through the row of big oeil-de-boeuf windows which, now that I saw them, I remembered seeing on the hideous façade left and right of the great clock at the top of the house. Obviously Mr Millar had created a private, and quiet, place for himself among the old attics. It was elegant, understated, cool. As indeed was the voice which turned me in my chair and brought me to my feet.

'I deplore unpunctuality more than I can say. And I am the culprit. Do forgive me.'

Brent Millar sat bolt upright in his wheelchair, a cashmere rug thrown lightly across his knees, hands folded in his lap. Joseph stood easily behind him. Smiling lightly.

'Do sit. I, as you see, am already sitting.' He indicated the chairs with one hand and manoeuvred his chair towards them and me. 'You see, I hope, why you had to come to me rather than I to you. It is less of a hassle. I manage this thing very well really; it moves like a Rolls, and Jojo here gets me up and down steps and things . . . we get through. But it is wildly frustrating. Huddled in a bloody wheelchair *long* before my time. Really very frustrating.'

'One can only hope it's a temporary frustration?'

'One would be a bloody fool if one did. It's for life. Horse fell on me. The supreme moment of exhilaration, the rush of wind through one's hair, the pounding of hoofs – do they "pound" in *mud*? One must suppose so – and then up! That heart-stopping leap soaring into the winter sky, the fence cleared.' He shook his head. 'Ah no . . . *Then* the fall.'

'Oh Christ . . .'

'Had nothing whatsoever to do with me that day, chum, nothing. He was very occupied keeping his eyes on his sparrows. *Wire*. We didn't see the wire.'

'I'm sorry. Futile remark. One makes a noise.'

'One does. However, I can move my arms, my neck, I can still write. And after all, a writer spends half his life sitting on his ass so what do I complain about? I am grateful I wasn't something dashing, like a climber, a runner, played baseball, danced, you know? Small mercies.'

'I had no idea. I never heard about it.'

He motioned to Jojo (for that is clearly who he was, I now gathered) and was instantly handed a glass of wine.

'There was a *great* deal of concern in the States. *Time*, *Newsweek*. And the *New York Times* was divine about me. It, of course, was certain that I was finished and wrote a sort of glowing obituary. They have *never* been so kind since. You probably missed out on my accident. I am not overly known in the UK. But continental Europe adores me. And Japan – my God! *how* Japan goes for me. Of course they are a violent people, and I tend to write fairly violent books . . .' He finished his wine in a single swallow and thrust the glass towards Jojo. 'I am *so* dry after all that tedium. Now, accident dealt with. Nothing killed me. I was merely maimed.'

Jojo replenished his glass. '*So*. Where are we? Ah! James, that is so.'

Jojo was now spread-legged in the zebra skin chair, one hand caressing his chest. 'That's what it *is*,' he said. 'We are at James right now.'

'You would appear to have lost your brother, Mr Caldicott? And that may seem careless to you, but James was always rather a wanderer. You knew that, of course? He never stayed put for very long.'

'No. I didn't really know that. I have been here a week trying to find a trace of him, to find out why he, well . . . wandered . . . if there is anyone who might assist me?'

Brent Millar sat back, a small smile on the lips of what had once been an exceptionally handsome face. Fine mouth, strong jaw, good nose, well-spaced eyes of an intense blue, a face which had been, just as Jojo considered his to be presently, 'patrician', but all the splendid attributes were now deep sunk into a marshmallow blubber of yellow flesh, chins flopping cruelly over his heavy-breasted chest. Only the brilliance of his eyes remained. Sapphires in putty.

'Tell me,' he said softly, 'just from the beginning. It'll all be so interesting; to know what *you* know . . .'

And so I told him in brief. As clearly as I could without stretching detail, trying to condense for fear of repetition and boredom. But my audience (for Jojo was now eagerly sitting forward) was very attentive. I only refrained from speaking at all about Florence. She merely figured in my story as 'his wife'. No more. When I had finished, there was a short silence.

'Twelve years' difference. It's a long time,' said Mr Millar.

'And all the years since he left England. It adds up to a lifetime.'

'Indeed. And why, pray, have you come to me? What led you to L'Hermitage?'

'In the scraps which he did not destroy of his papers he mentions a "Daniel". There are some Polaroid photographs of him. I recognized him the first time I saw him. James's wife said that he was often here and that he . . . well, she said that he was commissioned to paint . . . portraits, if you like, of Daniel, and she mentioned a couple of other names.'

'Mine?' Jojo was grinning.

'Yes. Yours.'

Brent Millar held out his glass again. Jojo sprang to his feet, took it to the bar.

'You say that he burned all his documents? Diaries? Papers? Nothing was left?'

'A few scraps. Nothing. Impressions of the countryside, the town. The light, colours. Nothing. Oh, there is a piece about his "wedding" in Porquerolles, and a photograph –'

'Which', said Jojo, handing the replenished glass to his master, 'I took my very own self.'

'That I guessed. There is a very tall shadow . . .'

'It was evening.'

'But nothing worth having. No clue as to what happened over all the years. He appears to have destroyed everything, obliterated his past just as he now seems to seek oblivion for the future. Everything has gone.'

Brent Millar ran a surprisingly slender finger round the rim of his glass, making it hum softly. He was still smiling, the startling blue eyes unblinkingly fixed on mine.

'Well, not quite everything, chum,' he said. 'It's here. Neat and tidy.'

I know that I looked idiotic. 'Everything?'

'Everything, as far as I know. Half a lifetime in fat "Agendas".'

'But why are they here? Why have you got them?'

'Because I bought them.'

'Bought them? I'm sorry, I'm being terribly obtuse.'

'Hardly surprising; you appear to know so little about your brother. He was desperate. Broke, with huge overheads.'

'But he had money. From our father. A modest legacy but –'

Mr Millar waved his glass dismissively. 'That all went. God knows where or how, but all your brother had to live on finally was his painting. And he was not, as I feel certain you will agree, a Monet, Cézanne or a Francis Bacon. He painted to exist.'

'I know. I have seen the stuff at the house.'

'That was all commissioned by Solly Aronovich, out of kindness and a very old friendship. He is building an hotel in Cannes. Somewhere . . .'

'I know that too. But, forgive me, why did you, as it were, bail him out? Buying all his diaries, "Agendas", whatever.'

'Ten thousand dollars is ten thousand dollars. It got him out of a lot of trouble, it paid part of the rent for that absurd house, it also was something he could put away for the unhappy child. He had a very strong conscience, you know. Very British.'

'When was this?'

'This? The sale of half a life? Oh, about the end of last summer.'

Jojo decided to join the conversation. 'It was the end of last summer. Right.'

Mr Millar suddenly snapped like an over-cosseted poodle. 'Shut-bloody-up, Jojo! Do *not* interrupt. I have told you before.'

Jojo uncoiled himself, meekly reached out for the emptying glass, and took it over to the drinks table.

Millar wiped his lips. 'He had it in mind, Mr Caldicott, as early as the end of last summer, to go away, to, as he always used to say, seek oblivion. He was beaten as a man: he had screwed things up for himself with an idiotic "marriage", landed himself with a house and a family, and fathered a disabled – I can say? – child. An event from which he never recovered. His guilt was unbearable to watch. He began to die.'

Jojo returned and handed Millar his glass. He put a finger to his lips, leant towards his master.

'Can I say a *little* thing?'

'What? What do you want to say?'

'That he was so damned sad, that man? So desperate, it broke my heart. And that "wife". God! She got so haughty. She was worse than the mother and *she* was worse than Medusa. James was destroyed. Right?'

'You have said it. Now hold your tongue. Yes, he was sad. But he was also aware that it was mostly his own fault.'

'Why his own fault? What fault had he committed in getting married?' I said. 'Or married in the eyes of God or whatever he preferred to call it?'

'The "marriage" was a piece of romantic tosh. Simply that. It was all his own fault for one simple reason. He went against his true nature. He was playing the wrong part in the wrong play.'

'I don't follow you, I'm sorry. In the little I have which he has left, he did not consider his marriage "tosh", he was radiant –'

'He was also gay.'

I'm setting this down just as I remember it. I suppose I sat there with a blank face. I could have heard the dew settling, a leaf fall, a worm turn. I was, frankly, dumb. Somewhere, as if from fifty miles away, I heard Millar's low, smiling, whispering voice saying, 'I'm sorry. Obviously you were unaware.'

I was able to reply in a reasonable voice. 'No. I did not know this. Not remotely. It's the last thing, the last thing . . .'

'It is not catastrophic! But for James, I fear, it was the *first* thing.'

Jojo decided to rejoin the act. He sighed heavily. It could have been regret but clearly was not.

'Gay as a carousel,' he said.

Millar smoothed the cashmere rug over the shrunken thighs. 'He was not absolutely certain of the fact himself, it must be at once admitted. It took a little time for him to come to terms with it all, but once that had been achieved, everything was fine. For a time.'

'Genes,' said Jojo. 'Genes, chromosomes, whatever. Like me being an "Abyssinian". You recall, Mr Caldicott?'

Millar's face was suddenly suffused with rage. The hand which was not holding his glass beat furiously on the arm of his chair. 'I told you! Do not interrupt me. If you can't hold your bloody nigger tongue, get out! Get the hell out! Get out!'

Jojo rose majestically from his zebra skin, his hands splayed along his thighs.

'An' if I do? What then? Who will fix the pills? Who wipes whose backside? Who does a million and one loving little things? Who *needs* this caressing nigger mouth? You tell me that.'

I got up. My mouth was drier than sawdust, more bitter than wormwood. I ignored the ugliness of the conversation around me, just blundered in.

'This "everything" which you have belonging to my brother . . .'

'It belongs to me now. Remember?'

'Can I see it? As you will realize, I am a little battered at this moment. Not at all what I expected to hear, any of it, but if you could see your way to just letting me have a look at the stuff, just so that I can form my own opinion, so that I will at least be armed, for his wife . . . or perhaps discover some clue that might lead me . . . to know why and where he has gone.'

'He left in January. In a light snowfall. He came to say farewell. I can assure you that he left of his own volition, against all persuasion to remain. He went, and he never intended to return, or that anyone should try to find him. He was determined to go and no one, *no one*, I assure you, could have stopped him. It was no sudden caprice. He had reached a conclusion over time. He wanted out.' Millar threw his empty glass into one of the zebra chairs and began to manoeuvre himself out of the room.

Jojo watched cautiously.

'Mr Millar?' I said. 'May I see the stuff? Can I come back? I *am* pleading. For my family . . .'

He stopped in the doorway, his broad back towards me. 'Oh dear God! The utter *tedium* of it all! Ten thousand dollars and now this.' He half turned the chair with angry twists of his hands. 'Tomorrow. Come to lunch. You can have the afternoon with the stuff. After that no more. *No more*. Right?'

'Thank you. No more.'

He turned again and wheeled off into the other room shouting over his shoulder, 'Jojo, buzz Millie. Our guest is leaving.' He went noiselessly away.

Down in the hall, Millie Millar had just arrived, a little breathless, fixing her Alice band, eyes anxious behind the thick glasses. She stood at the lift; beyond her, at the front doors, a youngish man in a blue striped apron like a butcher stood with hands by his sides. The early-evening light was fading, spilling from the terrace through the doors, across the polished parquet floor.

'Was it a good visit? It's almost evening now . . . I mean night – there is no twilight here, not really. It just goes dark . . .' She offered her hand, we said goodnight, and I walked down the long driveway, the gravel crunching lightly under my feet. A bat was up, swooping, flittering, soaring.

At the lodge by the Simca a dog rushed out barking in a flurry of rage and surprise. I heard Martha Millar calling it to heel, and then she was there, one hand pulling at the choke-collar, the other raised against her good eye to shield it from the dying light. She had removed her eye-patch and the red scarf.

'All right?'

'I'm all right, thanks. Thank you. Not a long walk. Up or down. As you said.'

'Breathless? I also said that. Remember?'

'Breathless. Yep. Pretty winded.'

'I thought you might be. I have a bottle of Jack Daniels here. And I pour a generous measure, they tell me. Could you use it?'

'God, I could. Thank you. I really could.'

CHAPTER 10

AFTER THE SECOND Jack Daniels it was suggested that we drop the 'Miss' and just use Martha. This I did. Easier, familiar, relaxing.

She was altogether comforting in her movements, slow, deliberate, calm, unfussed. After my trip up the hill I felt disjointed and unsettled. Bewildered, I suppose, is a better word.

Anyway, Martha, and Jack Daniels, sorted all that out comfortably.

The room, as far as I remember it that first day, was white, uncluttered, clear. Simple furniture, soft colours, flowers, books scattered, one or two old prints on the walls, a terracotta plate over the big fireplace of a Madonna and Child.

The dark, as always in Provence, had taken me by surprise. It would seem that quite a lot of things in Provence took me by surprise, but the fall of night was extraordinarily rapid, ravishingly lovely. A vague suggestion of twilight steals upon the brilliance of day, the sky slowly bleeds away from intense blue to bleached blue, to softest mother-of-pearl streaked suddenly with the faintest lemon tendrils, and then the sun begins to die in a ripple of tiny scarlet and orange waves of vapour. There is suddenly a perfectly tangible silence, a breath held, the evening fades away and night has fallen.

The air was still warm, the tiles of the little terrace beyond the open front door retained the heat of the sun; the dog, a Dalmatian, lay in a wide-legged sprawl, the scent of wall-flowers mingled with the freshness of damp earth. She had been watering the pots and urns when I arrived and from a distance, somewhere in the valley, the frogs began to fiddle and cry. A star appeared, bats swung silently against the dark sky attracted by the beam of light which spilled out across the terrace as Martha lit an oil lamp on the small table at my elbow.

'This time of day,' she said, setting the glass chimney over the wick, replacing the white floral globe, 'this time of day I always call "l'heure verte". The green hour. It's a kind of sad time. I don't honestly know why. Here, in France, it's called "Between the dog and the wolf".'

'I thought that was known as "l'heure bleue"?'

'It's verte, in *my* vocabulary.' She carried the taper across to a lamp by the windows, for a moment shadows danced against the white walls, then were steady. 'Sometimes, in New England, it's called "taper time". But, frankly I don't know. I stay with "verte". I feel a sadness. The Jack Daniels helps. I do have, in case you are wondering, electricity. But I prefer lamplight. I admit it's a bore to trim wicks and polish chimneys and get the kerosene but, and this is important, it is a very kind light for ageing faces like mine.' She sat in a large, stuffed chair covered in black and white ticking amidst a swaddle of cushions, her glass in one strong-fingered hand.

'You have your wind back, I think?' she said.

'I do. Thank you. I really did need a stiff drink. God knows why. I mean, well . . . I don't know what I expected up there. I mean, nothing: "Just drop by for a drink at six-thirty." Easy. But I really wasn't prepared for the scenario, so to speak. I found the show a little surprising.'

She grinned, sipping her drink. 'As well you might.'

'I suppose that, really and truly, I lead, or have led, a very sheltered life. Mummy and Daddy and two little children and a typewriter.'

'With which you write your books. You *do* write? I mean, you aren't into meditation or weaving, throwing pots or running a sanctuary for stray members of the clergy? I mean, you have been about? Seen the world?'

'Been round it. Been about. And I don't think that suddenly discovering your baby brother is "gay" – that god-awful word they have stolen – is that big a deal. Lots of little boys have funny brothers.'

'Sure. And sisters; leave us not forget.'

'And sisters. But, well, it is like, you know, like murder, plane crashes, train crashes, ships sinking. Happens to other people. Not you.'

'A limited vision, William. You just walked into a new experience. Nothing as catastrophic as a plane crash or a sinking ship. Or a murder.'

'No. Indeed. But it was just, well, not what I expected, although I don't know *what* I expected. But not that ugly house, the elevator, the jogging or . . . anything. It was a little surprising, that's all.'

Martha rattled the ice cubes in her drink, a moth zoomed around the lamp at the door, battered at the glass globe, fell to the floor. 'People live differently. That's all.'

'And I had not the least idea about James; that he had a . . . was queer. Not the least idea. Not at all.'

'Would it have made any difference to you if you had known?'

'I don't suppose so. Hardly knew him really. It would have explained a few things; his sudden angers, sulking, his guilt. I suppose. He was quite consumed by guilt, apparently.'

'Well, it takes people in different ways. Had he reason to be guilty? Apart from his, umm, instincts, or shall we simply call him an "invert" since you are opposed to the word "gay"?'

'There are reasons. Yes. A wife. A child with Down's syndrome. Reasons enough for guilt.'

Martha finished her drink, reached for a pack of cigarettes. 'Got you. I'm sorry. Christ, it gets darker and darker. I didn't know about wives and children. I don't ask questions, as I told you.'

'Yup. Those are the facts. But I honestly just can't see how being . . . "gay" can be applied to him. I can't believe it.'

'It's always possible. We are all apparently born half and half. Does his wife know, do you think? Was, is, she aware?'

'It's possible. Yes. Quite possible. I don't see how he could have completely concealed the facts. But I'm as green as a frog.'

Martha stroked her nose with a chosen cigarette. 'You will realize, of course, that my brother, that is to say my *half*-brother, same daddy, different mommas and a gulf of difference between us both, is also smitten by the same bug? He always has been. He was well mannered about it, extremely correct socially. Millie takes it all very calmly. There is no child. And never will be.' She fished about for a lighter in the pocket of her jeans, lit her cigarette, slid it back.

'I didn't realize he was a half-brother.'

'Our ages could have tipped you off, although I agree that Brent now no longer looks as once he did. Very beautiful, much younger than me, the traditional golden athlete, tall, charming, a vigorous body. Swam, rode like a god, drove very fast cars. He was greatly desired. By one and all. He has a good mind. That is still left to him. But you'd be hard put to realize how splendid he was. Since the fall, about ten years ago now, that good mind has been trapped in a wrecked carcass, strapped in a chair. Now *that*, in my opinion, is catastrophic for the man. *That.* Not discovering, fairly early in life, that he had a predilection for truck drivers and sailors. That he preferred Hansel to Gretel. It's really no big deal.'

'When did he and Millie marry?'

'She came into our lives just before the fall. She came as a temporary typist-secretary when Myrna, his regular girl, suddenly quit. Millie, even though on occasion she looks like a drowned vole, is exceedingly resilient. She is brilliant, not just at her job, coping with his dictation, his manuscripts and so on, but at arranging his life, caring for him. She took him over completely after the accident, cool, calm, controlled, fast at her work, correct. Causes no ripples, asks no questions and adores her cripple. She is rare. He married her. Men do marry their nurses, you know? And it's convenient. She knows that. She doesn't in the least mind "wearing the beard" for her man, part of the deal. In return she is unmolested, lives in comfort, travels the world – she is passionate about renaissance churches, wouldn't you know? – and wears the beard socially, types the manuscripts privately. She packs the suitcases, sacks the staff, orders the meals, and does for him everything that Jojo does *not* do. Do I make myself abundantly clear, William?'

'Abundantly.'

'I have talked myself to a stop.'

'My fault. I am the questioner. I apologize.'

She got up, and stood with her hands on her hips, the empty glass clutched in a fist. 'In a *frock* – I mean a perfectly ordinary girl's frock, floral, with puff sleeves and a Peter Pan collar, you know? – In a frock, a little bit of make-up, and standing defiantly, proudly, beside that ruin of a man, you know she doesn't look a bit odd. Just valiant.'

The Dalmatian heaved himself up suddenly, shook himself into a wild scatter of tail and legs, yawned, ambled slowly into the room, then slumped heavily on to the rush matting at my feet.

'Exhausted, you see? It's getting cool. It does up here when the sun has gone.'

'Can you bear another question?'

'Shoot.'

'Daniel Jacquet? Where does he fit.'

She took my glass, went across to the table with the lamp, took up the Jack Daniels bottle. 'In all the nooks and crannies.' She was grinning. 'Not gay. Absolutely not. *Obliging*, shall I say? Apart from that, he gardens. Well. Trims the cypresses, prunes the olives in season, does the lawns; he is very clever with machines. I nearly said, God forgive me, with his hands. My apologies.' She handed me my replenished glass, settled herself into the swaddle of cushions.

'So he is pretty useful?'

'*And* pretty. Obviously.'

'Yes.'

'There's another. A little older. Martin. He's pretty too. Millie only picks the pretty ones, which, of course, enrages Jojo, who is as jealous as a scorned woman. If he had a brain he'd be dangerous.'

'The accident was a decade ago? He was writing then surely?'

'Brent? Oh sure, he had nine or ten books under his belt. All successful if not overly erudite. Good, exciting reading. He was about thirty-sixish. Jojo was a kid then. Brent picked him up. He was a rent boy from a club in Paris on rue de Cayenne called Le Poisson d'Avril. Run by a gentleman from the Argentine with the proud name of Solomon Aronovich, I kid you not. I do not know him, I have never met him, he is fond of Brent, has been here often. I don't ask questions, as I told you. You do, I do not. I just heard his name here and there, dropped like crumbs at table, you know? And if you have more questions to ask, William dear, you had better get them all marshalled for tomorrow, because they pack up the house and leave for Paris on Monday. Work here is over until July.'

I emptied my glass. Set it down, got up. The Dalmatian instantly raised his head in inquiry, settled again. 'God. I have asked so many questions. Sorry. It must have been hell for you, over the years. I mean, *not* to ask?'

She laughed, a soft deer-bark sort of sound. 'Hellish!' she said.

At the car, standing in the soft light of the lamp in the window, she trod her cigarette butt into the tiles of the terrace.

'Christ!' she said. 'What a bloody world we live in. Everyone gets hurt, we all get damaged. Who is there left to wound now, for God's sake?'

'A wife. A devoted wife. And some kind of a child.'

She was silent, standing looking into the dark. Far away the frogs were chattering in a crescendo. 'Yes. It goes on. I had almost forgotten that. The pain goes on. It's a shitty world, ours.'

'Thank you for your care and attention this evening. Kinder than kind you have been.'

'You are very welcome. Nothing to it. I enjoy company sometimes. I very seldom go up the hill there, as you know. When they go to Paris, and if you are around, drop by? There is plenty left in the bottle.'

She raised one hand in farewell, called the dog, snuffling excitedly in some bushes, and started for the gates.

I eased down the drive ahead of her, turned left at the gates, heard the gates clang and rattle behind me, headed for Bargemon and the Maison Blanche.

A squabble of magpies had gathered on the lawn below the ugly balustrade of L'Hermitage, but the instant that Millie arrived, bracelets clattering, a little out of breath, hastily smoothing the dun-coloured hair which had fluffed up like a hedgehog in her hurry from wherever she had been, they spread their wings and, still bickering, scattered up into the olives.

'Oh my! Good morning! I was so sure that I'd be late for you, I got a little behind with things, we leave tomorrow, and all the packing, and I thought, "I'll be late, and he's due at noon," so I had to speed up a bit but here I am. Welcome!'

'Thank you. You really aren't late. I'm probably early.'

'Well, excuse me being breathy. So many stairs.' She looked about the terrace vaguely. The insect chairs were, today, now arranged in an uneasy circle. By uneasy I mean that they looked as if a conversation had been suddenly disturbed. A conspiracy? The whole terrace, a table at one end laid for lunch, looked like a badly arranged set for a show which had had insufficient rehearsal.

'These awful chairs,' said Millie suddenly. 'We never use them. But do sit down. They are all we have here. We never come down to the terrace, not really. My husband finds it tedious. The elevator and steps and so on.'

She moved to the circle of chairs and sat down. I was bound to follow her example. We sat in silence for a moment.

'Martin – you maybe saw him yesterday evening? In the hall? – well, he'll be down directly with something delicious to drink. And cool. You must be warm after that walk up the hill, and it's a warm day too. My! It's warm for so early in May.'

Millie was wearing a frock. Just as Martha had suggested last evening. A floral frock. Bluish, pinkish, puff sleeves, a Peter Pan collar. Neat, trim. Not high fashion by any means, but pleasant, feminine, better by far than her tracksuit. Her pipe-cleaner legs ended in a pair of blue plastic flip-flops.

Suddenly she said, 'Do you care for lizards? Or do they scare you?'

'Lizards?'

'Yes. Do they scare you?'

'No. Should they?'

'Oh I don't know. But some people do get scared of them.'

'Not me. I won't.'

'Only there are a few scuttering about, quite near your feet. Your right foot. I just thought I'd warn you.'

'Very thoughtful. But they don't bother me.'

'There they are!' she said brightly. 'It's spring. The mating season. You know sometimes they have terrible fights. Roll around. Really bad.'

And then, mercifully, we were silent for a moment, sitting in the sun looking down at the distant view beyond the terrace. She was smiling a soft, abstracted smile. Crippled with shyness. I had made her shy, had made myself shy. She really was, in spite of her girl's frock, amazingly unprepossessing. Her nose was sharp; notwithstanding a blush of light make-up here and there, it succeeded in being very much like that of a vole, pink, wrinkling in the light. The pebble glasses glinting. Her lipstick, very lightly applied, had smudged, giving her the appearance of a hastily, and badly, painted wooden spoon. Millie, I couldn't help thinking, was a very fortunate woman. Whatever her problems.

Suddenly she turned towards me, her eyes wide, one fist clutched firmly to her breast. 'Did I say something? I was dreaming away there, looking at the view, thinking how I'd miss it in Paris, and then you were nodding at me! Agreeing with something. Did I *say* anything? No. Surely not?'

'No. Not at all, Mrs Millar. I was just nodding, if I *was* nodding, with pleasure at the view myself. That's all, really.'

'I am so glad it pleases you too. I love to share it. I

seldom do. And – do you mind? – could you just call me Millie? Mrs Millar is so formal. It's so stiff. Don't you think? I mean, I know you British are very much more formal than we Americans and so on, but, look, it's such a lovely day, so let's be happy. Right?'

'Right. Of course. Then I am William.'

'And I am Millie. Millicent, but everyone just says Millie, so that is done.'

She clapped her hands with pleasure, her eyes beaming behind the thick glasses and at that same moment the youngish-looking man in the apron whom I had seen in the hall the evening before arrived on the terrace as if summonsed. He carried two plastic buckets.

'Why, Martin! I clapped and you arrived,' Millie said in French. He just shrugged, looked about for somewhere to set his buckets. He was about thirty-two or so. Not bad looking, muscular, dark.

'Mr Caldicott here is longing for a refreshing drink. Do you have the white wine?' And, turning to me, she said that everyone preferred the white wine at noon. Rather than spirits. Didn't I agree?

I agreed. Martin set down his buckets, which were filled with bottles. Vodka, whisky, gin, vermouth, cognac, and, mercifully, I saw the slender neck of a Hock bottle. This he grabbed and held out to me like a dead goose.

'Bernkasteler Graben Riesling Eiswein. Eighty-three. Is German.' His English was thick, heavy.

Millie said it was just fine, told him to pour it, placed a tentative hand on my sleeve and said she had to tear away for just a moment; she left flopping across the terrace.

I took my not-overchilled glass and wandered across to the balustrade. Martin called out to me that he was going to go and get the Toy Box. I was obviously expected to ask what that was, so I did.

'The Toy Box? Important for Monsieur Millar. The ice

bucket, the knife, the lemon. All for his martini. He make hisself. Very important.'

I didn't notice him leaving, but heard him come back; he carried a bowl of sweet-peas, which he dumped on the table, and a lacquer box with ice, lemon and knife. He stood looking at the table, counting the things carefully. Under the long apron all he wore was a pair of red briefs. 'Is all fine. All fine. I forget nothing. My English you say is fine? You think I speak good?'

'Very good. But if you prefer, I do speak French.'

'I like speak English. I wanna go America USA. To my uncle. He is in New Jersey. He works a place in the city. La Bergerie. You know this place?'

'No. I don't know New York.'

'Is good place. I wanna go there. Right? He say, "Get your green card, you come to me." I try. Is famous place. Frank Sinatra. You know this man? Dean Martin? Liza Minnelli? They all go this place. I wanna go.'

'I am certain that you will.'

He came towards me slowly, head and voice lowered, a secret to impart. 'You know this Travolta? John Travolta? He dances. Jesus! He dances! All in white suit. I got the video. I see maybe fifty time already! So *sexy*! My goodness, yes. Such an ass! Is amazing –'

Millie's voice, now sharpened like a blade, cut the morning. 'Martin! You are half naked! Put on your pants! Mr Millar will be down directly. Where is his Toy Box?'

Martin's face was splendidly sullen. He indicated the Toy Box, grabbed bottles from the buckets and set them up like ninepins along the table. Millie hissed at him to go and dress and he left, as Daniel, with almost as few clothes to cover *his* glowing body, clumped about in his wellingtons, setting up a couple of big umbrellas while Millie put the bottles neatly, with the Toy Box, on a small marble-topped side-table.

She smiled nervously at me. 'He's a peasant that man. Half Italian. A poor mix. I don't even think he's true Provençal. Maybe Yugoslav.'

'He wants to go to the US, I gather.'

'He does. He listens to the American Forces Network all day. That's how he learns his English. You think he'll make out?'

'He seems fairly determined.'

'He's certainly that all right. But he's good in the kitchen.' She was busy rearranging the sweet-peas on the table, checking the place settings, examining a wine glass, holding it to the sun. 'Sometimes,' she said. 'He leaves fingerprints all over.'

I don't honestly remember much about the arrival of Brent Millar, except that suddenly, it would appear, he was on the terrace. Straw hat, dark glasses, cashmere rug, not for warmth but concealing twisted limbs. He raised a hand, an elegant hand as I had noted before, in greeting. Jojo hard behind him, smiling his dead-eye smile. Crisp white jeans, a T-shirt, silver chains glittering.

Millie said, 'The Toy Box is ready. You'll be longing for your drink? It's just after noon.'

I don't remember all the details of that morning. I do remember with blinding clarity, because it was so perfectly performed, the ritual of the Toy Box.

First, the chilling of the crystal glass with a handful of ice cubes, the slow peeling of the zest of the lemon skin, a scrap no larger than a fingernail, the violent swirling of the ice in the glass, the clatter which it made, the sudden hurling of the cubes hard across the terrace. The merest tear from the Martini bottle, swirled round the glass, discarded, and finally, with ceremony, the topping to the brim with gin, the gentle slipping of the finger-squeezed zest into the icy liquid. The perfect martini had been made.

Did we speak? We must have done so. Easy platitudes

about the sun, the calling of the first cuckoo . . . Millie made that contribution. Sounds: the scrape of metal chairs on the terrace tiles, the clatter and clink of cutlery on plates. Martin, trousered now, efficiently serving, silent, quick.

I don't remember much else until Millar said suddenly, 'You were late down there at Martha's? We saw your car parked for quite some time. She is a good hostess. She tell you about her travels?'

'Yes. We just talked, about places we had been to. How they had altered today . . . She serves a generous whisky.'

'She does indeed. One can become quite loquacious, after a couple of her glasses. We were working up in the office. Preparing for the move back to Paris. That's a bore but essential. Proofs read, all tidy. And we were attending to a little job for you. I do hope that you will be pleased with our effort. Millie, in particular, was exceedingly hardworking.'

Millie bobbed her head like a nodding duck on a pub bar.

'Trying to wade through close-written agendas is difficult. We have saved you time by copying a few pages. At random, you understand, at random, here and there. We have all the facilities: scanners, copiers, paper, computers. Very efficient.'

I mumbled thanks. Cheese was served, bread in a basket, butter in a terracotta crock standing in iced water, biscuits. Millar ate well, dropping crumbs and cheese rind all about him which Jojo, without any overt movement, removed neatly and carried to his own plate.

A second bottle of Domaine d'Ot was offered, but I covered my glass with my hand. Millar laughed, his teeth rimmed with cheese and bread.

'Keeping a clear head? You'll need it. Coffee, Martin.'

Across the terrace, below the balustrade, there was a puddle of water where the scattered ice cubes had long since melted. Far away, the cuckoo. Three calls. The chink of coffee spoons. The rattle of the elevator gate and I was in the white and yellow apartment with Jojo.

'You go and sit down,' he said. 'I reckon you know the way?' He eeled back into the cage and went down to collect the wheelchair.

For some reason I preferred to stand, not to sit in the zebra or pony chairs. Just to wait until they arrived. I felt, perfectly idiotically, as apprehensive as a child at the dentist.

Millar was silently at the elevator door fanning himself with his hat. Jojo behind him, closing the grill.

'You have about three hours. Understood? It can't be any longer, we are on our way tomorrow and there are things to pack. Sorry about lunch, it was almost a picnic.'

'It was fine. I usually have mashed potatoes and piccalilli . . .'

Millar looked at me flatly. 'I can see you are not gross. Everything is in the small study, so you won't be under our feet.'

'I am most grateful.'

'Why not wait until you have finished? Wiser.' He turned himself and rolled quietly away.

The little study was booklined, a desk, a pile of notebooks, a closed box-file. There were assorted pens and a ream of paper. A bottle of Evian and a glass.

Jojo was smiling his dead smile.

'The file is yours. To take away. You'll find that Mr Millar has put little markers here and there in the books. To save you time. You might miss something wonderful.' He raised his hand, one finger extended. 'If you faint or need something, just holler, we are right across the hall. Ciao!'

And he left.

A pile of well-thumbed notebooks, with the word 'Agenda' printed across the covers. Each numbered, none dated. They did not contain a daily journal; rather they resembled, riffling through them hurriedly in the first few moments, a writer's notebook. Items sprang out, were cancelled in heavy felt pen; pages were, as Jojo had said, slipped with coloured little cards. It would be impossible, I knew as I touched them, to sit and read them through. They covered years.

How, then, can I best get it over to you? How can I avoid the ugliness? Keep to the basic essential? To paraphrase is wisest obviously. And like all stories, to start at the beginning. Okay. We're off.

It may be as well here to note that I did jot down, at the very start, some of the leading points.

The first important entry is in retrospect. School. Sixteen, and a certain Mr Worth discovers his secret cache of:

perfectly splendid Beardsley drawings and some quite exciting muscle-men in California. Worth insists they are corrupting. I am to be beaten!

Bent over a chair in Mr Worth's study, James is given six of 'the very best he can muster' and, unfortunately, shouts out in apparent pain.

Not pain! But delight! Worth driven to a rage strikes again!

James finds it difficult to move after this beating. The pain, if such it was, and a sudden, and embarrassing, physical development force him to remain prone. Worth, enraged apparently, grabs the youth and is greatly disturbed by what he sees:

His glasses misted up, and he just took hold of my body as if I was a frying-pan. I exploded!

And so we have started. The glory of sado-masochism has been discovered and James embraced that particular side of life at Loggwood School with alacrity. Presumably driving poor Worth mad as a result. But school is school, college is college, and there came a time when James put aside childish things. Nevertheless the seed had been sown.

To Paris then, a young painter discovering the glory and joy after

the drabness and boredom of London. A small studio, meals on the run, painting, arguing, discussing, meeting, doing, in fact, just about everything one does do as a creative creature discovering life.

The allowance from Papa just about covers this life, but he manages, now and again, to augment his money by selling little pieces here and there. A great deal of time is spent in the Louvre and various other galleries, now and again a girl slips into view, and into bed, and as easily slips out again. Life, student life, is all as usual. Apart from the fact that James is extremely vain about his 'beauty', as he calls it, there is really nothing of interest in the very beginning.

In the second, or third, I've forgotten exactly, he is still chirruping away about his looks.

I am, I realize, the perfect Beardsley model. I have the height, colouring, elegance. Except for the flounces and the frills which I would never affect. Or the wigs! I am more the Greeks and Gods whom he draws and all the other licentious fellows. Prefer boots to bows, belts to buttons. Bonds above all!

In spite of his splendidly normal life as a student, the little seed long since planted still lies dormant. Almost.

And then, halfway into one Agenda he makes a startling, to him, discovery.

René takes me to an utterly amazing place. A very à la mode club called Le Poisson d'Avril. Exhilarating! Amazing! All sexes present! Dark, pools of light, noise, crammed. My eyes stand out like those of a lobster. I have never seen such sights, heard such sounds. Great music. I could paint here for ever.

He burbles on, comparing himself to a

very minor Lautrec. The faces, the bodies, cry out to be captured on paper.

His modesty stuns. This is the first of many, many visits, he becomes a regular and is accepted as such. But he continues painting and even has a small, 'very tiny display' in a gallery, which sells.

A little green card, thoughtfully slipped into one of the following Agendas, alerts me and saves my eyesight. James's tales are banal, his handwriting minute but a story line is developing. The green card points the way.

An unexpected, and for that reason amazing meeting at the Poisson. Solly, the patron [Aronovich clearly] *takes me to the private loge of Brent Millar, the writer. He is being treated like an Emperor! Everyone is staggered by his looks.*

Including James, who describes him thus:

Tall, golden, bronzed, obviously very *athletic, with slender hands like a pianist, but above all blue eyes which are incandescent.*

First arrival on the scene of Mr Millar. More to follow. Seeing James he goes into the Agenda with the following immortal lines:

Dear God! Just look! Here we have Narkissos to the life. Safe and well and living in Paris, France! I assume that you have *fallen in love with your appearance already? Or is that still to come?*

No. He had fallen in love with his reflection and so, it would appear, had Brent Millar for, before long, James is a regular visitor to the 'glorious apartment on Île Saint-Louis' and meets another regular.

Such books and such paintings! Dufy, Miró, Modigliani, Sisley! Flowers everywhere, and a black manservant, about my age, who is ravishingly beautiful, called Jojo. He once worked at the Poisson.

And so it goes on, this story. I almost forgot from time to time that I was reading about someone I knew. Well, *thought* that I had known. But obviously this was a James no one beyond the Île Saint-Louis and the club did know. Millar bided his time, he did not force his attentions on his pupil; he merely let him look, listen and learn from watching. The club became his passion, even though he continued with his work, and had another modest exhibition, which, again, was a success and brought him some money which, living as he now was, was clearly needed. Papa's allowance was not elastic. He had to work. But another coloured card alerted me to another key moment in the life of my brother. Apparently at the Poisson there was a small private room for select members. This room had a small stage, rows of seats, and was strictly a private affair. Here 'demonstrations' of various sexual kinds were given. Sometimes with poetry readings to accompany the 'demonstration' or tableau or tableaux. These, as might be expected, all glorified maleness, sex, violence, brutality, pain, torture and, above all, the 'glorification of extreme humiliation'. In short, this private club was a bondage club.

The first time there, James was merely a privileged spectator at the express invitation of Brent Millar, who was dressed, apparently ready to take a hand in the proceedings, thus:

Booted, breeches of impeccable and close cut, white silk shirt, a little whip with a swan-head handle.

The heart sinks. One ploughs on. Everyone present is suitably attired, some as Nazis, some as motorcycle police, or soldiers in the cavalry. The others, and there have to be others, are sailors, boy scouts or just wear riding-boots and a cache-sex. There is smoke, there is very soft blues music, and the sound of Solly (Aronovich) reading poetry.

He announced the performance we shall presently see. My heart thuds. Brent had his hand on my thigh and stroked me urgently. His eyes burned into me with the force of an electric drill.

Well, you may imagine with all that drilling it was not very long before young James had been hypnotized. Stoat and rabbit stuff. Gently, with a good deal of flattery and cajoling, one must suppose, James was persuaded to partake of the rituals one evening. To take part in one of the exclusive tableaux himself. As a victim, naturally. And therefore very soon after this initiation, James, naked as the day he was born, shaved, oiled, as smooth and suggestive as a Canova marble, was carried, chained and securely bound, over the shoulders of his Master, one Jojo. The tableau was called, as you might guess, 'Le Blanc et le Noir'. James, high on coke, limp and submitting. Jojo gleaming, armed with a whip, began the dance of humiliation and bondage. James's fate (as well as his lips – he was gagged with a belt) was finally sealed.

I reckoned, about this time, that enough was quite enough. The books, or Agendas, lay before me, the box-file remained untouched. I didn't even drink the water. But I had made use of the pens and paper.

I walked out of the little study. Jojo was lying on a sofa in the white and yellow room reading a magazine. He sprang up when he saw me.

'You through?'

'Through. Is Mr Millar awake anywhere? I mean, before I leave.'

Brent Millar was wheeled towards me, head to one side, the eyes, the incandescent blue eyes, half lowered. Questioning.

'You finished? It was quickly done.'

'I have seen enough. Thanks.'

'Don't hit me, I'm a cripple.' An uneasy smile.

'I wasn't about to hit you. I'm grateful to you for letting me see what I have seen. But it's all I want. I don't want to know *who* James Caldicott was. I want to know *where* he is presently.'

Millar raised his arms, spread the elegant fingers, smiled with a degree of weariness.

'There I cannot help you. None of us can, I think . . . Where in the movie, so to speak, did you come in?'

'I came in at the old-school story. Left on your arrival.'

'You have missed the best parts.' He was smiling. 'Why don't you sit for a moment. I have time if you have.'

I sat, in one of the zebra chairs. Jojo, I think, must have sighed a little sigh of relief, for he resumed his posture on the settee, picked up his magazine.

'I am not astonished. I just find it all pretty tacky really. It's the same old bit of porn. Starting with the thrashing from the teacher which set him on course; he would have us believe . . . But how long did it go on for, that life? I know that he continued painting – there were exhibitions here and there, that much he did leave in his notes which I have here. But when did it finish? When did he get to Bargemon?'

Millar ran a hand through his still blond hair. 'It all broke up after my mishap in Ireland at a wired "bullfinch". After that a cloud descends. We all went our separate ways. James was really only half and half, you know? He was fascinated by it all, he longed for domination. He simply adored sex and was very, very good at it. But, truthfully, he did want a different life. It was really a kind of delayed adolescence. I used him cruelly. But when my lamp went out, James decided to quit. Aronovich suggested Bargemon. Silence, calm, beauty. And not too far away from me. Should I ever recover. You follow?'

'Perfectly. And then?'

Millar shrugged. 'And then? I was considered dead. He began a new life down here, with the assistance of the amiable Aronovich, and he apparently began to paint again.'

'And the marriage?'

'Oh *that*. Well, when I was able to return here, and that took a very long time, James was a fairly frequent guest. Totally changed, radiant, in love, cleansed of his earlier lusts and longings, a rebirth. One *thought*. And I was utterly useless. There was no further temptation, no desire. I was a faithful old crippled-father-figure. It was fine. Absolutely understandable. I was very happy that he had managed to find his, shall we say, way. And until the child was born, that unfortunate error for which he blamed himself quite brutally, I really hardly ever saw him.'

'And after the child?'

Millar sighed, shook his head. He might have been sincere when he said, 'After the child it would appear that he felt that he had to atone for the wickedness of his act. He appeared always to blame himself for, shall we say, past demeanours? *Quite* absurd of course, nothing to do with his sexual frivolities in the past. But he sought punishment again, very modestly. It seemed to ease him to feel that he was guilty and could atone. I can't explain why. I didn't really try to understand. He spent most of that time with others. I stayed away. Not very much I could do stuck in a chair. Maddening. But I always was a good *audience. I* didn't have to perform, I did not crave the limelight in that direction, I get it through my books. My work. I am sure you will understand that?'

'Yes. But why would James start to write a book? For that is what those Agendas all amount to, don't they? A rather wearying pornographic book.'

'In one. That's what they are. Ready, almost, for the typist. So clearly written, don't you agree? Detailed? Good construction.'

'If you like that sort of stuff.'

'Lots of people do. You have to be very clever to write like that. You must have a tremendous amount of imagination.'

'But you bought them? Right? You surely must have felt that they had some kind of promise?'

There was a silence: Jojo laid down his magazine, Millar looked at the back of his hands, and then up at me. He was smiling gently.

'You *have* heard of blackmail?' he said.

CHAPTER 11

I DROVE BACK to Bargemon in the evening sunlight. The lodge was firmly shuttered. No dog. An elderly man, his bike leaning against the carless shed, nodded to me to wait, tied in the last sweet-pea, came across the little garden to open the gates. Madame, he said, was in Sainte-Brigitte.

At the hotel, a scatter of people sitting about at the tin tables on the terrace, children running with a balloon, parasols with 'CINZANO' on their frills flapping in the soft breeze. A ball was thrown, a dog barked, camera clicked, someone dropped a saucer.

Sunday. Shortly they'd leave, the day was almost over. I had lost track of time, day, hours. Everything. I had only one urgent desire and that was for a drink. I hadn't lost track of my way to the bar.

In the hall Madame Mazine greeted me pleasantly, gave me an envelope. 'Madame Annette left this. Half an hour ago. Will you be dining in the hotel?' I said I would and went through to get my Scotch; I was as dry as an oat-cake.

The bar was full, laughter, the till ringing, the pintable clattering. On the television, high up in the corner, Johnny Halliday writhed in copious sweat hitting a guitar.

I took my drink and the box-file over to the little table in the corner. The note was from Florence. Odd that I had never seen her handwriting before. It was almost childish, but neat, sloping forwards, not backwards, modest loops to the 'l's.

'Sunday: If you have time, can you call me at Dr Colin's surgery in the morning? Between 8.30 and noon. I am helping the new girl to settle in. Sincerely.' And she had signed it 'Florence Caldicott'.

Later, up in my room, under the raised eyes of Jesus and the patting paws of the kittens, I changed my shirt, washed my face, stared at my reflection in the speckled mirror of the wardrobe. Even allowing for the speckles, it was a fairly ordinary face. Pity.

From the window the dying sun was turning the clifftops to vermilion fire, a swing of swallows swept upwards against the fading blue of the sky and scattered. I felt a strange loneliness suddenly. A feeling of isolation. I had an overwhelming longing to go off right away to the rue Émile Zola and not to wait until tomorrow for contact with Florence. I wanted to see her, touch her, or at least feel her near me. I wanted to see those steady grey eyes, be comforted by her calm. After the operatic nonsense I had just read, and more of which lay, I was certain, in the box-file on my bed, a little sanity would not come amiss. Banal ordinariness would be balm.

But there were problems in such urgent desires, Thomas for one, Madame Prideaux for another. And anyway, perhaps they had friends in for tea or lemonade or something. Such a fine evening.

So, set desire apart, get down to work.

On the white counterpane of the hillocky bed the box-file looked like a black coffin.

Inside, a bundle of papers, the copies from the Agendas, neatly held in a metal clip. Beneath them a sealed brown envelope. Stapled on the top, a card:

I trust that these random pieces will be sufficient to satisfy you and your curiosity! They are, I would venture to suggest, self-explanatory. It might be useful to you if I point out that the Lodge gates are at all times locked against exits and entrances. You might well speak with the lodge-keeper. If you have any queries.

There was no signature. But that didn't matter.

The first page, on top of the Agenda copies, was a copy of a letter. It was undated.

Jericho.

My dear Master,

How wretched it always is when I return here from the pleasures of your retreat! The depression in this house is appalling. The mournful face, the whimpering child, the greyness! Oh! For light! For glory! For excitement and the touch of hungry lips! To pleasure myself I have been re-reading some of my Agendas. Remember them? I have kept them faithfully since our first encounter all those years ago, as you know. It is quite fascinating to watch the development from callow youth-unaware to – I trust! – faithful and experienced servant. How much *I learned from you. You who made me aware for the first time that the Oxford Dictionary is sometimes short of a meaning and that the word penetrate does not only apply to 'thought' or 'thicket'! What fun! Could you perhaps give me some advice on where to place these little pieces of erotica? Seems such a waste to leave them rotting in a drawer in the studio. I think* Stern *or* Spiegel *in Germany, and others in France and Holland, would be quite interested. And I desperately need the money. Solly has been generous, but I want so much to get away. To start anew before it is too late and I am too old. Perhaps you could advise me next time I am 'summonsed'?*

Your trusting slave, pupil, and ever-humiliated servant.

This ugly piece of work was signed simply with a 'J.' Must have caused a ripple of unease in the white and yellow room up on the third floor. I was not amazed that Millar had kept it. Copied it, and attached it to the pieces which Millie, and obviously he himself, had chosen for my education.

How much of all this did Florence know? Did she have the very least idea of her 'husband's' other life? Of the whips, the belts, the chains, the desperate need for 'humiliation' and pain. His need, as these pages showed so clearly, for domination and degradation, when only the screamed word 'Pax!' could bring torture to a stop. Did she know? *Could* she know? She had once said that sex had an odour. She had practically ripped a thumbnail off when she had spoken of Jojo and Daniel Jacquet. She must have known something.

He writes of

the supreme excitement of being straddled by your black glossy boots. The slippery delight of that oiled plastic sheeting . . . tied and helpless, waiting your command to Jojo to administer my punishment.

Now then, come on! Surely she *must* have known? How could he hide his cuts and bruises, for God's sake? I assume there had to be some? Did she ever see Daniel

all in his leathers, so tight that you could not have slipped a playing-card between the taut black skin and his hard flesh. Feeling the heat of him straining against my lusting mouth . . .

And so on.

She did know Jojo. He had gone on the false honeymoon. Now, why? Had she the very least idea that in the early days Jojo had been the one who readied the complaisant

James for Millar's savage whip? Did she know, much later, after the famous fall, that James, bound and spread, was dragged (of course willingly, that was all part of the fun) to the eager hands and greedy mouth of Brent Millar? Paralysed from the waist down but sexually capable if manipulated and his prey was brought 'struggling' to his side.

Did she have the least idea of any of this? Could she? Was there only a deepening silence after the birth of Thomas? She said so; said that they had lain side by side in the barren bed. But could that possibly be so? There was, I recollected, the empty room next to Thomas's room. Did he seek refuge there? Or in the studio perhaps? When Jojo and Daniel came to pose, it would appear, for their portraits or whatever they all did together up there.

Impossible to guess. Impossible, equally, to ask Florence. How could I?

I only skip-read this stuff. The light had gone completely and I had put on the elephant-lamp and sat and stared at the secret James in my hands. There was also the envelope.

Photographs. One or two. One large one which so surprised me that I did catch my breath. Quite loudly. Loud enough for me to hear myself say, 'Oh! Christ!'

The nightmare had come true. There before me was the same image of James, golden, glowing, white, brilliant, naked and crucified. Arms and legs wide, head lowered, the remembered fall of blond hair tumbled, trussed in an aura of shimmering light, a gleaming naked Jojo kneeling before him, one black hand placed on a white thigh, the other holding a thick whip. All in vivid Technicolor. Eight by ten.

There was no sign of a Jojo in my nightmare, only the hideous image, glowing, pulsating, it had seemed, in an explosion of light. But otherwise what I presently held in my hand was precisely what had awakened me in a sweating terror of hatred. The unfinished crossword puzzle of my life finished by the tidy filling in of the final word.

Hate.

And I sat there on my bed, slumped, exhausted by ugliness, by the shock of discovery, of revelation.

How had this come about? How had a photograph, taken years before it seemed by the look of his youthful body, suddenly been imprinted into my sleeping brain?

Here I was looking at the darker side of a golden moon: and dark, God knew, it was.

There was a little scatter of black-and-white photographs in the file. Postcard size, some almost sepia with time. Some taken, it would appear, in the early days of the 'Paris sequence', when James's body was more supple, slender; others, and there were only a sparse half dozen or so altogether, were far later. He had become adult, muscular, firm.

I held the gathered photographs in my hand like a loser's hand at a bad game of poker. Weary with distaste. Brent Millar had, indeed, a great deal to be ashamed of: his quiet remark to me at L'Hermitage, 'Don't hit me, I'm a cripple', was well said. Of course I should have struck him. Too bloody English to do that. His corruption was clear in every line of the sordid little Agendas, every one of the photographs held in my hand.

But why panic and settle such a sum for blackmail? No magazine, wherever it was, would contemplate the stuff.

Would they?

Perhaps they might just keep him 'in sight', as it were; he'd be followed about, wheelchair or no wheelchair.

My sad, funny little brother ranged before me in a series of very unfunny situations of extreme degradation. Humility, humiliation, bondage. Why? Florence had said that I would find the results, at L'Hermitage, and indeed she had been right. But she had said that I would never find the reason. I wonder?

I wonder if the reason for this extreme, abject desire for punishment, for pain, for abuse, was because as a golden 'ewe lamb', as a creature adored, cosseted, spoiled, pampered, treasured from unexpected birth, he suddenly felt the desperate need to be brutalized, to be treated savagely, dragged *from* adoration and defiled before witnesses. For, it would appear, his degradation had to be *observed.* A form of public vandalism: sullied perfection. Rip the Frans Hals, smash the Michelangelo, defecate on the altar. The uglier, more profane, the better. Punishment for the years of being too well loved.

At school, at sixteen, Mr Worth had thrashed him. The first time that a violent hand had ever been laid upon him. And he had reacted accordingly. Could this be possible? Had I perhaps found the reason after all? The church clock struck the half-hour. I chucked the photographs and copies into the file, went over to the window. In the yard below someone with a wagging torch was locking up the hens. The sky was as blue as damson skin. Far above the shadow of the cliffs, a star blazed with a diamond light; so brilliant was it that for a moment I thought it might be the lamp on some idiot hang-glider coasting down. But it was motionless. The torch bobbed back towards the house, someone was whistling 'La Mer'.

So I knew *who* James was now. I did not know *where* he was. Yet. But it was just conceivable that I might have stumbled on 'the reason'.

Tomorrow, when I called her, I'd tell Florence.

I'd go to Jericho and destroy this stuff in the open fireplace. Then take up Millar's suggestion to go and pay a visit to the lodge-keeper.

If she was there.

Florence was abashed.

'I forgot to write the number here. How did you find me?'

'In the book. There is only one Pierre Colin, Dentist in town.'

'I'm so sorry. It's a long time since we spoke, I wondered if all was well? After your visit, I mean?'

'Well. I mean *I* am well. The visit was pretty bizarre. Can we meet?'

'Yes. I would like that. You can be free?'

'Can you?'

'Oh yes. I finish at twelve. I have done what I had to do.'

'I have to go over to Saint-Basile-les-Pins first. Could you come over to Jericho? About three?'

There was uncertainty in her voice when she replied. 'I think so. It's just . . . Thomas, you know? I can't leave Céleste with him all afternoon and all this morning. It's too much.'

'Bring him. He likes the garden. Likes me. All right?'

'You are certain? Céleste can come with us. We can't talk and amuse him at the same time. I want to talk to you. Importantly. You know why?'

'How could I?'

'I got a telephone call from Mr Aronovich. In Cannes. He wants to know when it would be convenient to collect the canvases after all this time. He has to have them framed.'

'I see.'

'Perhaps we can discuss this when we meet?'

'We must, Florence, we must. At three? This is *very* interesting news.'

I replaced the receiver and looked at my unmade bed.

Mr Aronovich indeed. What could I gather from him? And when, and where? It was going to be a busy day.

After leaving Bargemon-sur-Yves the road begins to wind down to the plain, and I was stuck behind a large cart, pulled by an ambling ox, which creaked down the slight hill. An old man, sitting on a pile of sawn logs, waved cheerfully and spat from time to time into the stone walls which ran alongside. He was not about to hurry; nor, for that matter, was the ox. I had learned early that the one essential word one had to learn in Provence, and accept instantly, was the word 'patience'. In the post office I had only once become greatly frustrated, wanting only one stamp, by an aged woman in black who was paying for a parcel in every tiny coin she could find at the bottom of a crumbling leather purse. Each coin when found was very deliberately placed on the counter, counted, steadied, and then the search would continue. Frustration mounting I tried to lean over her humped figure to gain the attention of the postmistress for my single stamp to England. The crone grabbed my arm and hissed furiously, 'Patience!' I decided to ration my letters to Helen and the children from that day on.

I finally passed the trundling cart and went through the greening pines, shimmering now with pea-green buds, and reached the gates of L'Hermitage.

Martha was there. Beyond her, far up the drive, Daniel was slowly raking back the gravel scattered by a convoy of cars.

I pulled into the gateway, caught Martha's attention with a wave. She was planting in a large stone urn, eye-patch, red handkerchief in her hair. She looked up, recognized me, came slowly towards the gate.

'They've left. Three hours ago. For the airport at Marseilles.'

'I want to see you. Not them. Possible?'

She shrugged, rubbed her forehead with the back of her hand, a plant firmly held. 'I'm putting out the bedding-plants. Petunias. Early, shouldn't do it before the 25th in case the iceman cometh. Okay, come on in.'

'No. Don't open the gates. I can speak through them.'

She started to unlock them. 'I refuse to talk to you through bars. We aren't in prison. Yet.'

I followed her and watched her dig in the last petunia. Then she sat on an upturned crate. Reached for a cigarette in her jeans pocket. 'You haven't come to sell me a subscription to anything. Of that I am perfectly certain. Sit down. Take that box, it's empty.'

I upended the box she indicated and sat in front of her. She lit a cigarette, slid the lighter into the breast pocket of her shirt.

'If,' she said, carefully removing a thread of tobacco from her upper lip, 'if it has anything to do with up there, or him, the Adonis with the rake, I don't want to know. I *don't* know, and I never *have* known. End.'

'Indirectly, it has.'

'I dislike enormously anything which is "indirect". So don't bother.'

'You knew James. My brother. You opened and closed the gates for him, you said.'

She raised a hand to the Dalmatian which had come lolloping round the side of the house. '*You* are supposed to be my guardian, idiot. You know, they used to run under the carriage, in pairs, in the old days? Very chic. Yes, I opened the gates for your brother. On occasion. Sometimes not. If I'm away someplace I call old Berthe to come in and help out. He has a hideous little villa down the road. Useful.'

'The last time James was here, it was January.'

'Am I supposed to remember January? It's May already.' She turned away and pulled a narrow wooden box towards her; it was filled with plants. 'Nemesia,' she said suddenly. 'Blue Gem. And behind them white Nicotiana. Do you like gardening?'

'I wondered if you could remember that time?'

'I have just stuck in twenty heliotrope. Royal Marine. Dark blue. It is supposed to smell of cherry pie. Did you know?'

'James. January?'

'It was a long time ago. Let it rest. I am not involved with your little brother, and I don't want to be involved. I get this place rent-free, no one bothers me. I have had a very active life; now I want rest, peace and oblivion.'

'So did he.'

She picked up a small plastic pot, pressed the soil with her finger. 'Tough tit,' she said. Then, 'This is bone dry. They all are. Never buy anything in the market at Sainte-Brigitte, they'll swindle you.'

'Your brother told me there was a light snowfall that evening.'

'You really hang on in there, don't you? So? So what if there was a light, or slight, snowfall? Would I be out in it?'

'To open the gate.'

'He was on a bike. He could have opened it himself –' She stopped abruptly. Set the pot and the plant aside.

'He was on a bike. Correct. So you knew? I mean, you saw him?'

She sighed, dragged on her cigarette, blew a long feather of smoke into the warm air. 'Okay. I saw him leave. Yes.'

'Thank you. Really, I mean it. Thank you. Look, I didn't want to get into this either. I didn't want to get involved. I didn't even *like* James, I hardly knew him. I have enough problems of my own. But I suddenly found myself getting caught up in things, in spite of myself. Things take on a force of their own. You kind of get led, if you know what I mean. You start to walk across the beach, so to speak, find that you are on quicksand and the more you struggle the deeper you sink.'

She was smiling at me. Not with me – *at* me. 'What a metaphor!' she said. 'Clever old you. Neat. I've been there myself.'

'What I now have to ask myself is this. If there was a light fall of snow, if he was on a bicycle, apparently ill-dressed for a winter trip, what the hell was he doing? How did he expect to go anywhere. At dusk? In snow. In January?'

'You use the past tense all the time when you speak of him. Deliberate?'

I shuffled about on my upturned box. 'I don't know. Instinctive, I suppose. I have no proof of "was" or "is".'

The dog, who had slumped down beside her, raised his head, rose to his feet and trotted slowly up the drive.

'Daniel has finished that part of his labours. Does he know that there is more to do down here? Avoiding us perhaps?' She suddenly shouted up to him in French. 'Daniel! Don't forget down here. It's like the army came through.'

I did not turn to watch him, but heard him whistling, the boots crunch in the gravel, the prongs of the rake rattling through the little stones.

'I have filled these pots', Martha said, 'with petunias. Blue and white. The blue ones have a sweet scent. In the evenings . . . Don't just sit and stare at me, William! I don't *know* any more. Really I don't.'

She began to stuff her shirt-tail back into her jeans, the cigarette hanging from carmined lips, good eye squinting against the smoke. I rose. The box clattered over. Daniel was raking away; a small silver crucifix hanging from a chain glittered at his throat.

'He left. Just like that. In the dark. In snow? You saw him go?'

She patted her stomach, took the cigarette from her mouth, trod on it and then bent to cup it in the hollow of her hand. 'With the beady-eyed one I can't really scatter litter, can I?'

She began to walk slowly towards the gates. 'There was a car,' she said, and threw the butt into the road.

'A car?'

'Parked beyond the gates. It was there for an hour or so before he came down. Not riding the bike. Pushing it. When he got halfway down he switched on his headlamp. The car started up.' She was standing with her back to me, one hand on the left-hand gate.

'What kind of car, Martha?'

'I don't know what kind of car. Solid. Probably a Peugeot 604.'

'What happened to his bike? No room in the car surely? A roof rack?'

Martha swung wide the gate to let me pass through. The meeting was over.

'He left the bike by the wall here. Just here. It's in my shed. You want to test it for fingerprints? Some other time, William.'

Out on the road I said, as the gate closed, 'Which way did it go? The car. Right or left?'

'To the left. Where you have come from. It had an 06 registration.'

'Shit. Where is 06?'

'Alpes Maritimes. This is the Var. *We* are 83. It is very glitzy, 06: Nice, Cannes, Antibes.'

She leant against the gate, her face pressed through the bars. 'That's all, William.'

'I am deeply grateful.'

'You're a nice guy. A good fellow. I mean *you* wouldn't microwave a kitten, would you?' She was smiling, her good eye sparkling.

'No. Never.'

'But we both know people who would. Right?'

'Yes. We do.'

'Sad. But good luck. I hope you find him, *if* that's what you want.

'Thank you. That's what I want.'

'Well . . .' She turned away, one hand raised in half-salute. 'Be strong,' she said, and walked back to the lodge.

Daniel looked up from his work, shook his rake at me as

once he had done before, but this time he was grinning broadly.

As I started the engine, Martha was pulling on her gardening-gloves. She didn't look back.

I only just got to Jericho in time. It was a few moments to three as I pulled the car into the driveway by the mossy pillar.

The house looked, as houses always do when they are shuttered and left, forlorn, unwanted, awaiting life to return. A dry rock awaiting the flow of the tide. I burnt the contents of the box-file on the open hearth. When I had finished I went out, locked the door and sat in the car to wait for Florence.

Wondering, in a mild turmoil of thought, exactly what to tell her, how to tell her, if I should tell her.

Consider: I had not seen her since the afternoon up at Jericho village. Since than a whole new, astonishing world had been revealed to me. How much of this world did she know? Where to tread, to avoid pain, how to probe, to get her to reveal what she knew without actually having to get her to face the unpalatable truths?

And then I was pushed into action as the green Renault bumped up the track, the sun glancing on the chrome, a podgy fist waving at one of the black windows.

Dragging Céleste behind him like a bulky kite, Thomas ran, stumbling, half falling, twisting in her iron grip, towards me. Florence called out above the slamming of car doors.

'I told him we were coming to see you. Look how pleased he is!'

He grabbed me round the knees with one strong arm, bringing Céleste and myself uncomfortably close together. She laughed, and tried to get him to let me free, but he crowed with pleasure, blowing and puffing his 'Ppppf' word, and only relaxed his grip when I stooped and kissed him. Then, in an instant, he relaxed, raised his stubby arms towards me to lift him smiling, laughing, his eyes screwed tight with pleasure.

Céleste stood back holding, of all things, the red and silver trumpet with which I had been greeted the very first time he and I had ever met. I held him close in both arms. He was not what one might call light but Florence was smiling, happy. Amazingly adjusted to our affection.

'You have a magic touch. He knew we were coming, he brought the tin trumpet for you. It's his most treasured possession. A gift to you.' She took it from Céleste, pointed it at me. 'Thomas. This is for William? Yes? Your trumpet?'

For a moment he was apprehensive, he swung round in my arms, reached towards his mother, his fingers wagging for the toy. She handed it to him carefully, he took it, held it, and then pushed it at my face. He was beaming with pleasure, bent his thick neck to mine, pushing it at my face, dribbling with joy.

'It's for you. You have to take it.'

I took the thing, handed it to Céleste, who was very watchful, and quickly spun him round in my arms so that for a moment he was bewildered, then got the idea of a kind of game, and shouted incomprehensibly for me to do it again. I say 'incomprehensibly', except that I understood.

Florence started up the track towards the gate and I stopped her with a shout.

'Let's go for a walk. Up this drive. To the château ruins? Under the cedar trees. The garden is a bit dreary. Okay?' She nodded, changed track and the four of us turned about and set out for the orchard and the abandoned park of the château.

'I thought these were apple trees. When I first came here.'

Céleste said no, they were olive trees, and badly in need of care. 'They must be cut right back. There will be no fruit for two years.'

Thomas was rather heavy. I set him down and, while he was complaining, explained why I had done so, and holding his hand walked up through the soft May grasses to the cedar trees. The tumbled tower of the château was busy: a pair of ravens circled about the ivy-covered stones, with shrill cries.

Under one of the trees, in warm shade, I sat down and pulled Thomas with me, holding his trumpet. He watched, eyes brimming with delight, to see what would happen next. Nothing did. I told him I was tired, that we were all going to sit down for a while, and he hit me smartly with his trumpet, laughing.

'He perfectly understands,' said Florence. 'The trouble is that he is so energetic. Poor Céleste. Céleste!' She patted the grass beside her. 'Céleste, sit! Take the weight from your legs, and take Thomas off his uncle.'

But this proved harder to do than say. It was some time before they could make him relax his grip on me and go off, unwillingly, turning back from time to time, with the stalwart Céleste dragging him for a walk. Only then could Florence and I relax enough to look at each other.

'So. A moment of peace. But I had to bring him. She can't have him all day, it's too much. She's not old, but you need a lot of strength for him.'

'I can tell. Well, I have been to L'Hermitage.'

'I knew. And?'

'And . . . it was very strange indeed. I don't know how much you know, of all that part of James's life . . . it is difficult for me.'

She pulled a long blade of grass, smoothed it between her palms. Flat. 'I think I know almost all. And you?'

'I know all.'

'More than I do, I imagine?' She had a dust of tiny freckles across the bridge of her nose.

'I imagine. I know things that only a witness could know.'

She looked at me directly, threw the blade of grass aside. 'But you were not a witness? How?'

'As near a witness as needs be. I have heard his story from Millar, read his papers, which Millar has. You know that? Millar has all his diaries or notebooks, whatever you call them. Did you know?'

She shook her head slowly.

'I think I might as well tell you exactly what I know, when I think it all began, how it all started, and what happened up until the evening he went away. Do you want me to?'

She looked away across the parkland. Thomas and Céleste were sitting, picking buttercups. They'd be out of the way for a very little time.

'Yes. Tell me quickly. Later tell me all. But for the moment tell me what you saw. Heard.'

'It will be difficult.'

'I know.'

And so I told her. It's easy to say that so simply. It only takes up half a line, less, written down, but I condensed hugely. I began with the essentials. I did not go into intense details, nor did I mention the photographs, or my own feelings or my dream, and when I had come to the end, having got as far as defining a possible reason for this cruelly destructive aberration, Florence was sitting, head bowed, hands over her face, weeping, as well she might. I apologized, as far as I could, as far as was needed, and went down through the fields of buttercups and spring grass to Céleste and Thomas.

When we wandered back, Florence had pulled herself together a bit. She looked wan, exhausted, battered. And obviously she had wept. Céleste looked at me anxiously, touched Florence on the shoulder.

Florence said, 'I'll be all right now. It's good to cry a little. A relief.'

Céleste nodded, jigging about uneasily as Thomas pulled and swung himself in her grip.

'Give him to me,' I said, and settling back on the grass beside his mother, I took the struggling body into my arms and forced him to sit. Which he did instantly, leaning back against my side, thumb to his mouth, the trumpet forgotten in the trodden grass, his head heavy against my chest.

Céleste sat down slowly, a bunch of wilting flowers in her hand, not too close, near enough to come to my assistance if needed but just out of earshot. Tactful Céleste had seen the residue of tears. She knew distress when she saw it.

'Florence, just how much of what I have told you did you know?'

'Much. Not all. At the beginning, not at all. Not even with the faux wedding, with . . . Jojo. I was suspicious. He always hinted that his life in Paris had been . . . different. That he came to Bargemon to escape, I knew that. I believed that I could make it right. Could make it work. I suppose every woman thinks that? It is in our instinct to heal. To help. And I was . . .' – she shrugged, wiped her face with her hand, touched Thomas gently – 'impossibly, wonderfully, in love. Alas. Idiotically in love. The very first time in my life: there had never been another man in my remotest dreams. I was poor Florence, the sister of the wonderful brother Raymond. My life would be to remain at home, look after my parents when they grew old, become the spinster daughter. You know? Raymond was the idol. I accepted that perfectly easily. Girls do.'

'And then James?'

She was holding Thomas's hand, raised it to her lips, kissed it. 'Then James. I had never known anyone like him before. I was lost. Quite lost. He made the world so light! So brilliant, so possible . . .'

'And then Thomas.'

'Thomas. That was a terrible time. At first, just at first,

we did not realize what had happened. There is a test – it is called the four-finger-palm test. Then we knew. In the beginning – oh, I don't know – we were hopelessly inexperienced. A baby was a baby. All babies are the same? My mother was uneasy. In Algeria she had seen a lot of children: she was in a children's crèche. She had suspicions.'

'And when you knew?'

'When we knew, when it was certain, from that time on James began to die. He was convinced, as I told you before, that he was to blame.'

'But it was a question of chromosomes. It could be in you, in him. It is not certain.'

'James was *certain.*'

'And he went back to Millar? To Jojo, to his previous life?'

'Yes. After that we separated. He moved to a little room, apart.'

'But you must have known what was happening, seen him?'

Thomas's head was suddenly heavy against my arm; he had fallen asleep.

Florence looked at her watch. 'I must take him back.'

'You said that you and James shared a "barren bed". Your words.'

'I lied. Of *course* I lied! Would you confess that to anyone, to a stranger of all people? I never asked questions, but I saw his . . . well, I saw his wrists. I watched his face, the pain, the greyness, but I never again saw his body. It was "Do you want salad?" or "Have you brought in some logs?" or "I am going to the village, is there anything you need?" He wept very much at first. Then he came to terms with our "life", but he never touched Thomas. He almost never acknowledged him. He was a terrible reminder to him, he was ashamed and afraid. That was the end of things.'

'He did love you. In the fragments of stuff he did not

destroy, he says so. You know. You have read them. His life was radiant with you.'

'It finished.' She hugged her knees, leaning forward, hair falling loosely about her face. 'The Agendas that Millar showed to you. Why does *he* have them? What sort of Agendas are they? It is so strange. Why Millar?'

'He bought them.'

She looked up instantly. Startled. Brushed hair from her face. 'Bought them? Why? The Agendas?'

'To avoid blackmail.'

Thomas was suddenly awake, perhaps his mother's sudden movement. He thumped me in the chest, laughed.

'Blackmail?'

'That too. And cocaine. You knew that.'

She reached out towards Thomas to take him in her arms, but he pulled back, shaking his head, holding me.

'I knew. At first after Paris, but he fought. We won. Until Thomas.'

She got briskly to her feet. Céleste got up at the same time, moved towards us quietly.

'Take Thomas, Céleste. He is tired, we must go.'

But Thomas struggled, screamed, was finally subdued by us all, and we walked back to the cars, I carrying a shouting, furious child waving a trumpet. Not the happiest of afternoons. Not by a long chalk.

We drove back to Bargemon in a convoy of two. Thomas, calmer now, waved the bunch of wilting wild flowers from the back window, I waved back. At the cars, Florence had asked me to come to rue Émile Zola at about six. Madame Prideaux was away playing bridge. There was more to talk about, she had more questions; it was already late, well after Thomas's time for his milk and biscuits, or whatever he had.

There was no one in the hall of the hotel, and I took my key from the hook behind Madame Mazine's desk, washed, changed my shirt, and was at the door of number 11, rue Émile Zola, as the church struck six.

We sat together in the conservatory among the plants and in the last of the evening sun. And we just talked. Florence was strangely calm. She too had changed quickly, combed her hair; there was no suggestion of stress or anxiety. She explained very easily, as if she were discussing a complicated stitch in tapestry work, why she and James had not, in fact, married. He was unsure of himself. His past life could, he told her, return. She must help him fight back to total normalcy, and with her help he'd win out. That was his reason anyway, and she appeared to accept it.

For a virginal, doomed-to-be-a-spinster young woman, she had made amazing steps in coming to terms with the problem. But, as she said, she was totally bewitched, completely in love, certain that with love, understanding, care and patience she would succeed. The cocaine had frankly worried her more. It was costly as well as dangerous, and he felt, at first, that he could only 'see' how to paint if he had had a sniff or two. Colours were brighter, patterns swirled into shape, the structure of his work was more easily defined. But, gradually, he came off the stuff. Money dictated that. Or lack of money. And, Florence was certain, he was not 'addicted'. He took it for the stimulation of his painter's imagination. Anyway, she believed that. And if he said so it was so.

She was a little uneasy about Aronovich. He very occasionally came to Jericho on his way, she presumed, to stay up at L'Hermitage. He was pleasant, in his late fifties, helpful with James's painting, and had commissioned a collection for his new hotel. This we knew. The call at the weekend signified that the hotel was ready, or soon would be ready, to accept the works. He had, after all, already paid for them. A large sum which had helped them greatly. Five thousand dollars.

It was about this time, when we had been discussing the paintings and Aronovich, that Annette came in bearing a tray of glasses and a plate of biscuits with a small jar of pâté and some olives. She set these down and went away. The goldfish drifted about aimlessly. For a moment we just sat in silence, a silence broken only by the hum of the oxygenator in the aquarium. So still were we that it sounded like a vacuum cleaner and made us suddenly, idiotically, shy. Florence laughed, rubbed her nose.

'So much more to discuss. I don't know what to ask next. Do you?'

I confessed that I'd be better with a little nourishment at the same moment that Annette returned with four tins of beer and a can of orange juice. She put these down, stood for a moment looking about her, turned and, just as she was about to leave, suddenly stopped and patted my cheek. Blushed, hurried out.

Florence opened a beer for me, handed me a glass. 'That's her way of saying "thank you for being so kind to the child". Céleste thinks you are a magician with Thomas.'

'It's so odd. Because I'm not terribly good with my own children. I have hardly ever held my son, Giles, hardly ever carried his sister.'

'You seem to love Thomas.'

'I do. I love this beer too. God! I needed it. Are you going to stick to orange?'

She had a tin of beer in her hand, pulled the ring opener, poured it into a glass. 'A beer too. I need it. The revelations of a life are exhausting.'

'So you have five thousand dollars in the bank at least? That is a help for you. A boost anyway to what remains of James's legacy from our father.'

She wore a little white moustache of foam across her

upper lip. She took an olive, shook her head. 'Ouf! The legacy. That went a long time ago. Long time ago. Boff! Why do you think that I got a job with Colin, the dentist? Thomas is a very expensive child. Oh, not because he has Down's syndrome, not that, but he has to be looked after. Mama does not charge me rent. She pays for Annette and for Céleste, and food for us all. I'll have to find another job very soon. I just hated sticking that water-thing into ugly mouths.'

'Florence, I told you that Millar had bought the Agendas? Remember?'

'Of course I remember.'

'For ten thousand dollars.'

There was a silence, save for the hum of the oxygenator in the tank and from somewhere outside, in the square, the angry voice of a boy shouting, a tin kicked along the gutter. The silence held, apart from that, and then she said, in a voice so low that it was a whisper, 'Ten thousand dollars? For his Agendas?'

'Millar told me. He bought them just before James went . . . away.'

She placed the olive stone carefully in a small brass bowl at her side. 'I never heard of these dollars. They are not at the bank. *That* I do know. I have Aronovich's money for the collection, plus a little bit more from what I have saved. Not much, a little bit. That is all, William. All.'

'It was probably a cheque. No one, not even Millar, wanders about with ten thousand dollars in his hip pocket.'

'If James had cashed a cheque at the Crédit Lyonnais in Sainte-Brigitte I simply would not know. He didn't tell me those things. Sometimes, at the start together, I asked him. Tried to get financially sound. But he would never discuss things like that with me. Never.'

I poured out the last of my beer, went over to the tray and took one more. The pop and hiss, when I pulled the metal ring, caused her to look up.

'Christ! I am sorry, Florence. Inadequate, okay. But I am. My family, and James is a part of it, have been pretty bloody awful to you.'

She looked away, across to her mother's wretched banana tree. Laughed. 'Mama's tree. How she cares for it. As I do Thomas. Cherish is the word. Your family, if you mean James, as you do, has not always been "bloody awful". There were wonderful times, glorious happiness, magical moments which we shared together. I would never have known them without him. I won't forget them. Never. But I have to forget James because I know he is dead. I know that. I told you. He will never come back, I would know if he was alive. He has gone. Just gone. I settle for that. In the war they say that women knew, quite suddenly, that their men had gone. Not taken prisoner, not just missing. But dead. We know.'

I sat down gently facing her; here came the cruncher. 'I spoke to Millar's sister. She lives in the little lodge. She saw James the evening that he left. In January. In the snowfall. He got into a car with an Alpes Maritimes registration. The bike is still in her shed.'

'She said that?'

'Said that.'

'Oh sweet Jesus! Oh help me –'

'He could be anywhere. In Algiers, in Tunisia, a boat from Nice, or from Marseilles. Even in America by now. Argentina, where Aronovich came from. He is still around.'

'No. I would know. I would *know*. Why do you persist?'

'Because I have to be certain. I have to know for sure if he is alive or if he has, as you feel sure, died. I must know.'

'Why! What difference can it make to you? Go back to England, to your family, your work, leave me. Why won't you leave all this?'

I poured my beer steadily into my glass, watching the thin head rise slowly up the side. It was almost full before I told her what I had wanted to tell her for some days.

'Because I have fallen in love with you. I don't "love you", I am "in love" with you. A very different thing. Do you understand?'

She stared back at me; her eyes were as wide, as dead, with shock as those glassy ones in the head of a porcelain doll.

'I am in love with you, Florence.'

'Please don't be. *Please*. Don't be. It is impossible, it can never be . . .'

'Too late for that, I fear. It is possible and it has happened. I can't alter the facts, I don't want to. I know it's a mess-up, a muddle, but you might as well hear the truth for once. I am in love, idiotically, stupidly, all the paradigms you like. I can't retract.'

Her eyes brimmed with tears, she lowered her head, stuffed a fist to her mouth, and when she asked me please to leave, in the softest, sweetest voice, I knew perfectly well that she could not look at me for grief.

At the hotel, Madame Mazine was behind her desk. She looked up as I went in, shook a finger at me.

'Your key is not here? It is lost? You have it, Mr Colcott?'

'In my pocket. I came in about five.'

'I was at supper.'

'I had some business to deal with.'

'There was a telephone call for you. About four o'clock. From London.' She handed me a slip of folded paper. 'They will call again tomorrow in the morning. The lady did not speak very good French. Tomorrow I am sure. About eight, our time.'

When I opened the paper I saw the number, and the name.

It was from Helen.

CHAPTER 12

I WAS AWAKE before the cockerel the next morning. It was just getting light.

I don't quite know what in-built clock functions in one's head and rings unheard bells to get one alerted for a telephone call which is not due until eight o'clock.

But I was ready.

The room was washed in grey mussel shell light. The wardrobe loomed in dark bulk; the two depressing pictures reflected merely silvery glass; my clothes, thrown over one of the chairs last night, a stooped figure, a vagrant frozen into stillness.

And then the cockerel started his morning with a raucous crow, a flapping of sleep-heavy wings, shaking and flustering of neck feathers, a furiously agitated scratching of his beak. A huffle and fluffle of feathers, then he settled and looked vaguely around at his wives wandering cautiously about the yard as if they had never seen it before, heads bowed, eyes yellow with inquiry. Quite suddenly he jumped on one, frightened the wits out of her, had his way, scrambled off, began his crowing, wings a-tremble. The hen ruffled her plumage, shook her head, recommenced the search for whatever it was she had been seeking.

I had left my hillocky bed, wandered across to the window to see the dawn come up behind the cliffs. A gentle breeze trailed through the lilac bushes, fluttered the washing on the line, bowed the tall peony tree which almost smothered the chicken shed.

The day had started: sun not yet up, but time for me to start adjusting to the idea of speaking to Helen again after so many weeks. Well, it seemed to me like many weeks. I had, after all, rather altered tack since arriving in the village. I had written, not frequently, but often enough to show a vague interest, which I frankly did not feel, and she had replied. Usually. Brief notes or letters on those blue air-mail things. She never had much to say: the house (she had moved back since the holiday with Mummy) was all right, the children were well, she had been to see this film, that play, and someone was 'amazing' on television. The name Eric Rhys-Evans arrived one day. He had been, before we married, a young and promising executive in television. He was now a Vice-President, Europe, for some American firm of commercial television people. He had sought her out in my absence, or perhaps it was more likely that she had sought *him* out – she was ever sparing with details like that – and they had spent various evenings here and there. Married and divorced in the fourteen years in which she had been, as she put it, 'out to lunch', he was edging back again, or she was edging towards him. One was never absolutely certain. It didn't really matter much to me. The children did; I was a little uneasy about their position there. But it would hardly be the children who would cause her to telephone me at eight in the morning.

It would be the first time.

Supposing it *was* the children? Annie ill, Giles hit by a car? Unease instantly swamped me. I telephoned down – it was not yet six, and I was a little surprised to get Eugène. He said that he would bring me some coffee, but the croissants were not in yet from the baker. Half an hour? Half an hour was fine. So I shaved, showered, and by the time I had finished my ablutions Eugène had a tray of scalding coffee ready.

I apologized for being so early, asked him if I could make a call to London at half past seven. He said he'd leave a message for Madame Mazine, who would be at the desk shortly.

So I had my coffee, watched the sun rise beyond the tumbled red roofs, and the light flood into my room, probing into every corner, glittering on the varnish of the wardrobe. For the first time I realized that the wallpaper was the negative colour of mashed turnips bordered with a heavy frieze of Cape gooseberries and honesty. Not altogether *House and Garden*. But clean.

Helen sounded, and probably was, asleep. She was flustered by being awakened a bit earlier than planned.

'What time is it with you?' Her voice was husky with irritation.

'It's seven-thirty.'

'Six-thirty here.'

'I know. I'm sorry, but I have to be out by eight, when you said that you'd call. I'm sorry about yesterday.'

'I got the hour wrong. Why can't we all be the same? It's so bloody silly.'

'Yes. Sorry. What is it? Anything wrong? Not Annie? Giles?'

'They're all right. Fine. And so am I.'

'I was just about to ask.'

'Liar! No, I'm fine; I had a bit of a cold last week. Nothing, all gone. Is it lovely and sunny with you?'

'It'll be a hot day. But you are all right?'

'Great. Never better. How's your house? Are you in it yet? Well, obviously not – you are calling from the hotel, right?'

'Right. There is a good deal to do to the place: new furniture, a coat of paint. I'm here until June-ish.'

'Super. Brilliant. What I wanted to tell you was . . . well, you remember Eric Rhys-Evans? Welsh? I mentioned him in my letters?'

'Yes. Yes, you did. And . . .'

'Well, he's Vice-President, Europe, lots of lolly, for Kraus–Kaufman–Levi, you know who I mean?'

'Splendid English firm. All solid names those.'

There was a short silence.

'You haven't changed, sweetheart, have you? Still got your arse-breaking wit.'

'Sorry.'

'A bit early in the morning for jokes. Eric has got the Marks and Sparks contract and wants me to do P.M. for him for the spring. *Next* spring. Kiddies' gear. Twenty little darlings plus mummies or chaperons, and me in charge.'

'Sounds great. Next spring?'

'Yes. But the shoot is pretty soon. He wants me to go on the recce soonish. Look for the backgrounds. You know, sand, sun, swimming-pools, and so on.'

'How soonish?'

'About a week . . . Marbella. Brilliant! Well, it's better than Blackburn.'

'And so?'

'So what?'

'So why call me? I mean, you want to go, don't you?'

'Naturally! But who looks after the children? Mrs Nicholls is not into being a nanny.'

'Helen, dear. I can't get back just yet. You know that.'

'So I miss the chance of getting back myself? To work again after all this time? I won't get the offer again, you know. Annie will go down to Mummy. They get on wonderfully well. Love each other. Very alike. And she goes to boarding school. No problem. Anyway, she's all right. It's Giles.'

'What about Giles?'

'Well. He *doesn't* board, my dear William, he can't cope on his own. He's nine, not nineteen. And I can't take him with me. So . . .'

'So? Can't he go to your mother, with Annie? Just for the shoot, or whatever you call it. It can't be for all that long, surely?'

'Mummy, William, is not twenty-one. She can manage a girl, that's easier, and she's at school all week, and it's company for her anyway. But Giles is a boy, and boys, in case you have not had time to notice in the last nine years, are different. *Giles* is different anyway. He's sullen and sulky. I don't know what's wrong, he won't say. I'm at my wits' end sometimes.'

'He wasn't like that. He was quiet, but never sullen.'

'He is now. I want you to take him over. See what's wrong.'

'Helen, I'm not at home and I can't get back to sort out a small boy –'

'You don't have to. I'm sending him out to you. You take charge for a bit, sort things out. I've booked him on a flight to Nice on the sixteenth.'

'That's this week, for Christ's sake!'

'So it is. This is true. Clever you. It has to be then because there is the Film Festival in Cannes and this was the only seat I could get. Actually, Eric wangled it, through the firm.'

'Very good of him.'

'I thought so. He really wants me to have a shot at this Marbella thing.'

'Nice airport is miles from here. Marseilles or Toulon are much –'

'I got him to *Nice*. You pick him up. He's got a label, got a handgrip, he's on flight 950, Air France. Two-fifty.'

'On the sixteenth?'

'The very day. Be sweet for once in your life. It's not much to ask. He *wants* to come out. It was *his* idea. So don't let the child down. Right?'

We said goodbye. I hung up and heard Eugène knocking at the door with my hot croissants. Well, well. Old Helen absolutely true to form. Eric, and Marbella. Fine. And don't let the child down! Ball severely in my court. Typical.

At La Source, Madame Yvonne looked only vaguely interested when I told her that there would be two of us for lunch. She set a Cinzano before Florence, a large Scotch before me, and asked if we wanted ice. Her expression indicated that to obtain this she would have to venture forth to Alaska. And back. But, with a helpless shrug, if that was what we needed then she would go.

We saved her the journey and she looked around the gloomy little restaurant for the menu, which she located under a pile of old *Télé-Sept-Jours* and *Elle* next to the TV set, which was, mercifully, off.

'It's always the same. Never changes. Tinned cassoulet, a cut from some joint with frozen peas, or cod à la grecque. There is packet fish soup to start with or home-made pâté, which could be highly dangerous looking at the cook's fingernails, and an apple or cheese to finish. Okay?'

Florence was a bit pale, not 'greenery-yallery' pale, just pale from not enough sleep the night before, and strain. I was surprised, *delighted*, that she agreed to come with me. I had a feeling that, after my having blurted out the intensity of my devotion and all that, she might shy away.

But here she was; only not hungry.

'Would she make an omelette fines herbes? A little salad?' she said.

'Oh! Christ, Florence! That's pushing things. She'd have to break the eggs.'

We sat at a table in a far corner. There was only one other client, and he was spooning his way through a double portion of cassoulet with intense energy.

His truck was parked outside.

We weren't, perhaps, the most light-hearted pair that had ever been in La Source, but we were surprisingly comfortable with each other, except that it was perfectly clear to me that she did not want me to start up again on my protestations of love. Tact was now essential. I had made my declaration, she had heard it, and she had accepted it. Otherwise she would have refused to join me for this sorry meal. I had assured her, on the telephone, that it was not a conversation about James which I sought but, more urgently at the moment, her advice on the impending arrival of my son.

That had intrigued her greatly; I could see that. And when I pointed out that she was, in fact at least, his aunt, she was doubly intrigued. So I scored a little there.

Madame Yvonne looked anguished when an omelette was asked for and said that *she* couldn't do it but Marcel could. Marcel, apparently, made excellent omelettes. So that was all right. I ordered the cod à la grecque, and she wandered off shouting the orders through the plywood door to the kitchen. The door click-clacked.

The truck driver wiped his plate with a piece of bread, and Florence said suddenly, 'What *is* cod à la grecque? I mean, apart from being frozen?' She was making a valiant stab at idle conversation.

'It's a piece of cod. Quite square, with two black olives and a sliver of tomato. In a sort of sick-sauce.'

There was a flick of a smile across that calm, sad face. I longed to take it in my hands and kiss it. But refrained. For a time we sat in thoughtful silence.

Madame Yvonne came back, a tearful child straddled on one hip, a bowl of nuts and olives in her free hand which she slid on to the table. On her way out she just avoided collision with Marcel, her husband, who had served me on occasions and who set down a chipped plate with a large pale omelette fines herbes. At least, there was some parsley in the mixture, and with it a blue plastic bowl of salad. He extolled the virtues of the frisée which he had wrenched from his own garden soil, and set the oil, vinegar, sugar, mustard and spoons before us. Wishing us an excellent appetite, he went over to the truck driver who was picking his teeth with as much energy as he had consumed his cassoulet. They were sharing a carafe of red.

Florence began to mix her vinaigrette. 'Your cod?' she said.

'Eat that. Before it gets cold. The cod is still frozen, I reckon.'

But Madame Yvonne arrived with my meal, shouting at Marcel to put on the TV for the Film Festival news. Which, unhappily, he did.

'What day did you say your son arrives?' Florence was forced to speak loudly to overcome the chattering woman with a lollipop-microphone talking to a busty blonde girl wearing diamonds in the sunshine.

The cod à la grecque was as disgusting as I had thought. I ate the bullet-olives, smeared the tomato around generally, forked at the sodden lump of fish, so that at least the plate looked as if I had made an effort. To complain would have meant a conversation; so I decided to carry on with the cheese and the bread. The cheese was a good Coulommiers, the bread fresh. We ate in silence.

Silence broken by the TV, of course, but after a short time it seemed that the constant chatter and twitter drove Marcel to anger; he was discussing some very hand-involved subject with the truck driver and suddenly sprang up and stopped the wretched thing. I thanked him. He looked bewildered, sat down again, casting uncomprehending eyes in our direction from time to time.

'When does he arrive? This child?' Florence had half finished her pallid omelette, set it aside, started to peel a wooden Golden Delicious.

'Friday afternoon, I think. The sixteenth. Nice.'

'Where will he stay? With you, obviously . . .'

'With me obviously. Madame Mazine has a room. Almost next to mine. She was about to shove him in my room on a folding bed. But I drew the line at a nine-year-old sharing. With the lavatory down the corridor.'

Florence laughed. The first time in the morning. 'He would probably sleep far better than you. At *his* age. At your age . . . well, the nights are broken, eh?'

'It depends. Anyway, he's got a room.'

'I'm surprised. They are usually full at this time of year. Walkers. The elderly come here before the heat, you know? Archaeologists . . . there are places in the hills.'

'She was full. I agreed to pay for a double room. It is the season. That was made clear.'

She had peeled her Golden Delicious in one long, curling wriggle of unbroken skin, held it up proudly on the prong of her fork.

'Clever old you. Lots of practice?'

'My father taught me. Useless information. He said it would encourage me to be patient. And diligent.'

'Did it?'

She looked up at me quickly, the grey eyes steady. No smile. 'Yes. It did. Both.' She cut her apple into quarters, speared a piece and offered it to me. As it could very likely be the only thing she ever would offer me, I took it. Wood or no wood.

'How long will he stay? You can't keep him in a hotel for weeks?'

'I'm going to have a real try at getting Jericho ready. I don't know how long he'll stay, or if he'll like it, or me for that matter, when he gets here.'

'You said your wife says he is sullen. He is?'

'I don't remember that at all. He was quiet, wrote, read a great deal, he was very pleasant as far as I remember. I was not the greatest father. I don't mean that he was my little burst of pride and glory, or that Jesus would want him for a sunbeam. He was – is, I mean – a perfectly nice young man. Something must have gone wrong . . . he's not extrovert at all. His mother and his sister are. Perhaps they have swamped him?'

'Perhaps. Is that why he is coming?'

'Florence, I told you. I don't *know*. I have to find out. That's all.'

We drove in glorious sunshine, under a brilliant blue sky, all the way through the pea-green pines to Jericho. The house, not the village.

Walking up through the rusted gate bearing its sign, Florence said suddenly, 'I am sorry about my behaviour yesterday. I was idiotic, weeping, like a shopgirl. I apologize. You caught me off balance, you know?'

'I think so.'

'It had been a long day. First the clinic, with the new girl, then to the château. I expect I was over-tired. And the conservatory . . .'

'I expect so. I took you by surprise.'

'Yes. But I remember what you said and what I said. Nothing is forgotten. I am very, very grateful that you were so gentle, so kind.'

'Oh for God's sake, Florence! You make me sound like a . . . like a vet or something! I *meant* what I said, still do, I always will, and you can't avoid the fact. I do love you. Am in love with you. I won't embarrass you, I know the situation. But I am not going to give in. Now, today or ever. Understand?'

Along the path going towards the house, the peonies were in fat bud, the vine now green. A flash of brilliant yellow streaking across our path brought us to an instant halt. Florence had her hand on my arm, holding me.

'You saw?'

'A bird? Yellow.'

'The golden oriole. They are so shy. The song is marvellous. I always used to wait for them. Every spring. And then the hoopoe.' She let go of my arm and we walked up to the terrace. I took the key, the fatal key, from my jacket pocket, dragged the two tin chairs into the sunlight on the terrace. Already the vine was thick enough to freckle the tiles with light and shade.

'School is the problem,' I said. 'For Giles.'

'He is called that?'

'Giles. Yes. In French it is "Gilles".'

'I know. He is nine?'

'Ummm. If he is to stay here for a while, well, I mean more than a couple of weeks, he'll have to get some education. What I need is a tutor. Someone to get him interested, working his brain. To learn French perhaps?'

'Schools here finish for the summer next month, you know? Until September.'

'I wonder if there is a teacher, someone local, who might be interested in a little spare money? To tutor him? Do you know?'

Florence had kicked off her sandals, thrusting her bare feet into the warmth of the sun.

'I don't. Most of the teachers go away for holidays, you know. My mother might know of someone. She plays bridge with so many other people. I'll ask her.'

I got up and unlocked the front door. She did not move, or turn round. I opened the shutters, opened the windows, let the air course through the shaded room.

'I hope that Monsieur Simon and his sons will come tomorrow. To take away the bed and that wardrobe,' I said.

She pulled on her sandals once again, got to her feet. 'Annette's brother wants both of them. And anything else you want to get rid of. He has a brocante shop. Secondhand shop you call it.'

'Simon clears attics and barns. It said so on his truck, which is why I got him to come over. You are certain you don't want anything . . . it's all right?'

'I don't want anything. And the canvases? Mr Aronovich's canvases?'

'When I go over to Nice to collect Giles I'll go and see him. Do you know his address?' I was extremely casual.

'Telephone number. Not his address.'

'Perhaps I should call him? Tell him the canvases are all ready. He can take them, they have been paid for. And I would use the studio to work in. One day.'

We stood together on the threshold of the house, looking about the long room. With a few things changed, dust sheets and newspapers removed, with some pleasant paintings, flowers in jugs, new covers on the settee, the place could look different. Would, in fact *be* different. A change of atmosphere would work wonders.

'A coat of paint everywhere,' I said, 'upstairs and downstairs. As soon as Simon carts the bits away, and Aronovich takes his loot. Too many canvases for me to carry in the boot of the car.'

She wandered back to the terrace, leant against the vine trellis, tearing a leaf into fragments. A habit of hers in stress. 'Thomas's bed, the cage, is that going with Simon?'

'Of course. Unless you want it?'

'No. No. We have one. It's too small for him now anyway.'

'I thought, with a new bed, Giles could have it. While he's here. That room.'

She threw the stalk of the leaf into the air, wiped her fingers on the hem of her skirt. 'That room. Don't put him in the empty room. That was James's private place. Everything that was in there I burned. It was full of unhappiness.'

'I think we'll bring happiness back here again. It's an old house, it's used to change, to moods. Ready now for something new again. A renewal. You agree?'

'Oh dear, William! I don't know. It's your life, your house now. For the time being anyway. I have my own life ahead. Ours do not join. Anywhere.'

She turned and walked slowly down the dusty path to the gate. I followed her, and when I caught up with her, just as she reached the gate, I took her hand. She looked up at me without expression.

All I could find to say, holding her hand, was, 'But we *must* join! I will need your help. You can't ignore me. Not after yesterday. I mean, I remember all I said. I've told you, I shall need help here: Where the fuse-box is. Is there a well? – I'll need a well for watering – Where is the cesspit? Where do you suggest that I go to buy some beds – Sainte-Brigitte, I imagine?'

She withdrew her hand from mine, leant against the gatepost, a half-smile on her lips.

'It seems not to have occurred to you that once upon a time, not so long ago, this was my house. Full of promise, of joy, happiness. Laughter even. Yes, there was laughter. It's empty now. Stripped of love and joy. You have told me that you were certain that James was "around still", that was your phrase, I seem to remember? That he could be in Tunis, even the Argentine, anywhere, with a large sum of money. You insist that he exists still. And yet you can happily ask me about fuse-boxes and cesspits and beds for your new house? I don't give a fig, William, not a fig. You go it alone.'

'A *part* of your life, Florence, has ended. I agree. It's like a book coming to the end. Closing the covers. But there are other books to read, to take up. We must go ahead. A phase in *my* life has ended, but not my *life*! I knew that when I came here, but I am not going to sit down and say all is over, that I have had my turn! Not me. I am starting again. I need you to help me, I want to help you. We will try to set out again. Together. It won't be easy, it won't be smooth. There are terrible hazards ahead, that I know. As firmly as I know that I love you very, very much indeed, that I want you, that I will wait, be patient, and always be near you to help you "cross the stile". Do you follow me?'

'I do.'

'That I love you, and that I have told you – that was the one thing which you omitted from your list just now.'

'I omitted it, William, because I must discount it entirely. Like garlic in a recipe. It is "optional", you know? That means it is not necessary.'

'It is necessary. I am deathly persistent.'

'And so am I. When you go to collect your son at the airport, will you contact Aronovich? He knew everyone at L'Hermitage: the Jacquet boy, the black man, Jojo . . . Perhaps he might know something that you, or we, do not. Will you try?'

'If you give me the telephone number, I'll call this evening, until I get him. Explain who I am, that I now have Jericho, the canvases. Would that be in order?'

'Perfectly. I'll give it to the hotel desk. I haven't got it here.' She pushed the gate idly with one foot; it squealed in protest. 'It needs oiling. So much to do. The garden looks much tidier. You have been busy.'

Wallflowers flourished in scattered clumps, insects droned and zinged about. Along the uneven path, through the potager, clumps of chives, bright with purple pompoms, and the tall, unfolding stems of fennel lined the edge. At the far end a flowering currant, hung all-about with tassels of coral blossom, shook and trembled under the onslaught of a hundred bees.

The air was still, warm, scented. Dust spiralled from a scrabble of sparrows bathing in a dip of the pathway, and far across the meadow at the château came the dulcet, suggestive call of the cuckoo.

We looked at each other, content. Strain ebbing, tact restraining.

Florence said suddenly, 'Your son. Does he like the country? I mean, this place will be very dull for him if not. So silent. Nothing to do.'

'No. He likes the country. On holiday he was always very happy. With me anyway. Not that I gave him much time somehow. We used to take a gîte in Cognac, and in Normandy. He enjoyed it. My wife, Helen, loathed it! She hated the silence, insects, the outdoor privy, that sort of thing. Loved people, the market, the cafés and the bars. But the rest, she hated.'

'But why go to the country if she hated it so?'

'For the children. Healthy. Good for us all. Being together, a family. A total disaster always.'

'Do you think he'll like being in the hotel then? Stuck indoors.'

'I've got him a room, paid in advance. We can come here every day. He can do what he likes while I'm getting the place in order.'

'Will he like that?'

'Florence! How the hell do *I* know? He'll have to put up with it. After all *he* asked to come out here to me. Not the other way round.'

'He asked to come?'

'I told you.'

'No. Not that part. That means he wants you. Like Thomas, you see? A boy needs a father.'

We started to walk back towards the house slowly. I kicked a pebble into the chives.

'He's happy. Helen is a very good mother. She does drive

me mad sometimes – not to-suicide-mad, but just impatiently insane. She and my daughter are the two extroverts in the family, as I told you. My son and I are rather dull, I fear. He likes reading or fishing, or sitting looking into space. Thinking. You know?'

She had stooped down to pick a bunch of mint.

'I'm thieving your mint,' she said. 'Some for me, some for Annette, and some for Céleste. You must take care with this, it will spread everywhere. I had no time in the autumn. There was too much to do . . .'

'Of course there was. I'll come to terms with it all. When I move in here.'

'We'll have to see how your son feels about the house. There is a stream up at the top, did you know?'

'Full of toads, frogs and marsh marigolds. I know.'

'You found it. Good.' She got up and started to separate the bunch of mint into two small ones.

'And later on I'll find the cesspit, won't I? And the fuse-box?'

The small cloud of depression which had settled over my head down at the gate lifted. The fact that she had referred to 'we' when she spoke of Giles and his reaction to Jericho had given me infinite pleasure, but I contrived to look perfectly casual, ordinary, calm.

There was time. It would all take time. Aronovich, the canvases, James, always James, Jericho and then Giles.

After that, when I knew more or less precisely where we all fitted in this uncertain scenario, I could start the wooing. That would take longer, and be strewn with problems – the path to it – but I would go ahead.

Softly, softly . . . I wonder if you follow me?

By Thursday evening, just as the sun was about to slide into a threatening cauliflower of cloud in the west, M'sieur

Simon and his sons Marc and Georges, who had long worked for James and had, indeed, assisted in the building of the wall which had given Jericho its false sense of security, sat down at the big table in the long room with me, three six-packs of Kronenbourg beer and a big bowl of potato crisps. We all shook hands, or rather they offered their elbows because their hands were grimed by moving furniture, carting things about, cutting back old bramble and nettles to find the well and the cesspit, and with caps pushed to the backs of their heads they sat, legs akimbo, arms on the table, and we laughed and congratulated ourselves on the amount of work and effort we had put into the two days. It had been a major achievement to get the three of them free – free that is for the *time*, not financially. I paid in 'paper', and that made a tolerable difference to things. Beds had been removed and taken away, then chairs and wardrobes, desks and tables, the long settee, a selection of odd wooden chairs, all had been dragged about, resited, approved or changed. They had even managed to slosh some whitewash over the walls in the kitchen, find the fuse-box, reconnect the oven, and generally, except for two beds, make the house almost, not quite but almost, come alive again.

'And your brother, tell me,' said M'sieur Simon, 'will we ever know where he is? How sad for Madame Colcott, with the child . . .'

'Perhaps he is dead? It's possible,' said Marc, the younger brother. 'On the other hand, maybe he just went away. I know the feeling myself . . . to be alone.'

This suggestion we considered in silence, each with his own thoughts, until M'sieur Simon made a gruff remark about Marie-Louise being a good wife, even if she did nag. All French women nag, he said. It is normal to them. Marc shot a sideways look at his father under thick brows, drained his glass, reached for another bottle of beer.

'The range,' said Georges suddenly. 'If he went up to the range – and he liked to be there to paint, you recollect, hein? – If he went to the range, well, maybe . . .' He shrugged.

I looked across the dim room in the fading light. The sun had gone. 'Where is the range?' I said, lighting a candle which we had stuck on an old tin lid on the table.

'Up there.' Simon jerked his head towards the back of the house. 'At Jericho, the firing-range. Military zone. It's very dangerous because you can trip over a grenade maybe, or an unexploded shell. They litter the place. Dangerous.'

Marc took a handful of crisps and stuffed them into his mouth. Through a spray of crumbs he said, 'The range is closed. Between April and May the 26th there is no action there. They suspend training.'

'Why? Why then? There is a reason?'

Simon scratched his head, cap between finger and thumb. 'Sure. It's the lambing season. The shepherds have to collect their lambs, it's a big effort. Then they go up to the high hills for the summer. But there will be no firing until the end of this month.'

At that moment there was a deep rumble of thunder, the room had grown dark. We got up and walked to the door. Marc hurried down the path to cover the back of their truck just as the first rattle of hail spilled down into the vine and clattered across the terrace.

'A treacherous month,' said Simon. 'Some people are foolish and impatient and plant everything out without waiting. Now look! Regardez! Catastrophe!'

The hail was tearing down in a white curtain; through it the scurrying body of Marc, head bent, hands covering his face, weaving and leaping towards us. Another crash of thunder, the hail thrashed into the tender new leaves above us, the cherry tree shook and swayed in the sudden violent wind. Marc stood shaking his head like a dog on a duck-shoot, brushing his jacket, his face streaming with water.

'Malheur! Hey! That is the end of my broad beans. Merde!'

I lit another candle, and we went back to the table to wait for the storm to pass, which, thankfully, because the beer was running short, it did in a half-hour when the whole sky suddenly cleared, the great cauliflower cloud moved elsewhere trailing veils of hail behind it, and the Simons made their way to their truck, my money safely stowed away in M'sieur Simon's pocket.

At the truck we all shook elbows again, and they climbed aboard, advising me that if I needed anything, two beds for example, I should not fail to go to Futurama on the road to Sainte-Brigitte, where I would be able to purchase all I needed, from nails, tripes à la mode de Caen, double-beds to good nylon socks. With much laughter, grateful thanks once more from me, they bounced down the track and went off waving arms through the window.

The garden was still. Water dripped from the trees, from the eaves, and somewhere I could hear it running fast. The little brook at the top of the garden where the toad had lived was now a modestly foaming cataract. The air was sweet, cool, washed; far away, beyond the great gashed cliff-face, the storm rumbled off to the north.

I started to close the shutters. At least, after two days' toil, there was a possible place to offer Giles as a future home. If he cared for it. He might not care for the idea at all, but I did. No question of that.

I drove back to Bargemon, splashing along the roads, high-heartedly, to call Aronovich. Once again. He had not replied for two days. Perhaps tonight?

I thought, quite suddenly, that although the Simons had asked, most anxiously, for James and had, apparently, deplored the fact of his departure, not one of them had asked me if the police had been notified. Naturally enough. No good peasant in Provence would dream of such a thing.

The police were more disliked than the German tourists who posed for photographs on the war memorials in every village. But I began to wonder if perhaps it was time that I notified someone official? Against Florence's wishes, her mother's and, indeed, James's.

But there would have to come a time when I did. After I had spoken to Aronovich. See what he had to say to me. If anything.

By the harsh light of the elephant-lamp I dialled, for the fourth time in two days, Aronovich's number in Cannes. This time, taking me by surprise almost, there was a reply. After a couple of rings a voice with a very thick Arab accent shouted, 'Allô! Allô! Oui?'

I gave my name – the French version, Colcott – and was told, 'Attendez'.

Which I did.

In a few moments I heard a low, clear, smooth voice, controlled, polite, with no hint of a question in it. 'This is Aronovich. What do you want?'

I explained who I was and why I was calling, apologizing for disturbing him. I probably spoke too quickly in my borrowed tongue because he suddenly halted me mid-stream with, 'Excuse me. One moment. I have not understood you perfectly. You are the brother of James Colcott. That is so? And you are now living in his house. Is that right?'

'Quite right. Actually, I am staying in an hotel in Bargemon, but apparently the house is now mine.'

'How "apparently"?'

'Well, I have a letter from my brother, and he also mailed me the key.'

'When was this, Mr Colcott? Some time ago, I assume, for your brother has been absent, shall I say, for some many months, as you no doubt are aware?'

'I am aware. I got his letter and the key at the beginning of April.'

'Ah yes. That is possible.'

'It is fact. His wife sent it to me on his instructions.'

'And what has that to do with me?'

'I understand that you are ready now to collect the paintings which James has stored in the studio.'

'That is so. I want to get them to the framers. They take so long.'

'I wondered if you could help me? I am here trying to find out what might have happened to James. Where he might have gone. His family are desperately worried, as you will understand.'

'How could I possibly help?'

'Brent Millar suggested that you might.'

There was a singing silence on the line for a moment. Somewhere in Cannes a brow might have beaded with fine sweat or merely wrinkled in bewilderment.

'Brent Millar said that?'

It was an absolute lie, but before he could check that out with Millar, who was presently in Connecticut, I hoped to get his agreement to help. I decided to play a good card.

'He said that you had been very close to James, a marvellous and generous friend, especially in your interest in his work. And the very fine sum of money you paid out for these canvases at a difficult time for him.'

'And you are here to find out what happened? For his family?'

'I am his family, as well. But that is so.'

The fact that the family had long since been 'gathered', and that only I remained, I ignored. He need not know that part. Obviously Aronovich was not a fool. But an apparent helpless appeal for assistance from a worried foreigner might perhaps sway him.

'It is difficult for me, Mr Colcott. I am extremely busy, you know. I have no time for meetings at the moment. I know nothing about your brother, only that he has gone away somewhere. It is common knowledge.'

'Common knowledge to whom?'

Caught him off guard there. For a second his boat rocked gently. He steadied it adroitly.

'Perhaps, "common" is an unhappy choice. French is not my mother tongue. His wife knows of course, and as you will be aware, so does Mr Millar.'

'And you?'

'I knew because Brent Millar advised me . . . oh, long ago. In January, I think? His wife verified this fact when I telephoned her at her mother's house to say that there had been a very little hold-up in the building of my hotel. Nothing grave. A spring in the foundations. It meant drainage and so on which had not been anticipated. I told her I would collect the canvases when the time was right. She said that was in order. The works would stay at the house. Voilà! The time is now, and that is all that I can possibly tell you.'

I tried a stronger line.

'I have seen the Agendas which James sold to Brent Millar. They are, as you will obviously understand, of exceptional interest. They are extremely detailed and cover such a long time. From Paris up until Bargemon. Which you so very kindly guided him towards. Could we meet, just for a moment or two? Perhaps you have a tiny clue which could be helpful to me. I do need your advice.'

'If Brent Millar has the Agendas, you can be perfectly certain, Mr Colcott, that they are in very secure hands.'

'I can only be certain that he has the originals. I have seen those . . .'

The silence once more. This time there was the sound of not heavy, but simply breathing on the line. Somewhere I had a feeling that Aronovich was not quite sure of things.

'Originals?'

'Yes. James was very keen to earn some money. I expect you know how strapped he was for cash? Wretched business.

But he thought that perhaps he could do well if the things were offered on the open market. You know? France, Germany, the US, where Mr Millar is a rather popular writer. There is a brisk demand for stuff like that, I gather.'

'You say there are copies of the Agendas?'

'One can't be totally sure, can one? I know that I would keep a copy of anything I valued in the way of writing. I write myself. Essential to have a copy or even copies, and it is easy now to do that.'

'It is highly unlikely, Mr Colcott.'

'So, Mr Aronovich, is life on Mars. But who knows?'

'What do you want?'

'A meeting, very short. I have to be in Nice tomorrow to meet the afternoon flight from London. Would that be any good to you? If I am in Nice?'

'I can be in Nice. Yes. Very well. Noon. The Pullman Bar on the observation floor at the airport. For a few moments.'

'You are more than generous. I am sure that we will recognize each other, but alas! I am not a blond like James . . . and older . . .'

Suddenly Aronovich was at ease. He laughed lightly. 'I know that. You have dark hair and it curls, eh?' He hung up abruptly.

My turn for a silence as I replaced my receiver. How did he know that I was dark-haired and that it did, indeed, curl? James, I suppose, or Millar? Someone had probably warned him. Be aware! The brother is hunting his sibling. Take care. If care were needed.

I had taken a risk in my modest bedroom under the roof. I had, however, not lied. Implying is not the same as lying. Although one can hope that it has the same effect when needed.

Downstairs by the desk Eugène was sorting out the menus for the evening.

'Tomorrow evening my son will join me. He's nine.'

'Certainly. Madame Mazine has told me. Room number 5.'

'He likes food. Amazingly. When he has the chance to eat anything decent.'

'Ah. There is something particular? You think of a celebration dinner?'

'Well, in a way, yes. He, I remember from our last holiday in Normandy, loved a really good poule au pot. Is that possible? Just for two?'

'Quite possible. De la béarnaise? That is rich but delicious.'

'Or . . .? I'm not worried about the richness. Strangeness. My son hates baked beans, detests fish fingers and won't look at an English sausage. He knew a boy at his school whose father was a very respectable butcher who told him that they mixed sawdust, anal refuse and finger-stalls in the blender. It rather put him off.'

'It would. Sure. Or' – Eugène suddenly gleamed with pleasure – 'a Navarin of lamb? Spring vegetables, the new broad beans, baby onions, carrots as thick as your smallest finger, potatoes like pearls! A gloriously garlicked gigot – he will eat garlic?'

I may have lost track of life in general, but I knew the way to the bar, which I most desperately needed at that moment. I remember that I agreed to the poule. If Giles refused it I'd eat it all. I went determinedly to the bar and Claude with his bottle of Haig. Tomorrow was going to be a difficult day one way and another.

At that moment it was as well that I didn't know just how difficult.

Ignorance is sometimes bliss.

I recognized him immediately. I really don't know why. Possibly because I was a little over-aware. Perhaps it was just the way that he had placed himself, right in front of the entry to the bar, sitting quite alone in an alcove of buttoned-black-leather and steel walls. And he recognized me: there was a slight hesitation, then a smile, a languid arm raised, inviting me to sit beside him, across the little round table on which stood a bucket of ice, two glasses, and, above all, a bottle of Cristall.

I sat, he offered his hand. 'I am Solly Aronovich and you have to be the older Colcott. Right? I don't actually remember your Christian name. I do remember it is very English.'

'It's William.'

'Ah! Norman, as in Conqueror. Will you take champagne? Frankly, after a bloody morning on a building-site champagne is essential from eleven until whenever.'

'Champagne will be perfectly splendid. It is good of you to see me.'

He flicked fingers at some waiter who arrived to pour the wine.

'I thought so too.' He was smiling so there was no rebuke. Not that I would have, as Florence would say, given a fig. But I needed his goodwill, so he got thanked.

'What can I do for you? I know *nothing* of your brother, you know. Years ago, yes. You have read the famous Agendas? So of course you know . . .'

'I know. I equally know that you persuaded him to come to Bargemon. To get back to a . . . to a more seemly life. Right?'

'Perfectly right. He is a good fellow. Wild, emotional, very vain, but he has a talent, I knew that. It needed to be contained, encouraged, given time to grow and develop. In Paris the . . . temptations, shall I say, were too great. Here he could breathe, start again. It took courage, you know? But . . .' – the helpless shrug – 'but the boy is now a man. If you grow old in the environment in which he thrived you die at forty.'

He was smiling at me, his glass held in a strong hand. I

suppose I had expected someone in a blue suit. Or a black raincoat. A hat certainly. With a hooked nose and a bald head like a vulture. Aronovich was not at all like those fleeting images. Mid-fifties, possibly, but looked an early forty. A full, glossy head of black hair, a good face, brown eyes, a generous, but not slack, mouth, a firm nose, perhaps 'fixed', but altogether a good-looking man. He was tall and slim, in a pale blue shirt, his initials on his breastpocket, blue jeans, sneakers and a silver belt with a fat dollar coin for the buckle. He watched me as I took stock of him.

'I don't *look* like Fagin? Do I? Sometimes it worries me. But my mother was from Pisa, in Italy, my father from Cracow, I was born in the Argentine. We were very fortunate. And you' – he leant with folded arms on the table – 'are quite unlike James. It's true. He was so fair! So different in complexion, he really could not be a brother to you –' And then he stopped, and without altering his look he said, 'One gets so confused with "was" and "is". I should, I suppose, say James was so different from you that I would never imagine you were brothers at all.'

I had noted the change in tenses. Perhaps because, again, I was over-aware. But I suddenly liked him. He was easy, he was calm, he was not at all what I had thought he would be.

'There are over ten years between us. He was the changeling. Is. Was. You see I am in a muddle too. You have no news of him at all?'

Aronovich shook his head slowly, moving his flute of champagne about in tiny circles on the table, spreading the melting ice from the bucket.

'Not a word. Not hair nor hide. You can say that? Since . . . oh, well before he disappeared. Before January. He just went away. People can do that, you know? If life becomes intolerable to them they close the shop and go away. It is easy for them, hard for those left behind.'

'Desperate for his wife. She is in constant anguish. Wondering where? If? I feel certain that we should go against his wishes, in his letter, and inform someone officially. The British Consul. The police . . . Someone. There should be a search. He can't have left the country after all, he must be somewhere around.'

Aronovich was nodding in agreement, but suddenly looked up at me with curiosity. 'Why do you feel sure of that? He could be miles and miles away by now. In Germany. Italy is easy from here. Anywhere.'

'On a bike?'

For a moment we held each other's gaze. Mine of inquiry, his of belief. He broke it finally by saying, sadly I thought, 'We'll never know. I feel certain of that.'

'*I* am equally certain that he did not ride a bike to Rome or Naples or Berlin and Hanover.'

He refilled our glasses with expert grace. There was no spillage, no head of foaming bubbles. A perfectly poured glass of champagne. Which, after all, I thought he ought to know how to manage by now. After the Poisson d'Avril days.

'It's all humbug, isn't it?' he said suddenly. 'I mean, about the Agendas? There are no copies, are there?'

'How can we tell? I would have copied them if they had been mine. For safety.'

'They were James's. And he did not. You used it as a bait to lure me to this meeting. Confess!'

'I confess. Yes. But it was imperative that I see you. You are the last hope I have. You knew him, you were, I gather, fond of him, you wished him well. You may know where he has gone to. Why.'

He shook his head again. 'I know neither. He was a friend, I agree, but he did not confess his innermost thoughts. And if he left, then he left. I can't tell you.'

'Am I to really believe that?'

'It is up to you, Mr Colcott. I paraphrase: I am not your brother's keeper. I am sorry. Why do you persist so hard? Why not accept the fact that he has fled? You know perfectly well, I am certain indeed, that he was never actually married to Florence Prideaux. All that was just a happy bit of romantic nonsense. There is no marriage.'

'There is a child.'

'Sure. That does not constitute a marriage, my friend. In Africa, in Jamaica, in all those liberal or backward countries, whatever you choose to call them, no one gets married just because there is a child! If so, there would be fifty million priests conducting services every moment of the day!' He drained his flute, set it down, looked at his watch on a bronzed wrist. 'I so much regret it. But I have to go. I have to be on the site all the time, otherwise they sit about reading the paper or playing boules. It is not at all amusing to own an hotel. Half ready, half not. We are nearly there, not so long now.'

I rose with him. 'And then you'll come over to Jericho. For your canvases?'

'That would be most kind. Can we speak? You have my number. When it is quite convenient to you I'll send a truck.'

'Or come yourself? To see what changes I have made? I would like that.'

'Very kind.' He pulled himself into a white bomber jacket. We walked down to the swing doors which led to the elevator.

'The champagne? One can't leave a half-bottle of Cristal in the bar!'

He put out a hand, which I took. It was strong, as I had seen, firm. 'If you will, *do* finish it. You have a plane to meet at three? Then stay up here and watch the airplanes landing! Order a club sandwich from Antoine there and enjoy the wine. I really *must* go.' He pressed the elevator button, a red light flicked on.

'Fifteen minutes on the autoroute. It doesn't take long. But at lunchtime . . .'

The elevator arrived, staggered to a halt. Two women got out carrying plastic bags and a small dog.

'What are you driving?' I said.

He got into the elevator, turned to press the button for descent. 'A good solid car. What one must have on these autoroutes, in case one gets hit. A good old Peugeot.'

'A 604?'

'The same. Fast and safe. Goodbye!'

I stood thoughtfully watching him spiral down to the mall.

The International Gate was crowded with people waiting for the London arrival. Placards waved with the names of hotels, car firms, or the names of travel couriers and film companies. The Film Festival was in full swing: journalists, thin girls in thinner dresses, fat men with jackets over their shoulders, briefcases in their hands, people who had drunk enough on the flight, elderly women pale and disoriented by a first journey at 36,000 feet.

And among them all, among the waving arms, embracing bodies, the cries of 'Here you are!' and 'So *brown*! *Aren't* you brown?', I saw Giles. Taller than I seemed to have remembered him. He couldn't have grown so much in a month surely? He was looking about him perfectly calmly, lugging a large blue handgrip.

I waved, caught his eye. He raised his arm and shook a cheerful fist in the air, turned to someone beside him and pointed me out.

It was his mother.

CHAPTER 13

I PUSHED THROUGH the crowd, touched Giles's head, took his handgrip and gave Helen a preoccupied kind of kiss. That is to say a bob at each cheek. She was carrying a green and white bag from Harrods food halls, thrust it towards me. She had a bundle of newspapers under her other arm.

'Here you are! A pound of farmhouse Cheddar, Cumberland ring and a delicious Arbroath smoked haddock. All wrapped up in tin-foil.'

I juggled a handgrip and Harrods, muttered thanks.

'If you looked in a mirror now, my dear, you'd recognize extreme shock,' she said. We were walking through the chattering throng without direction.

'Not shock. Not that. Just surprise, that's all.'

'Well I was coming down anyway. Eric's at his place at Valbonne. We're off on the recce. In two days.'

'You said a week?'

'I said soonish, dear. Remember? So I just brought Giles. He wanted to come. And here we are.'

A seedy little man in jeans and trainers pushed towards us, a piece of white card with 'APHRODITE PRODUCTIONS' chalked on it.

'It's Ron!' said Helen brightening considerably. 'Dear old Ron. You got here then?'

'Last evening,' said Ron. 'Got your baggage tags? How many pieces?'

'This is my husband, Ron, Mr Caldicott.'

'Hi,' said Ron indifferently. 'How many pieces? It's down here; watch the steps.' He turned us left, towards the baggage claim, hastening ahead to get a trolley.

'I don't know about accommodation, my room is a bit cramped for two.'

'William, dear. Those days are over! No mummies and daddies now. I am staying with Eric at Valbonne. Easier. We leave together and there is a lot of, you know, preliminary stuff to do before, so . . .'

We had reached the carousels. Rome, Ajaccio and London at the far end.

Giles said, 'I'll take the carrier, shall I?'

'Well, it would be kind.'

'If I had told you on the telephone what I was doing you'd have made all kinds of a fuss and excuses. I know you. So I decided on a fait accompli, right?'

'Obviously.'

'As obviously as you are absolutely ill with delight that I'm at work again. Your face! William, *really*. What news of your Treasure Hunt? Hot on the trail, are we?'

'If you mean James, no. Not at all.'

'Good grief! What did he do? Evaporate or something?'

'Something like that.'

Giles said, 'Our flight's gone up. On the notice thing. And it's started to move.'

Helen was fishing about in her handbag. Someone was making an announcement over the sound system, an appeal for a Mr Hackenburger in two languages. Then Helen found a card and gave it to me.

'Where I am. From today until we leave on Sunday afternoon. I've got yours, so we are in touch. Mummy is *thrilled* to have Annie, Annie likes being with her, and you –' she prodded Giles so hard that he almost stumbled off balance – 'and you wanted to see Daddy and Daddy you've got. That right?'

Giles looked up at me uncertainly. I smiled inanely, but I hoped I looked encouraging. He just nodded, and Ron arrived breathlessly.

'You did say all tartan and a white cross of camera tape? Okay?'

'Yes. Christ! Don't say you've lost them?'

'*I* haven't lost them!' Ron was indignant. 'I just asked. They are only starting to come off now.' He pushed away again.

'This is the drag of travelling. *God*, I hate it.'

'You've only just started, Helen.'

'Take the gleam of triumph out of your voice.'

'No gleam. Observation, that's all.'

'Look! Ron's waving at us. He's got them. Come on.'

She grabbed Giles and I followed them through people with autograph books, photographers, banners, laughing holiday-makers and movie buffs. There was an immense 'Welcome to the Film Festival' in the form of a plastic Mickey Mouse and a Snow White tower in the centre of the concourse, starred with flashing lights, revolving slowly.

'Have *we* got a car? I mean you and me?' said Giles.

''Course. I have borrowed one. From the Mayor.'

'Wow! The Mayor of Cannes?'

'No. Idiot. The Mayor of the village.'

'Oh.'

Helen, who had sorted out her baggage with Ron, waved to us to come down to the Customs and the exit. Nice is an odd airport. I looked at the Harrods bag in Giles's hand and vaguely thought how easy it would be to smuggle in a pound of coke instead of Cheddar. No one would be any the wiser – *we* would not be leaving through the Customs area. French logic.

Outside in the heat of the sun, under the palms, among a milling crowd, Ron started to cross the road. Helen shouted to him to wait. He turned and came back, his face flushed with irritation.

'What's up?'

'Well, how far is your car? My husband isn't coming with us. He's got his own.'

'First floor down. I'll wait then.'

'Look, call me, or I'll call you if you'd rather, this evening? About six? We ought to have a talk. It's been over a month now? Saturday?'

'I can make Saturday. Yes. Would you come over to us?'

'Well, if I can get there. How far is it?'

'About an hour on the autoroute, a bit longer. An hour and a half.'

'Oh Christ! Can you send a taxi?'

'Easier if you get one. I'll pay, naturally.'

'That *is* kind. Goodness. Don't call me. I'll call you. At six sharp.'

'Unless you'd prefer me to come and get you? I could?'

'No. That's silly, I don't know when I'd be ready. Depends on Eric . . . I'll call you.' She bent to kiss Giles, her handbag swinging, under her arm the London papers slipping.

'It's the Hôtel La Maison Blanche, Bargemon-sur-Yves. You know that?'

''Course I know that. Goodbye, Giles. Have a super time. I'll be back soonish. I'll keep in touch, let you know where we are in Marbella. Aphrodite Productions will get me, I reckon. It's a long address. All in Spanish.'

'If you've read the London papers, I'd be very grateful –'

'Oh William! I'm *sorry*, lovie, I bought these for Eric. He goes spare without the sports news.'

'I see. Okay.'

Ron called above the rush of traffic for her to hurry. She pulled a paper out of the bundle and pushed it at me.

'Don't look so miserable, William, really! Take this *Financial Times* – that do? Eric likes his *Mirror*. I must go.' She kissed me hurriedly, waved to us both.

'You look like the Bisto Kids!' she shouted and was lost behind a roaring surge of traffic.

In the Simca, Giles fixed his seat-belt, settled back comfortably. 'Funny feeling, sitting on this side. Terribly near, I mean *you* are. The traffic. In the middle of the road really.'

'Cheer me up. Thanks.'

'You looked as if you needed cheering up.'

'Did I? Why?'

'When you saw Mum.'

'Well . . . I only expected you. With a handgrip and a label round your neck.'

'Well, you don't mind, do you? I mean, me coming?'

'Of *course* I don't mind! I'm really pleased. You've got a decent room, and a super dinner tonight, specially ordered for you.'

'Which is what?'

'Your favourite. Poule au pot.'

'Brilliant! How long can I stay?'

'How long do you want to stay?'

'I don't know.'

'What about school?'

'Look! It says Marineland, that big poster. Dolphins . . . could we go there one day?'

'Yes. About school, what do we do about that?'

'I don't know. It's nearly end of term, you see . . .'

'Not till July, Giles, they'll have me arrested.'

'Who will? The school? Mr Davenport?'

'No. The education authorities. Someone. I don't know.'

'But we can go to Antibes? To Marineland?'

'Yes. We'll go.'

It was after five by the time we got to Bargemon-sur-Yves. Helen's flight had been delayed, there was more traffic than I had expected, and we stopped at a service area for petrol, a pee, then a tin of orange for Giles, a beer for me.

After that, I turned off the 'Provençal' towards the distant hills and Bargemon. I drove slowly so that he could see the vines in their immaculate rows, the groves of olive and almond, and the red-tiled farms and barns scattered about the wide fertile plain, and then we started, gently, to climb.

He was, I was comforted to see, perfectly content, silent, watching. And when we did speak we spoke together easily, relaxedly. As if we had done this kind of journey often, when, in fact, it was about the first time ever, by ourselves. He had his hands folded in his lap, head craning about on a slender neck, looking, watching, missing nothing.

'Are those sheep? Up over there? With the man on a horse?'

'Sheep and goats.'

'Why goats?'

'Sheep follow goats. They are good leaders. Don't ask me why, I don't know.'

'And *cows* pulling the plough-things?'

'Oxen. Not cows. Like percherons – *they* are enormous horses. Very strong.'

'Brilliant. Do they always use oxen?'

'Not now. Farmers who can't afford a tractor do, and some do because they are easier to hoe with through the vines.'

'Are we going into the hills then?'

'That seems to be the general direction I'm taking, wouldn't you say?'

'Yup, I did say. That's what I meant, I mean.'

'Bargemon is up there. You'll see the cliffs in a little time.'

'Awesome. What's Valbonne like? Do you know?'

'No. Never been there. Why?'

'Uncle Eric's house is there. It's got a huge swimming-pool.'

'"Uncle" Eric?'

'Yup. That's what we have to call him.'

'But why? He's not your uncle.'

'I know. Mum says it makes him feel more welcome. More at home. Belonging.'

'More at home?'

'They are all called Uncle.'

'Who are? Who is "all"?'

'Well, you know. Mr Price, Mr McKenna and Eric. It gets a bit funny.'

'I should bloody well think it does. Do you like them, you and Annie?'

'Oh, they're all right. Really. Eric's a bit . . . well . . .' He turned away and looked out of the window.

'A bit what? Eric's a bit what? You said. Something, what?'

'Well, actually, it's a bit rude to say really.'

'You mean he farts?' This was a deliberate attempt to disarm him. It worked.

He collapsed into a heap, giggling, sniggering, helpless, rubbing his face with his hands, burying his head in his chest, avoiding my look.

'Giles! If he doesn't fart, what *does* he do? Something awful?'

The laughter had subsided, he was still hiccuping, eyes rimmed with tears of sheer pleasure, hand to his mouth. Conspiracy in the look he suddenly shot at me.

'You wouldn't tell if I say?'

''Course not.'

'It's his breath! It's amazing. So awful. I don't know how Mum can bear it.'

I heard myself saying flatly, though I had not intended to let it show, 'Bear what, Giles?'

He looked straight ahead, ignored the question.

'Flies all over the windscreen. Millions of them, all squashed. We must have been going very fast. A flies' cemetery. Brilliant!'

'Bear what, Giles?'

'His breath,' he said.

He was hanging out of his window when I went into his room, one foot kicking the heel of the other.

'Don't fall, not the first night.'

'I won't. It's pretty good here. Look at the cliffs. All pink. Are they really that colour or is it the sun? It's the sun, right?'

'The sun.'

'Can we go up there?'

'It's miles, you'd have to be a mountain goat.'

He turned from the window and hitched up his jeans, fiddled with his belt.

'You don't mind me being here, do you?'

'I told you. I'm *terrifically* pleased.'

'Really?'

'Really. You'd know otherwise. I just hope it won't be boring here for you.'

'Why? Do you think I'll be bored?'

'You could be. Countryside. Nothing to do. No Safeway's or Tesco, no movies, video. It's very dull.'

'I don't think it is. I don't like Safeway's and Tesco and those things. I have to go with Mum. That's boring.' He turned and looked out of the window again. He was avoiding confrontation when he said, 'What do I call you? I mean, if I do stay? You might send me back. You could, couldn't you?'

'I could. Yes. I probably will if you keep your back to me.'

'Why?'

'Bad manners. You want to ask a question, ask me to my face; don't ask the chicken run.'

He turned back into the room, eyes on the worn carpet. I was sitting on the edge of his bed. I didn't help him out. He started examining his thumb as if he had just grown it.

'Well. What do I call you?'

'What do you call me anyway? I mean behind my back? Dad, Daddy, Pa, Him . . .?'

He half laughed, put his hands in his pockets, faced me directly for the first time. 'At school . . . sometimes . . . I call you . . . Will.'

'Okay. Do you want to call me Will here?'

'You mind?'

'Why should I? If it makes you comfortable.'

'I would feel comfortable.'

'Frankly so would I. I don't care for the Daddy bit. Too ageing.'

'You mean it makes you feel old?'

'Yes.'

'Well, you are, aren't you?'

'Yes. "Will" will do very nicely.' I got off the bed. 'Have you unpacked all your stuff?'

'Two of everything, Mum said. Where's the lav? I forget. You did show me but I can't remember.'

'Bottom of the corridor. It's got a large WC on it. Water closet.'

He bent over, snorting with pleasure. Typically English. Any mention of anything scatological brought all life to a sniggering halt in suppressed, or otherwise, laughter.

'When you have recovered your wits, I want to talk to you. Okay? There will be a guest tonight to share the poule au pot. She's very nice, I like her very much, and, you may be astonished to know, she happens to be your aunt.'

His look of amazement almost made me laugh out loud.

We just stood and stared at each other in a bemused way. I felt almost as idiotic as he looked.

'I didn't know I had an aunt in France.'

'Neither did I. She's quite young, younger than me, and her name is Florence, and that's what you call her.'

'Where did you find her? I mean, if you didn't know about her. I mean, who is she actually?'

So I told him. Sitting down again to do so, and cutting out all the detail which he didn't need and would not have been able to take in, let alone understand. When I had finished, by explaining that his Uncle James had just gone away and no one knew where, he looked as bewildered as I often felt. I had made the story as simple and straightforward as I could, from the arrival of the key to our arrival together at the hotel. But it was still a lot to cope with.

He looked at me in silence for a while, then turned on his heel, slowly, hands still thrust into his pockets, and walked back to the open window.

'It's getting quite dark. The sky is all red coloured,' he said.

'It's after six, and no call from Mum. She said six, didn't she?'

'I didn't hear her. Probably. Does she know about . . . about this aunt and that?'

'And what? Don't say "and that". It doesn't mean anything.'

'About your brother going away?'

'Yes. She knows that. She knows why I came here. To the house.'

'Is it nice? The house?' He was running a finger along the bolt of the window.

'*I* think so. We'll go over tomorrow. You also have a cousin. He's three, and his name is Thomas.'

'Brilliant! He's the first cousin I've ever had! That's awesome!' He was smiling broadly, had turned away from the window and stood half-silhouetted against the dying sky.

'He's a bit young for you. Three.'

'Still, he's a cousin. It's a bit good, isn't it? Will he come to the house, your house?'

'Yes. He does come. Often. There is one snag, Giles. It's a bit tricky this part: he's disabled.'

He came across to the bed, lounged against the bedpost at the foot, cupping the carved wooden ball on the top with his hand, not quite looking at me.

'In a chair, you mean? I know a boy in a chair. Purvis. He can play volleyball really well. He's fast –'

'Thomas is only three. He can walk all right, it's just that he doesn't really *look* quite like you and me. He's a bit, well, a bit backward. Do you know what I'm getting at?'

'You mean he's a bit funny? In the top storey? A bit weird?' He looked up at me directly.

The devastating honesty of children always takes one a little by surprise; I never know why. They are, it would seem, far better equipped to deal with some difficult problem in a simple, unsentimental, straightforward manner. So I replied in the same way.

'In the top storey. Yes. But he's *very* nice, *very* loving. I think you'll manage with him. Like him. Anyway, I know you'll try?'

'All right. And his mother is Florence, right?'

I got up again and went to the door. He'd got enough to digest for the moment. At the door I said, 'Yes. She's coming tonight because, and this will give you a thrill, she's looking around to see if there is anyone in the area who could give you a few lessons. A bit of French, you know? You should be still at school, you see?'

'Oh. Mum said it didn't matter. About no school.'

'Mum would. I'm going down to the bar for a drink. Want to come? I'll show you off to the barman, Claude, and then you'll know the way, and know who he is.'

'Am I allowed in the bar? You aren't allowed in England.'

'You are in France. Coming?'

'Yup.' He took his denim jacket and pushed his fingers through his hair. It was dark, and it curled. Like mine. He looked like me, tall, good nose, but Helen's eyes, well set, green-blue. Nice-looking boy. I closed the shutters, secured them with the iron bolts.

The room was suddenly dark, slits of crimson cut through the louvres in the gloom. Giles pulled on his jacket.

'This aunt, does she know about me?'

'Of course she does. She's looking for a tutor, I told you.'

We were walking down the corridor to the stairs.

'Yup. Forgot. I call her Florence? There's the lav, I see. WC. English?'

Going down the stairs I said that we had invented the thing, and when we got to the desk I introduced him to Madame Mazine, who came from behind her mahogany fortress and shook his hand.

'Do you speak French?'

He looked at me blankly. I answered for him, and said no. Madame smiled, smoothed her apron and suggested that he would in a very short time. He was a clever young man, she was sure. I told her that I would be in the bar if a call should come for me from Valbonne, and steered Giles on his way to Claude, my whisky and his first, as far as I knew, bar.

There was no fire in the dining-room. Summer had been acknowledged by a large Japanese fan spread wide in the empty hearth. On the tables little glass jars of sweet william and fern.

Eugène was busy – there were four other tables besides ourselves – and he hurried in and out of the kitchen like a shuttle, the door swinging behind him with a flash of light.

Giles was silent, eyes wide, watching, eager for every

move. The sight of the stuffed partridge had greatly pleased him and the several horned heads stuck about the rose-trellised paper on the walls. He was relaxed, smiling in a bemused way, swinging his legs, sitting on his hands, content. I rather liked his trust.

Florence watched him gravely. She was looking pretty in a new dress (well, new to me anyway). It was simple, with a little collar, a floral tie, white cuffs. She and Giles had been naturally cautious at first meeting. I had never expected her to accept a sudden invitation to join us for the poule au pot. I was aware that she had never dined in the hotel before, that the most she had ever done was to have an ice cream once or twice in the summer on the terrace. To come into the dining-room was something she had never remotely considered, until I told her that I had met, and spoken to, Aronovich; that her new nephew was savouring his first grown-up evening; and that I would prefer, for once, not to talk to her about important matters in the conservatory with the banana tree. This she had readily understood. Temptation was accepted, and she joined us.

Her English, though halting, was perfectly adequate, and although she clearly found it a little uncomfortable at first, she very soon settled down. A glass of wine had helped, and she even, at one point, made Giles laugh aloud. From this she gained confidence, I settled down, and Giles, with eyes all about him like those of a lobster, was so overwhelmed by everything that he determined to be perfectly underwhelmed even to the extent of merely nodding in agreement when a smug Eugène flourished the big copper pan before him, and the sight of a plump poule smothered in spring vegetables and stuffed with pork and chicken liver merely elicited a nervous nod of acceptance. Florence had already had it presented to her and had looked at me with an appeal of despair in her grey eyes. So much food at this time of night was not, obviously, something to which she was accustomed.

But we started off. Giles was so occupied that he took absolutely no notice of us speaking in French together. I told her, in a brief résumé, about my meeting with Aronovich, that I had liked him for some reason, that he had seemed pleasant, a little preoccupied under a thick layer of good manners, and that I had gained absolutely no information on James at all. At this point I did not say anything about a Peugeot 604 or anything else in that area. Until I was perfectly sure of my facts it was better to remain mute on that subject. That could come later. If there was a 'later'.

'So. When will he collect the canvases?' She was obviously disappointed.

'When I call him, really. Next week sometime. Building an hotel is a very time-consuming business, I gather. It's getting near, but not yet.'

'And he had no ideas to give you? About James?'

'Nothing at all. He said that he knew that he had gone away, as he called it, but had not seen "hair nor hide", in his words, since well before January. When do you last remember seeing him? Aronovich? In the summer?'

She set aside a bone on her plate, pushed her fork around.

'No. Later I think. There was a time in October. He came then. I was with my mother in the kitchen, we were making jam. He came then. I saw him walking up the path with the Jacquet boy. October. That was when I saw him last. James, I don't know.'

Madame Mazine was at my side, a whisper with head bowed, I was wanted on the telephone. Madame Colcott.

The telephone cabin was hard beside the desk, an accordion door, the walls lined in a faded chintz of parrots in laburnum blossoms. I slammed the door shut and took the receiver from the urgently ringing machine.

'William? Helen, sorry. But you didn't call. You said six!'

'*You* said six. I waited.'

'I gave you the card. At the airport. You *are* impossible!'

'There is no telephone number on the card, and your host is not listed.'

'Well. I couldn't call. It's chaos here, so much to do. One of the mothers is ill and can't come and we have to find a chaperon . . . *I* have to. Look, I can't make Saturday, it's just no good. You are miles away and I don't fancy sitting on my backside in a French taxi for four hours.'

'All right. Fine.'

'Well, see it my way. It's four hours out of my day. And the time at your house, you know? It's impossible. And Eric can't really do without me so near the recce. I was only coming over to see that Giles was all right.'

'He's fine. We are in the middle of dinner at the moment.'

'Having my haddock?'

'No. Actually not.'

'Oh.' Displeasure crept into her voice. 'It won't keep for ever, you know. Even smoked. It'll go off.'

'I have given everything to the kitchen. They'll cope.'

'*The Cheddar?* They'll freeze it!'

'Helen. It's all right, honestly. There are over three hundred varieties of cheese here in France, we'll manage.'

'I see. I needn't have bothered? It was just a thought, that's all.'

'A very sweet one. Thank you. But this evening is Giles's treat. There's a quite special pudding.'

'William, don't spoil him. He's been really a rotten little beast for the last month. Sullen, sulky, damned rude.'

'Seems all right to me.'

'You wait. Try and find out what's bugging him, will you?'

'I will. Don't you worry. He's having a tutor next week, until I come back to the UK.'

'And when will that be? Are you hot on the trail? I thought you'd drawn a blank?'

'Not certain. I'll try and get back, as I said, at the beginning of June, a fortnight's time. Okay?'

'Okay by me. I just feel that you ought to get your house sorted out, Simla Road, put it on the market. Summer is a good time, they tell me.'

'What about you? Won't you need a roof over your head?'

'Not really. Sooner you get rid of it the better. William, I won't stay there, you know? I'm moving out as soon as this shoot is over.'

'To your mother again?'

'No. To be honest, no. Eric has a lovely place near Burnham Beeches . . . You can't mind. You really can't . . .'

'I don't. Not at all. You go ahead. We'll talk lawyers in June, all right?'

'All right. Yes. As I said ages ago, there is nothing I want. You take it all, your house. I'll take just a few things, and my clothes. But otherwise . . . understand?'

'Perfectly.'

'Did Giles find his *Zoo Monthly*?'

'I didn't ask him.'

'Christ! It was a surprise, in his bag. I wrapped it especially.'

'I'll ask him.'

She placed her hand over the receiver, the line went dead for a second, then her voice again, thin and rushed. 'I have to go. I'm late already, Eric's taking me over to a favourite restaurant somewhere. I must go. I'll write from Marbella. Give you the address. Love to Giles. *Do* find out what's got into him. Must go. Sorry about Saturday.'

'You'll really be late.'

'This is true. Hugs and kisses. Bye.' She hung up and I leant against the parrots and laburnum, weak with relief. Gone! How quickly love dies, how little one chokes on the '*charcoal dust of passion*'. My italics. All over and done with. On a telephone.

I replaced the receiver, pulled apart the accordion doors, went into the hall. Madame Mazine looked over the top of her glasses.

'It'll be cold. What a time to do business.'

'What a time indeed.'

'Eugène will have saved it. Hurry.'

I walked back to the dining-room as if I had just had a reprieve. Which, in fact, is exactly what I had. Free! Breathing, alive. I started to whistle on my way back to the dining-room.

Giles and Florence had almost finished eating and were talking, in a halting but perfectly easy manner, as I rejoined the table. He looked across at me with slightly raised eyebrows.

'Mum. She's not coming on Saturday. Too much to do or something, and we are too far away from wherever she is.'

'With Eric.'

'I know that. Where he lives. She asked if you had found *Zoo Monthly*.'

'Yup. I've already got it. She doesn't know.'

Eugène was at my side with the copper pan, serving expertly my unfinished meal. Giles looked at the pan anxiously. Eugène caught his look. 'It is hot still? The vegetables are fresh? He would take some more?'

Giles nodded, handing up his empty plate.

'Leave the plate, Giles. You aren't in school. Eugène will serve you.'

Florence laughed, folded her napkin, and her arms, and leant on the table. 'I wish I was that age again. Lucky Giles.'

'You don't mind, do you, Will?' It was the first time he had used the name. 'It's brilliant. Really good.'

'You'll be up all night. Tomorrow we have to go shopping, remember?'

'Shopping?' Florence said.

'Beds. At Futurama. And one or two things. Then we'll

go to Jericho.' And then I spoke in French so that Giles would not understand. 'That was my wife, as you probably realize. But what you perhaps don't realize, as I did not, fully, is that she left me. Gone. Fourteen years wiped out.'

She looked at the table, smoothed the napkin as if she had just ironed it. 'I'm sorry. Did she just tell you?'

'I am delighted. God! I'm relieved. We agreed to separate some time ago, but now it's a permanent break. Another gentleman.'

'And you are pleased?'

I put my hand on her arm. 'I just might start singing!'

I finished the last of my meal, which I really didn't by now want, and set my knife and fork aside. Giles was looking vaguely about the table, his dish full of sauce, knife and fork clutched in his hands, sticking upright in anxiety.

'What do you want? Not more, Giles!'

He shook his head, grinning, made a spooning movement over his plate. Florence understood instantly.

'Bread,' she said. 'Use some of the bread for the sauce, it's so good.'

Giles looked a little startled, then looked back at me. 'Bread? That's rude, isn't it? To use bread . . .'

'Not here. Wipe it round your plate!'

'I like France. You can go in the bar, mop up your gravy with bread – great.'

'Not *mop up*. And it's not gravy. Sauce. You'll learn.'

'I have found a man. For you, Giles. A man to help. He's very nice, old, but nice, I think. He is a friend of my mother at bridge. Yes? He is English, so that is a good thing for you and he has lived near here thirty years. He was an English teacher at a big school in England.'

Giles looked glum, Eugène came to clear.

'Where in England? Do you know? It doesn't matter. I mean, if he was a teacher he probably still is one. I assume he would take Giles?'

Florence looked a little uneasy. I had spoken in English and too fast. I repeated it in French and she replied that, when I wanted to, we would have a meeting and arrange things. Times, money. The money, I gathered, was a useful inducement to the agreement her mother had made with Mr Theobald. An impossible name to try in French, so he was known locally simply as 'Théo', and he had a wife called Dottie. She had their telephone number, which she found in her purse and gave me as Eugène returned with the cheese board, decorated with fresh vine leaves.

In French I said, as he left to get plates, 'My wife! My nearly ex-wife! God! It's so amazing. I feel like an empty refrigerator. Do you know what I mean? All clear, tidy, gleaming, cold, no clutter, very surgical. All ready to take in the *next* chunk of my life. It is not often that you are allowed two chances at life, is it? It's a marvellous feeling. There is so much to do!'

Giles suddenly said, 'Will? I don't want cheese, all right? I'll wait for the other thing.'

'What other thing?'

'There's a pudding, isn't there? You said?'

'There is. Yes.'

He put his hand on his heart, rolled his eyes. 'Awesome!' he said.

After dinner and a pot of lime tea we walked Florence back across the square to 11 rue Émile Zola.

There was a sickle moon, sharp and clean as a curved slit in the sky. A single star was up, the air smelled fresh and cool, and of leaves and new blossom mixed with the drifting scent of wood smoke, probably from the ovens of the boulangerie next door to Le Sporting.

At her gate in the lilac we said goodnight. I was inordinately pleased to see that Giles shook her hand with a slight inclination of his head. Helen's hard teaching, at times, had caused irritation and also mirth in the children, but was attractive when put into practice. He did it well, without the least degree of self-consciousness.

Florence walked up the white gravel path. With a slight wave she closed her front door, and we started off on our walk again.

'A little exercise, after that bloating dinner? You overate disgustingly.'

For a second he walked in silence, head down, then flicked an uncertain look at me. A reprimand? A 'snap' from Helen? Or a good-natured comment on greed? He risked the latter.

'The pudding was brilliant.'

'So I noticed. Apricot soufflé. Not much left after you and Florence.'

He realized it had not been a reprimand, relaxed almost visibly.

'You know, she's really nice?'

'I know. That's the reason you should try to learn a little French. To speak to her. It's not so hard.'

'Well, I *can* talk a bit. Listen: "Savez-vous planter les choux, à la mode?"'

'Great. Clever old you. But what does it mean?'

'"Do you know how to plant cabbages . . .?"' He snorted with laughter.

'Won't get you far, will it?'

We had gone round the church and into the marketplace. In the centre a fountain, a fat swagged urn spilling continuous water from a brass spigot into the rimmed basin below. Across the square there were still lights in Le Sporting and the shuttered sound of radio music muffled across the empty square. No one was about. We were the only life apparent, save for a couple of cats hunched opposite each other on the church steps, growling.

The entire populace seemed to be trapped before the

turquoise rectangles of their TV sets shimmering through gathers of lace curtains.

We went on round the church again by silent, but mutual, consent, our feet striking harshly on the cobbles. Mine anyway – Giles was bouncing in his white trainers. When we passed 11 rue Émile Zola a light suddenly sprang up in one of the top windows.

'Florence is going to bed,' I said.

Giles went across to the little iron gate in the hedge, took two of the bars in his hands, stuck his face over the top and called out, in a quiet voice, 'Bonsoir, Mademoiselle!' And, turning to me, he smiled. 'She's really nice. Do you think she heard me?'

Futurama was a gigantic concrete block set in the middle of an immense car park.

Soulless, efficient, hideous in every way. Cheaper than anywhere else in the district. Inside there were thirty check-out counters, staffed by human robots in ill-fitting uniforms. There were aisles and aisles of shelving piled high with goods of every description, soaring off into vanishing points like vast cathedrals built of girders and breezeblock.

The trolleys were large enough to carry an armchair plus a small coffee table, or ten cases of vin ordinaire. I found, after a time, 'Bedding', bought two modest brass beds, mattresses, pillows, sheets and two – only – blankets. It was soon to be summer, after all. A wan youth wearing headphones, the sound of thudding music blurring through his scurfy hair, took down all my particulars, looked at his digital watch for the date and said that they'd deliver on Monday, before noon. How did I want to pay? Credit, cheque, cash?

We wandered through the thronging alleys of merchandise, struck dumb by the sight of desperate crowds surging about chucking everything from packaged children's underwear, garden umbrellas and mixed toolkits to deep-frozen tripes à la mode de Caen, as M'sieur Simon had said, to dead bleached chickens and plastic bottles of milk into their massive trolleys.

You could obviously buy everything in the world here from fishing-rods to Harpic, but Giles, made uneasy by the crowds and the unfamiliar language on every sign, hurried to the lavish bookstalls to see if he could find anything interesting, which, when he did, turned out to be comics as dull as his own at home, but harder to read. So they were left. Instead I bought four big reproduction posters of Monte Carlo, Cannes, Antibes and Menton in 1889 and we made our way to the mammoth *parking*.

Jericho, when we eventually arrived there, pleased him much more. As we turned into the track by the mossy pillar he stuck his head out of the window.

'Oh! It looks brilliant! Look at the cliffs up there. Is it all yours?'

'Not the cliffs. Up to the beginning of them. There's a stream.'

'She told me. Florence did.'

The house filled him with silent pleasure. He didn't say much about it, looked at the room I had chosen for him as his own, pushed the shutters wide and took a look at the view, and then sprinted down to the garden where, generally mucking about and looking, he spent the next hour or so until lunch at La Source.

I liked having him about. While he was damming the stream somewhere, I was tacking up the posters in the long room. They instantly gave the place colour, but I was vaguely thinking that, later on, if one ever did manage to settle into a way of life in Jericho (settle to write, for example), it was going to be difficult with a young boy banging about waiting to be fed. He couldn't be left on his own.

There was no school which could occupy his time, not at present anyway; and the man Florence had found to help tutor him in early French, Mr Theobald, or Théo, was not within walking distance. It was going to be a problem. But, on the other hand, he might grow bored with the idea of France as a permanent place to live. Bored with me, might very likely miss his mother, however cavalier her behaviour, and he'd certainly miss companions of his own age – and language.

But, in my usual way, I decided to shove all that to the back of the stove and let it quietly simmer for the time being. First things first. Giles was only here for a short stay. Until his mother returned from her recce. Or, on the other hand, if he chose to wait, until I went back at the end of May. It all hinged on James.

If by the end of the month there were no significant leads, if Aronovich had really no idea of what might have happened, then I would have to face up to the facts and report him missing; no matter who might try to stop me. The British Consul was in Marseilles. In a couple of weeks I'd report a missing person and hand it over to the authorities. I'd have done my best, obeyed James's wishes as far as possible, but I had a life of my own to live and to rearrange. Time to think of myself. Helen always said that, 'way down there at the bottom', I did anyway. 'Número Uno' she used to call me when a row began to rumble or an argument was in danger of being lost. By her.

So, I'd wait until the end of May and that would be that. Two weeks left. Meanwhile life had to continue as if there were no problem at all.

At La Source that lunchtime M'sieur Simon and his sons were clustered round the bar, a truck of logs parked outside. I was greeted warmly, which was quite reasonable because I had paid heavily for their services before.

'Logs! A good opportunity to buy! We have a whole

truck! Half olive, half oak, from a building-site across the valley. You can have them at a good price. It's May, who buys logs in May?'

'The boulangerie?' asked Marc mildly. 'Anyone with an oven will buy –'

'People in May forget the cold of November! A truckful! You will need fuel in the winter?' M'sieur Simon's gold tooth flashed persuasively.

We made a deal. My deal, which they did not quite understand until they had done the job, was to cart more stuff about Jericho: a dressing-chest for Giles, a wardrobe, things that he and I could not manage ourselves.

With encouragement, Marc and Georges unloading and stacking wood beside the house, and M'sieur Simon and I dragging things about, finally Jericho began to look habitable. When the beds arrived I'd have a house in which to settle, and to perhaps try a hesitant new life. Nothing ventured, nothing gained.

Giles, naturally, treated the whole thing as an extended version of an adventure holiday. Fact and fiction (that is to say his future) were conveniently blurred. For him anyway, if not quite for me.

We left the hotel early the next morning, going to the market first to get a picnic together, some flowers to stick in jugs about the long room, some beer, soft drinks and teabags.

It was Sunday. An important day for Jericho, an important day for Giles and, indeed, for me. Today Florence and Céleste would arrive. With Thomas, for the afternoon.

One wondered.

'What are all the flowers for?'

'To make the house look settled and comfortable. You know? Lived in.'

'When can we?'

'Can we what?'

'Live there?'

'Giles. Are you perfectly certain that you want to? It's early days. You've only been here since Friday. And, anyway, I've paid the hotel for our accommodation in advance.'

There was a silence. Suddenly, from the wincingly dainty garden of a little villa by the road, a dog roared out and ran beside us barking and shrieking, teeth bared, hair standing up like a scrubbing brush. After a moment it fell behind, sniffed around, lifted a leg, trotted back to the garden.

'Don't you want to say, really? Will?'

'Say what?'

'Well, about living here. For ever. I mean, it's his house really, isn't it?'

'His? James's, you mean? Yes.'

'And if you find him?'

'Let's just wait and see.'

'Perhaps he's dead?'

'Perhaps.'

'Then it would be all right, wouldn't it?'

'Giles, I honestly don't know, I can't be certain . . .'

'*I'm* perfectly certain. About staying here. Aren't you?'

'Well, yes. In a way. But not for ever. I mean for a holiday. But you'd have to go to school. Someone would have to look after us. You. Buttons. Iron your shirts. My shirts. Not easy, you know.'

Another silence; he fiddled quietly with his seat-belt.

'Okay,' he said eventually. 'It'll just be a holiday. For a while. How long?'

'Well, if I can discover where your uncle is, how he is, that will make a big difference. Otherwise we'll leave about the end of the month. I paid until the twenty-sixth.'

'I see. Am I a nuisance? I mean, am I in the way?'

'Do you feel in the way?'

'No.'

'Then shut bloody up.'

Later, when I was filling a couple of pots with water for the bunches of white stocks I'd bought, I heard him calling from the terrace where he was setting cups and glasses on a tin table he had found in the chicken shed.

'Car coming! It's them. Florence, I mean.' I carried a pot out on to the terrace, set it among the glasses. 'Another car. There are *two* cars. Did you know there would be two?'

There was a slamming of doors, a roar of fury from Thomas, recognized at once, Céleste's calming voice, Florence calling out, 'Don't park too close, Mama, I'll never be able to reverse. Move away a little.'

Madame Prideaux, obviously far too curious about Giles and any changes made to Jericho, had joined the afternoon gathering.

Thomas, tugging away from Céleste and Florence, straining towards me, stumbled and fell. I hurried to pick him up and discovered that he was laughing with joy, arms flailing about my head, the happy bubbles spraying the air.

'He likes you!' said Giles in wonder.

'Why shouldn't he? I'm very nice. Say good afternoon to Madame Prideaux, she is the mama of Florence, and that is Céleste, who looks after Thomas, when I am not.'

Madame Prideaux moved towards us in her unsuitable tweeds, pulling off her driving-gloves. In perfect, if accented English, she said, 'Florence said that you were a fine-looking boy. She was right. My name is Sidonie Prideaux, how do you do?'

Giles shook hands correctly, smiled nervously, shook hands with Florence.

'What do you say to your new cousin, hein? Thomas? Not what you expected?'

'Yes he is. Will . . . my father . . . told me. He's the only cousin I've got. Brilliant.'

'He can't speak to you,' said Florence. 'But he understands very well, so don't worry. Forgive my English.'

'Very good English,' said Madame Prideaux, sitting down on one of the tin chairs. 'We will all speak English until *Gilles* here can speak sensibly in French. Shall we be having tea today? The English always have tea.'

'We have beer,' said Giles. 'But Will, my father, bought teabags. I'll put on the kettle, shall I?'

It was all a bit like the Mad Hatter's tea-party. Thomas sat on my knee and Céleste helped Giles in the kitchen, which she had, obviously, known before, for she came out with a plate of biscuits and whispered something to Florence.

'Céleste says you have painted the kitchen! And there are pictures and flowers. She's very impressed.'

Thomas suddenly screamed, for no good reason, and clouted me cheerfully. I ducked and handed him over to his mother.

'I trust I do not intrude? But I was curious. Every woman is curious and I am more curious than most,' said Madame Prideaux. 'Also, it is an excuse to use my English, which is very . . . what? Not used – what is it called?'

'Rusty?' I said.

'Exacte.'

Céleste and Giles arrived with teapot and water in a china jug. After tea, which passed in reasonable comfort, Thomas, sucking on a ginger-snap, and watching everything eagerly, suddenly reached out and pointed at Giles.

'Look! Another pair of trousers,' said Madame Prideaux. 'He thinks everyone in trousers must be his father, you see. He can recognize trousers. Excellent!'

Giles said suddenly, 'I can recognize my father even without trousers.' He was grinning broadly, head ducked.

'Giles! Belt up.'

'In the shower. I can!'

'Thomas didn't really know his father, you see,' said Madame Prideaux.

Giles put out a hand. Thomas grabbed it, still holding the biscuit in his other wet-crumbed one, slid off Florence's lap and stood, slightly wobbly, looking up at Giles, grinning, offering the biscuit, and then threw it away. Quietly, wordlessly, they walked slowly down the steps of the terrace on to the path. Céleste was on her feet, watchful, ready to move.

'I think he quite likes me,' said Giles, almost to himself but loud enough for us to hear. 'He's got a very tight grip. Breaking my hand!'

Madame Prideaux was smiling, holding her cup above the saucer. The loop of grey hair had slipped down to her shoulder.

'Children are much wiser than we are. As we grow older, the more foolish we become. It's sad. Look at those two, such trust! We lose it, of course . . .'

Céleste moved slowly down the steps just behind them. Giles bent and found something on the path. He offered it to Thomas, who took it, held it, turned round to his mother, a great smile on his face. He held his closed fist up high. Florence went down and joined Céleste. It was a neat, tidy, careful little ballet. Thomas crowed with mirth, waving his hand.

'What is it?' called Madame Prideaux. 'A toy?'

'A shell. Giles found a shell in the stones!'

Suddenly Thomas sat down hard on the grass, Giles beside him.

'He really can't speak, can he?' said Giles.

'No. He's three . . . maybe one day . . .' Florence let the thought drift into the afternoon. No one pursued it. I poured myself a beer and another cup of tea for Madame Prideaux. It was, to all intents and purposes, a perfectly normal day, nothing was unusual at all.

Florence said, her eyes still on the tableau before her, 'I think he must know you are his cousin, Giles, isn't it?

Because he does not like people so much usually. You are very good with him. You know this?'

'He's a little boy, that's all.'

'That's all. But it is very hard for him.'

'Will he ever go to school?'

Florence shook her head, stooped to lift her son from the grass. 'No,' she said. 'No, he can't go to school.'

'Lucky thing,' said Giles, and came up the steps towards me, smiling, a look of inquiry on his face. I nodded at him. He picked up a flask of Orangina. 'Perhaps he would like some orange juice, would he, Florence?'

And so we sat, talking idly, Thomas eating another sodden biscuit, Giles on his haunches, the flask in his hand, which he poured into a cup and with which he 'fed' his cousin.

'I don't suppose I could take him to the stream, could I?' he said.

'Too far,' I said.

'He'd like it there. Kids like water. Do you want to come to the stream, Tom?'

Thomas stretched out his arm again, head to one side, smiling, bounced up and down on Florence's lap.

'He's getting heavy now for you,' said Madame Prideaux. She set her cup and saucer down, slowly got to her feet, brushing crumbs from her creased skirt, tucking in the loop of hair. Hands on hips she surveyed us.

'Can I look at the house? It is some time since I did? Curious, you see?'

At the cars Giles held on to Thomas, who was about to scream with fury at the end of his afternoon, but Florence opened doors and Thomas and Céleste were pushed into the back. Thomas by this time was howling his rage.

Madame Prideaux was pulling on her gloves. 'The house seems to me that it is smiling again. You understand? You have worked hard.'

'Not really. Just shoved things about with M'sieur Simon and his sons.'

'Get rid of all those canvases up in the hayloft.' She had lowered her voice, keeping one eye on Florence, who was talking to Giles. 'Then you will have a splendid room.'

We shook hands and she got into her car and began to back in a rather alarming way down to the turning-place.

'She's not very good at it,' said Giles.

Florence laughed. 'Not at all good. Very bad. We let her go first so that if she has an accident, you know? – we are not too close to her, but close enough to help if we must.'

'A huge bash in her mudguard.'

'We must paint it.' There was an agony of crashing gears, Florence covered her ears with her hands and, laughing, slid into her seat, started the engine, wound down the window and slammed the door.

'Thank you, William, Giles, for the tea.'

We stood watching Madame Prideaux ease into the road and then move off in a series of sputtering jerks towards Bargemon-sur-Yves.

We waved until they had disappeared behind the hedge.

'I'll have to do a bit of trimming one day. Oh lor' . . . Thanks, by the way. Very good, Giles. Not easy.'

'He's a nice little boy.'

'Yes. Rotten, isn't it, to be born like that?'

'He doesn't know, though. Does he? That he's different?'

'No. Don't think so.'

'I think he'd get quite used to me, don't you? Then we could go to the stream, I know he'd like it. The woman could come too, for safety, but I reckon I could manage.'

'I reckon that you could,' I said.

I asked Madame Mazine to get me Aronovich's number in Cannes, washed, found a change of shirt and was buttoning it up when the phone rang. To my surprise it was not the Arab voice this time, but Aronovich himself.

'It's William Colcott. I'm delighted to hear you.'

'Ah yes. Yes. You are surprised? Sunday, I am not at the hotel at seven o'clock on Sunday. Can I help you?'

'The canvases . . .'

'Yes. You would like them to be collected already?'

'Tomorrow? Or Tuesday? I have builders who can come to me on Wednesday, but if I lose them they can't come again until after August. The holidays and some other engagements.'

'It's very short notice.' He sounded preoccupied, almost vague, as if I had awakened him suddenly.

'I'm sorry.'

'I'll try. Try to get a truck tomorrow.' His voice was uncertain.

'In the afternoon, if you will. I have beds being delivered in the morning?'

He was silent, considering.

'Ah. Then let us make it Tuesday definitely. Tuesday morning. Will that suit your arrangements?'

'Admirably. About ten? There is a lot of carrying up and down, they will have assistance?'

'Naturally. They are experts in moving works of art.'

'Fine. Tuesday then.'

'They will be there. The driver, M'sieur Hubert, knows the way quite well.'

'Until then.'

'I will not be able to get there. It is a very difficult time for me here, but Hubert is very capable, you will see.'

'I'm sorry. Some other time then?'

'Some other time. Goodbye.' He hung up briskly.

And that's how it was on Sunday evening.

CHAPTER 14

THE BEDS ARRIVED just before noon on Monday morning. I felt vague surprise. But there they were, standing nakedly in the two bare rooms, pillows in plastic envelopes, plus sheets. Blankets folded neatly on top.

The two elderly men who had carted everything upstairs joined me in the long room for a beer, and signatures on this and that, and idle conversation about the state of the olives (unpruned for too long), the roses (neglected and left to make bad wood), the vine (a ruin, all leaf and no blossom).

Their self-satisfied gloom and sourness permeated the air like an odour. When I asked if they knew of anyone who could come to help, for a reasonable fee, once or twice a week, they only said that labour was hard to come by and that every local man had his own olives, roses and vines. Their time was fully occupied, but if I went to a firm they would charge me a *fortune*. So?

When they left, I went up to the studio to check the canvases. It had occurred to me, during a night of fitful sleep, that I had not really looked through the things and I could have overlooked an odd one here and there, which might cause a certain amount of interest, or consternation, among the removers Aronovich was sending the next day. Something from James's 'darker subjects' perhaps? There was, however, nothing. All was well, everything had been scrupulously arranged and covered with sheets of old *Var-Matin* and *Le Monde*. The abstract canvases of the cliffs and the ruins of Jericho hamlet were stacked at one end, the 'peasant heads' for which Florence had posed at the other, and apart from a neat pile of assorted empty frames, the rows of brushes in tidy order, the easel standing sentinel in the centre of the room, all was correct, safe for invading eyes. Nothing untoward. I still found the abstracts gloomy, and the 'peasant heads', with their suggestion of countryside backgrounds, pale and lifeless. Aronovich had made a poor deal.

Leaving the hotel that morning I had carted a large cardboard box full of junk down to the car. It is extraordinary how one can, so to speak, 'magpie away' a hoard of bits and pieces gathered together in a few weeks from market stalls and junk shops. There was a china swan with a chipped wing, a Victorian vase covered in blackberries and scarlet leaves, a tin alarm clock from Germany and a cheap Indian bedspread, a-glitter with chips of mirror, to throw over the sagging sofa in the long room. This stuff was intended to impose some kind of 'life' on neglected Jericho, and with this in mind, and a slew of paperbacks and magazines to scatter about, I began to 'dress the set'. Giles was busy, crouched on the tiled floor, snarling at me from time to time with mild irritation when I stepped on him.

On the long shelf which ran the length of the canopy over the open hearth I set the alarm clock, the swan and the vase in the centre, and in a frame which I had found in the studio the group photograph of the family at Dieppe.

It seemed to me in the room, with the settee now covered, flowers stuck about in the pottery jars, the clock ticking loudly, the Futurama posters on the walls, that a sense of 'belonging' had begun to invade the place, and with Giles fiddling about in the centre of the floor, the emptiness and feeling of loss had begun to disperse. At least to my mind.

Something clattered to the tiled floor, there was a muffled oath.

'Giles! Come on. Get up, go out in the sun. What are you doing there?'

'A lizard trap. I'm making a lizard trap. There are hundreds of them out on the terrace, little green ones, brown ones . . .'

'Well, go and make it out there. I'm busy here.'

'Too hot. Will? Look. If I put this flowerpot like this, and hold it up with this bit of bamboo stick, like this, and then tie a bit of string to the stick, see, and then sort of hide round the corner – well, when the lizard goes under the flowerpot I just pull the string, the pot falls down and the lizard is trapped. Easy.'

'Really? Why will the lizard go under the flowerpot?'

Giles looked at me patiently. 'I bait it of course.'

'Bait it? With what?'

'Oh. A worm, a grasshopper. Something wriggly to attract it.'

'I see. Well, good luck.'

'What are *you* doing?'

'Trying to make the place a bit more cheerful, lived in, you know.'

'Mum would say they were dust traps.'

'I am certain she would. And she'd be right. Get up.'

He got up reluctantly, stood rubbing the side of his nose. 'That photo. Is that Granny and Grandpa?'

'And your Aunt Elspeth who died, Uncle James with the crab. And me.'

'With a pipe?'

'With a pipe.'

'I've never seen you with a pipe.'

'It was my first and only. Made me sick.'

'It must be years and years ago. *Years*. You were *very* young then, weren't you?'

'Yes.'

'I'm glad you brought the radio. That'll cheer it up, won't it? Except it'll all be French, I suppose.'

'BBC World Service.'

'Yuck! Talk, talk. Are we really going to live here?'

'Well. It depends on a lot of things. Perhaps one day. We'll see.'

'Well, all these things you've put in the room. If we don't live here someone will steal them, won't they?'

'Who would want an old chipped swan and a tin alarm clock?'

'The radio. They'd pinch the radio. They always do.'

'That comes back to the hotel. I need it in my room.'

Giles pushed his flowerpot and the bamboo stick together with his foot. 'Funny thing to do. Making it all nice, flowers and everything, and then not staying.'

'Well, we might. We might. I'm just trying to see if it feels right, trying to make it feel more my place and not someone else's. Starting my "wooing campaign".'

'Your what?'

'"A Frog He Would A-Wooing Go . . ." Remember that?'

'Never heard of it.'

'Never mind.'

He laughed. 'Ha! That's what Mum always says. "*Never mind*."' He began to roll the length of string round his index finger. 'You know Eric?'

'Know *of*, don't know him.'

'Yes. Well, he's got a pony-tail. Pig-tail really. Down his back.'

'Very chic. They can pull him up to Heaven by that, when his time comes.'

Giles barked with pleasure, threw the ball of string into

the flowerpot. 'Not if he dies in bed, they won't. He hasn't got one in bed. His hair is all everywhere, yuck!, all over on the pillows, straggly, like a witch –'

He might just have butted me in the gut: if Helen wanted to know why he was sullen, sulky and rude, and what was bugging him, I could now tell her – unless I choked her first.

'Enough, Giles. That's it. I don't want to hear any more.'

He was quick to sense that perhaps he had gone a little too far. He began to collect his bits and pieces in silence. Face tight, brow wrinkled with worry. There was plenty of time ahead for wrinkled brows on Giles's face. I took his arm, and pulled him up.

'Be a good fellow. Let's not talk about Eric. Okay? Nothing to do with us, right? Not my business, not *your* business either. Okay?'

'Okay. Shall I go and undo our pillows, upstairs?'

'They'll get damp. Leave them alone, until the summer holidays.'

'You want to come and see me work this trap?'

'I want to see you wash your hands. We're off to see the Wizard.'

'Wizard? What Wizard?'

'Arthur Theobald. Forgotten him?'

'Well, when can we do this?'

'When you've got yourself the bait. Can't set a trap without bait,' I said.

The Theobalds were typical of their breed. They are usually to be found drifting quietly in the shallows of Guildford, Cheltenham, Bath and Tunbridge Wells. Ex-army, ex-Consular, ex-private boarding school. These were the latter. Dottie Theobald was pale, faded, wearing the same bemused expression which she had worn since leaving her mother's womb. She had a plait of fairish hair, a straw hat and a denim skirt, and English teeth, long like a sheep's. Arthur, her husband, a little older, scrawny, muscular, very bronzed, in a pair of floppy khaki shorts and laceless army boots.

They were welcoming and kind, offered instant coffee and Lulu biscuits and said what a devil Sidonie Prideaux was at the bridge table.

Then we discussed how best to help Giles in the short time available, and that perhaps it would be a good idea ('jolly' idea, said Dottie) if he arrived at nine-thirty in the morning, stayed for lunch, left at two-thirty when they took their naps. That way he would hear French spoken for five hours solid. Total immersion.

Neat and precise.

Giles stared into the middle distance with a blank face.

Arthur noticed this quickly. 'Well, you and Dottie chat away; Giles and I will go about our business, eh? Like birds? Feathered sort? Tropical birds, not those wretched budgerigars, *real* birds. Like 'em?'

'Yes, thank you,' Giles said politely.

'Come up to the aviary. Come along. Ever seen long-tailed weavers? Got a pair up there nesting. Marvellous thing, big as a football. Well, nearly . . . venez voir mes oiseaux.'

As they left together and walked up a little hill above the terrace, Dottie said anxiously, 'It'll only be rudimentary stuff, of course. Haven't the time for a real session, have we? Conversational stuff, just to help him cope. Things like "Où est le doubleve-se." You know?'

'I rather think he can say that already. But that's the idea. And I want a bit of time on my own, frankly. A lot of things to do . . .'

'Of course you have. There is a mother? I mean –' She ended with a flush of embarrassment.

'There's a mother, indeed. He's not an orphan. But she's abroad working, so he got sent to me. It's kind of you . . .'

Dottie got up with me and we started to walk towards

her white picket gate. When I turned to wave goodbye to Giles he was standing beside the ornate cage watching me.

'Will! You'll come back, won't you?'

'Always!' I called, and left Dottie in a little halo of nods and smiles.

The fine arts removal men wrapped each canvas in bubble-paper time and again and carried them down to the truck as if they had been newly discovered Monets. I was glad that I had been careful in my examination of the studio for nothing was overlooked, the work was thorough and careful, and they were carrying down the first of the 'peasant heads' (I could tell by the size, smaller than the abstracts) when to my surprise Aronovich walked up the path. I was raking up a pile of dead cabbage stalks. He looked pale and tired, not the bright-eyed boy he had appeared to be at the airport.

I laid the rake aside, rolled down my sleeves.

'Ah! Don't let me disturb you. I have to be here, apparently, to check the number of canvases and to sign various forms and things. The usual nonsense. I am so sorry.'

'I'm glad. My back is breaking. I'm not used to farm labour, but I have to be about while they work, so . . .' I walked with him up to the little terrace. He walked slowly, a notepad in one hand, a pen in the other.

'It's hot already. Were they on time?' There were dark hoops of fatigue under his eyes.

'Ten-thirty about. They took a wrong turning from Bargemon.'

'I'll go up and see M'sieur Hubert: he's efficient, but I don't remember just how many I have. Do you? The numbers?'

'No. I never counted them. Half are one thing and half another.'

He smiled wanly. 'Half for the main rooms, the other

half for the bedrooms, if there are enough. It's so long since we made the deal.'

'There are only the ones you commissioned, as far as I know. Nothing else. I mean, none of the erotic ones.'

He looked at me sharply. 'Do I follow?'

'I don't know. He did a number of paintings, of young men in the nude. I went yesterday to check before your people arrived.'

'It was kind of you to take the trouble. The things you are concerned about were drawings, actually, not paintings. They were all sold, fortunately, because they kept the household here going. I imagine you know that? He got a good price for his "nude fantasies". There are plenty of people along this coast who are delighted to pay a good price for things like that. Specifically drawn to order from their own suggestions. That is found to be most attractive.'

'Or even Brent Millar's, I gather? He sent little sketches over, ideas?'

'So I believe. James had a limited imagination in that respect. His Arab clients, and certainly his Japanese clients, had vigorous ideas. Rather cruel, but I suppose they found them stimulating. They paid enough for them.'

'And you were his dealer?'

'I prefer the word "banker". I sold them for him, I have the opportunity in Cannes and Nice, Monte Carlo above all. I took no commission, you understand. The proceeds all went to James. For that unfortunate child . . . If you'll excuse me, I will go up and get the list. I know the way.' He said that with a certain irony, stood aside as a red-haired man came past carrying two bubble-wrapped rectangles.

'How many, Hubert?'

'Thirty-three larger ones, and we have twenty smaller, the pictures of the girl, fifty-three altogether. Nearly through.'

Aronovich nodded, smiled at me. 'He did well, your brother. A lot of work. Not all done at the same time of course, but I bought them all anyway. No one really looks at pictures in hotel bedrooms, do they?'

'I do. Frequently.'

'You are an exception,' he said, and went into the long room. I heard him go up the slate stairs, call out for someone named 'Nicco'.

They came down together, each carrying canvases.

'I can offer you a Scotch – no Cristall, I regret – or a beer?' I said.

Aronovich paused at the threshold, looked about the long room for a moment, smiled. 'I hardly ever saw this room. It was always what one would call a hostile area.'

'You mean Florence?'

'I mean Florence and Sidonie Prideaux. Hostility emanated from them like a vapour. I would be happy to have a beer, thank you. I'll take these to the truck.'

I got some beer, a couple of odd glasses. Two men came down from the studio with the last of the pictures, said that the place was now clear and where was M'sieur Aronovich?

The studio was enormous. Empty save for the easel and the stool, the scatter of brushes, some trembling scraps of discarded bubble-paper, a roll of sticky tape. On one wall, which I had not noticed before, a page torn from a magazine of a Cézanne Sainte-Victoire pinned to the plaster. And that was all there was left of James's presence.

Aronovich was putting his pen away when he came up to the terrace, smoothed his hair, accepted his beer and we both sat on the little tin chairs looking down the garden to the gate and the truck, its bright orange paintwork glittering through the greening hedge, bumping down to the road.

'I am surprised that Florence appeared hostile to you. She is a reserved girl but never, I thought, hostile,' I said.

'You were no threat to James.'

'Were you? Surely not? With the help you gave him.'

'I was associated with his "threats". The Jacquet boy,

with whom he was greatly infatuated for far too long, and against all advice, and the wretched Jojo, who excited him. They were from the Millar stable. Not attractive. Attractive in one way, naturally, but dangerous in others.'

'And Madame Prideaux? The same dislike?'

Aronovich leant forward, his elbows on his knees, glass in one hand, a small smile on his lips.

'She hated me deeply. I was *part* of the threat. I am a Jew. I helped James, and the family indeed, to survive by selling his pornographic drawings to rich Arabs and inverted Japanese. Being indebted to someone like me destroyed her.'

'How would Madame Prideaux know about the drawings? Florence?'

He shrugged, shook his head wearily. 'I imagine so, yes. Daniel Jacquet and Jojo were often at the house. This house. In the studio.'

'To do what, do you suppose? Two louche young men?'

Aronovich wiped his lips carefully with his fingers. 'To pose for him. You could say.'

'I see.'

'I wonder if you *do*? Sidonie Prideaux was often here also. After the child was born and they had . . . separated. She was here to help with the child. It needed, as it still must do, constant attention. I came here very little. To collect work.'

'And she hated you? Because you were a Jew? Why?'

'My dear fellow. A Jew in France? The French are anti-semitic. Always have been. I was pretty shocked when I arrived here: I was so certain that France was the haven for the displaced, the unwanted and reviled. You know? Perhaps it is, but a fine line is drawn against Jews. They only hate the "pied-noir" more, the people from Algeria. Prideaux, with her class, her age and profession, army, was particularly loathing of Jews. Dreyfuss. Remember?'

'Isn't that extreme?'

'Yes. So was French behaviour towards us in 1940. Extreme! Oh yes. Extreme.'

He had reached to take up his beer from the terrace when a hoopoe suddenly swept down, alighted on the white gravel path feet away, and began to 'grit' with caution, its crest rising and falling like a feathered hand. We sat and watched, mesmerized by its beauty until, with a quick jerk of its head, eyes bright as boot buttons, it looked about, took fright, and sailed up high over the olives in the orchard and was gone.

'I have never seen one so close!' Aronovich had got his beer, pouring the other half into his glass. '*Never* so close before.' He set the empty bottle back on the tiles, eased himself back on his tin chair.

'Of course, she also hated me because she knew that I ran a reprehensible, but very fashionable, club in Paris. I had corrupted James. Voilà! But you know, James *was* corruptible. He could have resisted, stayed away. But he chose to remain. In my club, whatever you wanted you got. If you could afford it. Sex? You could have it in all its many varieties. Risk? I gave them risk. The chase? You would find the chase at L'Avril, and the hunt and capture? The field and the quarry? All there, all on offer. I supplied. Supplied well. My job. I am a Jew, I am good at marketing, know what people want, and what they will pay for. A girl you want? You get. A boy? Join the queue. Arab, Chinese, Christian, Black or Green. I have. Bondage? That too. Pain? If you demand. Humiliation? Ah! Who better to know humiliation and grovelling than an Argentinian–Russian–Italian Jew with a nose job! The club prospered, became famous. It was well run, everything supplied was all "kosher". They got what they wanted. For real. Simple.'

'And James was corruptible?'

'He was a bisexual. This you surely know? He wished to try his wings, taste all.'

'*I* didn't know. I didn't know my little brother very well.'

'When he was first brought to the club he was unaware himself. He just had to be encouraged, shall I say? He liked it. He spoiled as easily as the perfect peach which he resembled. Ripe, glowing, firm, golden, untarnished. What a fruit to be taken. I mean no pun! He bruised quickly, alas.'

'I can imagine that very well.'

'He flourished. Like a rare bloom in a tropical garden. One can say that?'

'You do. You introduced him to Brent Millar?'

'Millar was glamorous, rich, lusty, a splendid man. He was the brilliant lamp, the central flame, around which all the idiot moths fluttered. James was enthralled from the start. The money too was good. He offered the boy everything the silly youth thought he wanted. And got. He needed only a little encouragement.'

'And you? Where did you stand in this sad story?'

'Aside. I was bewitched by James. I did not lust for him, that is not my métier. I could not have run the club if I had so defaulted. I was never tempted. I watched, it amused me, I guided, but I always stood apart.'

'Close to the till, one assumes?'

'Always! It was my job, as I told you. I now have a new hotel opening here in July. All due to hard work. But that was that, and then, after Millar had that accident everything seemed to change. It brought us all to our senses: the club still went on as usual – why not? – but for James I think it had a profound, and lasting, effect. Like drifting out of a deep anaesthetic. He was very much a weather-house, you know? "Fair" on one side, on the other "Storm". I always hoped that he would one day seek the fair side and stay there. And strangely, with the help of René, and to some extent myself, he did. We managed to persuade him to return to life, to come here, to paint again. René knew the place, so did I, and many painters came here. He agreed. He was no longer the golden youth and the life he had been leading was the downward slide to destruction.'

'And he came away?'

'He came away. It was a world and a half away from the one with which he had grown too familiar.'

'And Brent Millar was not far distant? Right? You must have known that?'

'Sure I knew. You cannot take someone off "medicine" instantly. An amputation! Easing him off coke was hard enough, and it was considered that Millar, who was paralysed, could be no longer a threat. He was a ruin. No danger. And he was not. For a time. James began slowly to adjust, started to paint again. I gave him this commission which we have collected today, a guarantee of money, forcing him to work. And he did. And then he met the girl, Prideaux. And all was magically well, until the birth of the child. From that moment on, when he believed that he had been responsible for an imperfect child, that it was his fault and only his, then that was the fall into darkness.'

He finished his beer, cupped the glass in his hand, shook his head. He was exhausted, telling the story had distressed and drained him. He looked at his watch, something which I had noticed he did often, then he got to his feet.

'I must go. I have answered all your questions, I think? And all the others which you did *not* ask. I must get back to my hotel. A building-site is very like a battlefield. The general cannot leave his soldiers for fear that they will desert. One has to set the example, as you English say, people have to be led. Strangely, they *expect* it, alas!'

He collected the bottle, the glass, and went into the long room, setting them down on a chest by the door, looked about him, noticing the flowers, the posters, the Indian bedspread. He was smiling, nodding approvingly, when he said, 'You are intending to stay here perhaps? To settle?'

'I might. It depends on many things . . .'

'All life "depends" on something.' He had turned to leave and stopped. Looking up at the canopy along the chimney-piece. '*There* it is! Is it the same one?'

'The same what?'

'The family by the seaside. It was always in the studio, on a little shelf, like an altar almost. In Paris he had it in his studio. I was sad just now to find that it had gone. Is it the same one?'

'The same. Different frame, that's all. He destroyed everything else.'

'I know. I thought that perhaps this –' He stopped, thrust his hands into his trouser pockets, stood, head bowed, in silence for a moment, looking away from me. 'Would you let me copy it? Very quickly? I could get it done today, mail it back to you tonight. It is something I would treasure. He cherished it.'

'There are a great many photographs of James in the Brent Millar archives. I have seen some of them.'

'I do not speak of those things. *Or* of that time.'

'Is this how you knew that I had dark hair? That it curled?'

'That is how. It is much the same, after all the years.'

A little breeze rustled through the leaves of the vine, a warning perhaps of the mistral to come. It faded and as if from a distance I heard Giles's voice.

A lizard trap. I'm making a lizard trap.

I took down the photograph, wiped the glass with my cuff, gave it to him. 'Okay. But mail it back tonight? I have no other. You swear to do that?'

He held the frame between both hands, his fingers splayed. 'I swear. Thank you; *really*, thank you.'

'I can't imagine why I trust you.'

He shook his head. 'The wily Jew? But you can. I assure you.'

We walked together down the path to the gate, past

bee-ridden clumps of chives, the fennel, the first scarlet cups of the poppies shimmering in the long grass. At the rusty gate he stopped, the picture close to his chest. He turned to me as if to speak, thought better of it, shook his head, walked on.

'I wonder', I said, 'why he didn't destroy that photograph with all the other stuff? Or take it with him perhaps. I mean, if he so cherished it, as you said?'

'I don't know. He took very little, nothing –' He stopped quickly and, as if to divert me, like the proverbial lark who leads the intruder away from her nest by feigning injury, he said, 'Did you ever hear of the accident? Banal, not serious as it happened, but James was run down deliberately by a car. Near La Source at Saint-Basile-les-Pins. He was not hurt, nor was the bike. The car hit the iron railings of the bar terrace. All James had was a bad shock and very bad gravel burns on his hands and knees. Did you know that?'

I stood motionless looking at the poppies. From a distance, Giles's voice again.

A huge bash in her mudguard.

'No. No, I didn't know that. I didn't.'

'Madame Prideaux. James saw her, knew the car. He called L'Hermitage and Millar sent help. It was three months after the child was born. That's all.'

He walked away down the track, past the mossy pillar behind which, neatly parked, was a Peugeot. 604. 06 registration.

He unlocked his door, dropped the frame gently on to the back seat. 'I really am so grateful. Tomorrow, without fail.' As he started to get into the car I leant against the gate and called.

'Aronovich? When you collected James that night in January?' He began to get out slowly. 'Where did you take him?'

He stood on the track facing me. His face expressionless.

'I don't follow.'

'You do.'

'No. Not at all.'

'Where is James?'

'How could I know?'

'You were seen driving him away from L'Hermitage that night. Millar's sister lives in the lodge. His bike is still in her shed.'

He walked slowly towards me. 'You think it was me?'

'Know. A Peugeot 604. Alpes Maritimes registration. Torrent-green paintwork.' This last was invention. The car by the pillar here was green. I took the risk, the string on my bamboo stick was taut.

'There are hundreds of Peugeots like this.'

'Where did you take him?'

He raised his hands in supplication. I walked up to him.

'*Where* did you take him?'

'To Nice. To the port.'

The trap was sprung. The flowerpot fell.

'And?'

'I don't know. He did not confide that. He took a boat, I imagine. He had arranged it all before. He was desperate, he had money, I merely helped him there. He is lost to us! Lost! Leave him.'

He turned away and strode across the ruts to his car. Over his shoulder he said, 'Go to Nice! Why don't you? Ask at the Port Office what boats sailed that evening and to where? Calvi, Bastia, Corsica, Tunisia . . . they will tell you. I don't know.' He got into the car, slammed his door, started the engine.

I ran to him, leant with elbows on the roof, looking down at his tense, white face. 'In twenty-four hours from now, *exactly*, I will inform the police here and the British Consul in Marseilles of a missing British subject. Resident of France. Missing for four months. They will investigate thoroughly *every* detail I can give them. You have twenty-four hours only to tell me. Where is James?'

'That I cannot tell you. I have told you all that I can. I am desperately late. James is lost, Mr Caldicott, he is *lost*.'

He drove down the track crashing the car over the dusty ruts, spun left into the main road without stopping.

A general returning to his troops? But who were they?

Florence moved about the conservatory making herself deliberately busy with the little watering-can. She wrenched at the tap in the wall almost angrily. It was perfectly clear to me that she was not going to sit down to an eye-to-eye confrontation.

For my part, having told her all that I was able to of the meeting with Aronovich, I just sat on a cane chair and watched her fuss away, pulling at a leaf here, a pot there, dribbling water into the fish tank. Evading and avoiding.

What I had had to say had unnerved her, distressed her. When a diagnosis is confirmed it is extremely difficult to accept, even though, secretly, one has known that it would be so.

She was behind a huge pot of Lilium, rustling away at some dead leaves, when she said, 'I remember now. The last time I saw Aronovich was in October, the first day. The end of summer. We were making jam in the kitchen and I saw him coming up the path. Mama saw him. We didn't speak, we never met, but I remember that was the last time.'

She came from behind the lilies, the can in her hand, a quiet, defiant look on her face. We looked at each other through a lacework of mimosa and plumbago in silence.

Outside, the wind had risen, heralding the mistral, clattering at the rattan blinds on the glass, pulling and teasing the shutters, spiralling dust into high eddies in the front garden, the lilac bending stiffly like the bristles in an old broom.

'Tomorrow I will go to the British Consul in Marseilles,

tell him all I know, then to the Chief of Police at Sainte-Brigitte. I'll have done my job.'

She came across to me, knelt at my side, a hand on my arm. 'Don't. I beg you not to. Don't do that, William.'

'Florence. Don't be silly, darling, I can't leave a man to just fall off the earth without alerting someone! I simply can't.'

'You can. You can. Leave it, let it lie where it is, please.'

She apparently had not heard my use of the word 'darling'. It was the first time I had used it.

'How can I leave it as it is?'

'For Thomas, for me. Think of the pain it will bring. The questions, the police, the press. We have endured enough distress already. I beg you.'

'If you are convinced that James is dead the least I can do is to find him, his body, if there is a body, and I am not as certain as you are.'

'I am sure. Sure.'

'Why did Aronovich want that group photograph? What could it mean to him? A photograph of a small boy?'

'Perhaps he is sentimental . . .'

'As a hanging judge.'

'James always kept it. It was on his easel, by itself, the day I went up to clear the place.'

'Exactly. Aronovich knew that, I assume?'

'I don't know.' She got up wearily. 'Is Giles at the hotel?'

'Giles is with the Theobalds, at Marineland in Antibes. Florence?'

She turned towards me. I got up and went to her, my hands stretched towards her.

'I love you. I hate you to be so sad.'

'If you love me, stop. Please.'

'I do love you, and I won't stop.'

'James longed for oblivion. He has sought it, it was his own wish.'

'I lied to Aronovich, trapped him with the colour of his

car, but it did force him to a confession that there might be a chance of finding James.'

'It is too late. Too late now.'

'That is negative.'

'No. Positive. I know.'

'You are always so certain! Let us wait for Aronovich to call.'

She set the watering-can down, buttoned a cuff. 'Now *you* are so certain. When must he call?'

'Tomorrow by noon. He will. He can't ignore the facts.'

'And if you should find James, you clever ones, find him in Corsica, Tunisia, find him anywhere, it will destroy him completely. We were not married, he has no reason to return, why cause such grief and pain? What has he left but his own secrecy?'

'He has you.'

'Ah no! No longer. That love died a long time ago and there is nothing so dead as the death of the heart.'

She opened the conservatory door, indicated that I should leave with a slight move of her head. 'I am sure that you will call me? Tomorrow?'

I promised to do so, and crossed the dim hall, went out into the racing wind.

It was dismissal.

At breakfast the next morning in the empty dining-room with its trellised paper, the partridge and the Japanese fan in the empty grate, Giles was describing, for the tenth time, how amazing it was to feed a dolphin with a herring, when Eugène, carrying a pot of coffee, said that there was a telephone call for me, I could take it in the booth by the front door.

It was seven-thirty, early for Madame Mazine. Early for Aronovich.

The phone was hanging from its cradle among the parrots and laburnum. I took it up and dragged the accordion door shut.

'Caldicott here. Who is this?'

'Solomon Aronovich. I am doing as you said.'

'You are early. Thank you.'

He cleared his throat. When he spoke again his voice was rather higher, thin.

'I have the photograph here. I also have one passport, expired for two years, and what remains of ten thousand dollars. Not, I am afraid, very much.'

'I don't think that I understand you.'

'Your brother James died this morning at four-fifteen. Peacefully. I was with him. He had seen the photograph and was . . . was . . . Was very pleased.'

'How? How did he die?'

'He died from pneumocystis pneumonia. You know what that is?'

'I can guess.'

'He was aware of this a long time ago: it was proved positive at the end of the summer. By January it began to race. That is why he had to get the money from Millar, why I collected him that night and brought him here. He knew then that he was dying, but the clinic here is not cheap, you understand?'

'Yes.'

'And the disease is capricious. It takes its course.'

'I will come to you now. Right away. Where are you?'

'In Cannes. It is a private clinic, we do not discuss it, you understand? It is very discreet. The Villa Mimosa, in Super-Cannes, near the Observatoire.'

'I want to see him.'

There was a silence at the end of the line.

'Did you hear me? I must see him.'

'Only if you absolutely insist.'

'I do. I will leave right away.'

'*He is no one that you ever knew*. You realize that?'

'I realize that.'

'I will wait for you outside Cannes station; in the front *parking* in one and a half hours from now. That should be time if you leave immediately.'

'I am leaving.'

'I will lead you to the clinic. You will, of course, recognize my car . . .?'

I heard him hang up. The line buzzed. I replaced my receiver in its cradle and sagged against the quilted parrots. No sense of satisfaction, or relief. Just an almost overwhelming feeling of grief and distress. So that is that. Tacky, ugly, sad. No splendour, no medals for valour; silent, cruel death for the ewe lamb.

Outside the booth, leaning against the corridor wall, Giles, hands stuffed into his jeans pockets. He raised anxious eyebrows.

'Mum? Was it Mum?'

'No. Not Mum.'

'Okay. I just thought an accident. Eric driving. You know . . .'

I walked slowly down the hall to the closed front door. Through the glass panes, the terrace was littered with fragments of broken tile, torn leaves, whirling shreds of paper. The wind jostled and ripped at the lime trees, had already tumbled the smiling pink-faced chef, smashed a pot of Portugal laurel.

'It's still blowing. Terrific – the whatever you call it.'

'Mistral. Blows for two, four or seven days. Something like that.'

'Arthur told me. Was it something you didn't want to talk about?'

An empty plastic dustbin trundled, jigged and bounced down the street beyond the terrace towards rue Émile Zola. I'd buggered that part up.

'No. No. I can talk about it. They have found James. Your uncle.'

'Awesome! Brilliant! I bet you're pleased!'

'Yes. A bit shocked frankly. Look, we have to go to Cannes. It's a long drive, are you ready?'

'Yup. All ready for Dottie and Arthur. All that frog-talk. Yuck!'

'Not today. Okay? Let's get going. Mind your head: flying tiles.'

As I began to open the door I felt his hand push into my free one.

'Will? You all right, really? Was it bad news . . . something?'

'No. I'm all right, honestly. Fine. One day, when I can remember it all, sort it out, I'll tell you about it.'

He leant against the wall.

'Will I have to go back now?'

'Back? Where?'

'Well, they've found him. There. I mean home.'

'You want to?'

'No.'

'So? Stay here? With me? You mean that?'

'Yup.'

'Sure? Quite sure?'

'Really sure. Really.'

'Okay. It's great! You're on.'

We were suddenly laughing.

I pushed out, holding the door against the wind, on to the terrace. Giles was close beside me, hands over his head. I let the door go and heard it crash shut, clattering the glass in the panes.

'Will you write it down?' He was shouting against the tearing gusts, forcing me to yell back, laughing.

'Yes! One day.'

'Write it down? Just like a book?'

I put my arm round his shoulders and we staggered, lurching, towards the garage and the car.

'Yes. For you! I'll write it all down. Just like a book.'

Grasse, 14.7.86
London, 13.2.91